Adventure of the Mouhumes
Jack and Annie's new
Visitors

Adventure of the Mou
Jack and Annie'
New visitors

CW00383629

Acknowledgments

Elizabeth Reed, Lilly Mitchell for their help on this book. And also to Karen Henderson for her support with the other two books, again Elizabeth Reed on all the books I've had help with. Also Lillian Hall for help with The Mouhumes journey

With thanks

Created and written by I C Henderson

Adventure of the Mouhumes
Jack and Annie's new
Visitors

Chapter 1
Jack and Annie's
New visitors

IN A LITTLE village in the north east of England, there lived Jack and his wife Annie

Jack was in his late thirties but liked to think of himself as younger he had worked hard all of his life, he had always been fit and active, but just now, things were not looking too good.

Jack had been in a car accident and had hurt his back, when walking the pain was too much, so he used crutches, these helped him to push up and ease the pain in his back.

He spent most of his time in the conservatory at the back of the house.

They had had it built, just before the accident; so it had come as a blessing, as they never thought it would become their main room.

Over the next few months they would spend most of their time in there as Jack could not get comfortable on any of the other chairs in the house.

The conservatory chairs were comfortable, it was warm and it looked out over the back garden, down and out over the small patio.

At the end of the patio they had a bridge over a pond, this led down on to the lawn, at the bottom of the garden they had a greenhouse with a large shed beside it, at the side of this there was a small vegetable patch, where Jack, who was a keen gardener used to grow his own vegetables.

2

Adventure of the Mouhumes
Jack and Annie's new
Visitors

During the day lots of different types of birds visited the garden the bird table was always full, both Jack and Annie loved to sit and watch the wild life, where they looked out they could even see the fish in the pond. Jack was getting fed up sitting down all day, so he would try to get up and go into the garden, but it was too much too soon. Jack could not lie down for long, as this would irritate his back, so even during the night he would get up and go into the conservatory and look out at the garden, some times the moon would give the garden a little light which would help Jack relax.

This was Jacks favourite time as early in the morning he would often see a different variety of animals, some that he would not see in daylight. If he was lucky enough to see anything that he did not recognise, he would often look it up on the internet.

This would keep Jack busy and he could learn about other things when doing this, he would learn about all sorts of things that he had never thought of before.

This also helped Annie Jacks wife, as she could still go to work and not worry too much about Jack getting himself up to mischief, and maybe hurting himself trying to do something that he was not ready to do yet.

Annie would help him all she could when she was at home or even when she was at work she would phone him, just to make sure that he was alright

Jack would often wake her when he was trying to get out of bed, even when he was trying to be quiet; the moans he would make when he was pulling himself up out of the bed, often woke Annie

3

Adventure of the Mouhumes
Jack and Annie's new
Visitors

Chapter 2
New Destinations

IT WAS A DARK STORMY NIGHT. The moon was hidden behind dark black clouds; the rain was coming down hard. The weather had been horrible for three or so weeks: it had never stopped raining. The Mouhumes had been stuck in a small part of the park, in some woodland, for nearly two weeks. They had arrived there after being moved from the only home they had ever known. It had been in an area untouched by humans for years; there were plenty of fruits, berries and all sorts of other food.

The home the Mouhumes had once lived in had been turned upside down by big machines. Some Mouhumes had been sleeping, when their home was destroyed; many lost loved ones that night. It had been a large community, many generations and now, for all they knew, they might be the only ones left, moving from place to place, hoping to find somewhere they could settle down once again.

They had been on the move for what seemed forever, their leader, Tube, had taken ill so they rested and took advantage of the shelter in this small woodland. They had taken over a small rabbit warren on a sandy embankment. It was a good shelter from the wind and rain and because of the weather, food was in short supply.

The young Mouhumes wanted to go out on a hunting spree. They were dressed in fur from head to toe; Linden asked Ratty why they could not go out and gather food. Ratty could not explain why? However, he thought they should not go out hunting by themselves, he just knew something was not right. Why had the rabbits moved away from the warren? All he knew was that there was a strange smell, a smell he had never come across before.

Ratty was exhausted. He had helped to dig part of the sandy embankment; they needed to make the room a safe place, and protected them from the wind. The tunnel was larger than the Mouhumes would have liked, but it had belonged to the rabbits,

Created and written by I C Henderson

Adventure of the Mouhumes
Jack and Annie's new
Visitors

and rabbits are somewhat bigger than a Mouhume: Ratty just knew that it was not a night to be out in the dark, more importantly, they all needed some rest.

Unknown to them, this was going to be a night that would split them up forever. As they were resting some decided to go and look for food near the building in the car park. Some of the youngest had decided to go, they had often gone looking for food with Ratty, but this time Ratty was staying behind to rest.

Ratty, who was named due to the way he caught and killed rats when he was younger, would nearly always go with the younger Mouhumes to help them learn how and where to find food but also to keep out the way of humans and their pets. [He would sometimes take them into a human's house if they could not find food in other ways because he knew there was always food there] This also gave them the opportunity to watch the humans and discuss afterwards what they had learned.

The younger Mouhumes decided to sneak out and hunt for something to eat as they knew food supplies where running low. Ruddy and Mousey knew it would take more than just the two of them so they ran to see who else may be brave enough to go with them. Ruddy said Joy might go, but Mousey said the last time Joy went anywhere she ran off and Ratty had to end the hunting early. "What about Ellis?" "No" said Mousey, he had a fright and was always reluctant to do anything that might be risky.

They took some time before they decided who they would ask and would not ask. Now they had to go and bring everyone together. They had picked ten in total: a good number [so if they ran into trouble they had plenty of support to help each other] they separated to look around the burrow to save time.

Mousey was heading towards where he thought Woozy might be. Woozy had a good sense of direction in the dark but was afraid of heights. On his way down the warren Jumper jumped on

5

Adventure of the Mouhumes
Jack and Annie's new
Visitors

Mousey's back and they rolled around the floor. Jumper was always doing this to keep his jumping ability up to scratch; well that's what he said. Mousey just thought he liked to show off. Mousey told him what they had planned and Jumper, without hesitation, agreed to go along with them.

Then Mousey told him that Ruddy was also coming, "a girl, what's a girl coming for?" Jumper asked with disapproval

Mousey told him that she had proved herself more than any of the others and she would be good if anything needed bashing. Jumper knew this and he also liked her a lot.

Ruddy and Jumper would often have fun together, they would roll around to see who was the strongest, Ruddy often won, but most of all without saying it, they liked each other so much; to see each other and to touch each other was good. He wished her no harm. Ruddy also liked Jumper and that's why she had not mentioned his name when they were thinking about who to take with them.

They finally went around and spoke to everyone they thought would go with them. Some refused but others they had not thought of wanted to go with them. The ones who had not wanted to go said that it was too dark and wet and others said they preferred to go hunting and gathering food just as day was breaking. In the end only six in total would head out, not as many as they would have liked. "Six of them could do a fantastic job and bring a good meal" said Scallop who had also joined them.

Scallop was dressed in what used to be a uniform for a toy. It was from a toy soldier, a green camouflage outfit, the uniform was bigger than he was so he could put other undergarments on to help keep him warm, which made him look fatter than he really was.

Created and written by I C Henderson

Adventure of the Mouhumes
Jack and Annie's new
Visitors

Others had fur skins on from rats or other animals and like Scallop they would wear whatever they could find to help keep them warm and dry.

Ruddy was wearing a rat skin, she had helped Ratty kill it when they had gone out hunting. They did not like to leave anything they might be able to use, so the rat was skinned and the meat was eaten. Some Rats where a lot bigger than a Mouhume and they would kill a Mouhume if the Mouhume was alone, that's why they needed to go out in numbers to protect each other. With the fur pelt being bigger than Ruddy she found it easier to be able to move around and not be restrained in her actions, as some clothing slowed others down.

After a long discussion on where they were going to go hunting, they all agreed that the car park might be the best place, as the large green area had not had any visitors all the time they had been in the rabbit warren. So there was less likely to be any food left on the grass area by humans.

Woozy wore some leaves stitched together. It had been his mothers' idea; she would also use sap from the trees, rubbing it over the leaves to help give it strength. It blended in well against the shrubbery and it was also waterproof. His mother often tried different ways of making clothes, in order to see which materials were best suited for all weather types.

The car park was some distance away and it would take some time to get there. They would go along the riverside and keep in the hedge and under the foliage. The rain had flattened some of the plants; this would help to give them shelter from the rain and anything that was on the prowl. Owls often came out around this time of night; they would swoop down taking mice and any other small animals. The Mouhumes had to keep their wits about them; other creatures hunting for food also came out in the safety of the dark, away from prying eyes.

7

Adventure of the Mouhumes
Jack and Annie's new
Visitors

Jumper wore baggy clothing made out of what was once a bath towel. It had been a dark red but now had lost most of its colour. Ruddy had changed she was dressed, as ever, in a fur skin. This one was taken from a young rabbit, she said it was warm and waterproof to a point. Jumper liked his outfit; he said it would let him move without any restriction.

As they went along the riverside they played around. Like all young creatures they liked to have some fun. Ruddy, the youngest, was also the fastest she could climb a tree as fast as any cat. At the back of the group, she slinked away ever so quietly; she ran upfront waiting for the rest to come her way. She waited half way up a small bush, hidden away behind the leaves and slightly wet from the rain; she went as still as a statue. When the rest came beside her she leapt out off the bush and onto Jumper's back. He was the second oldest in the group, and true to his name, he jumped high with Ruddy on his back; she clung on, laughing as she did so.

Mousey ran and hid under an old log, Scallop ran the other way and hid under some shrubbery, the other two, Linden and Woozy ran into each other and knocked each other down, knocking the wind out from one another. This was not the Mouhume way: they had been told when they have to hide; they should always keep away from one another but always know where each others were.

Ruddy was still holding onto Jumper's back as he hopped and rolled around trying to get her off, he was still unsure what or who, was on his back. The others watched, but still hid away, just to make sure they had not got any unwanted attention. Linden and Woozy eventually got to their feet and scurried under some shrubs together. Woozy always said that sometimes it might be better than being separated from each other.

Jumper finally got Ruddy off his back and ran up a small young tree to see what and who had attacked him. Hidden away, he looked around and could see that Ruddy was lying on the ground,

Created and written by I C Henderson

Adventure of the Mouhumes
Jack and Annie's new
Visitors

laughing. He knew then that she had played one of her tricks on him and he would get her back later with a trick of his own.

She might be the only female in that food finding group but she was certainly one of the bravest. Ruddy would take on anything that she thought would harm her friends. He remembered the time they had been taken out on a hunting expedition with Ratty; they had come across a large and aggressive rat. It had Ratty in a corner and he had no escape, so Ruddy, without any thought for herself, ran up the side of a wall around the rat, almost pushing the rat with her hand before she landed on her feet then she stood in front of Ratty to protect him and screamed with such anger in her voice that the rat ran away quickly.

Jumper had seen this so many times from her that he could not count how many times she had saved one or more of the Mouhumes. Her bravery had often been talked about; however, she had one weakness, she often did things without thinking, things that could also put the others in danger.

Just then the others came out of their hiding places. Jumper knew he would have to say something, "Ruddy, if you don't stop fooling around you will be stopped from coming on these expeditions. Do I make myself clear?" Ruddy sunk her head into her chest and nodded slightly. She knew that danger was all around them but also she knew they had to have fun sometimes and finding the time for fun was hard.

As they approached the car park they looked around to make sure there was no risk to them. Near the car park there was a bungalow with a large garage joined onto it. They separated and scurried around, looking around but still in contact with each other. They went in pairs, one pair checked out an area, then the next pair moved forward so that they kept together. If they got into any trouble the others would be able to help, or they could make a quick getaway.

Created and written by I C Henderson

Adventure of the Mouhumes
Jack and Annie's new
Visitors

They could often find some food that the humans had thrown away if they looked in the bins around the car park, This time, however, all the bins had been emptied so Mousey decided to go into the building. They found a small hole in the brickwork and soon they were all in the building. But unknown to them a cat lay asleep in the next room. The door was slightly open so the cat could go out when it liked. They looked around the room [it had a large object with wheels they knew from past experience] Sometimes food had been dropped near these things when humans got into and out of them.

They continued to look around. There was a cage at the end of this room in the corner; an old carpet was draped over it. Then Linden stuck his nose in the air, he had not smelled anything like this before so he beckoned to the others. They all came together and he said, ever so quietly, that he was afraid this smell was something to be wary off.

Ruddy asked if they should have a look to see what it was. But Linden said not to look; he was beginning to tremble with fear. Mousey held his arm out and took hold of Linden, pulling him away from the rest of them he asked him ever so calmly what was wrong. Linden could not say for certain but he knew whatever lay behind that carpet would be far worse than anything they had ever come across before. They could hear something thrashing around in a cage. It was trying to get out. It sounded like it was becoming more and more aggravated. It also started to scratch at the cage door, as if it was trying to dig itself out.

Just then they heard a squeak from the door that was slightly open, they all hid in different places. The door opened, light from the doorway now shone into the garage. There were still dark areas but the Mouhumes could now see what was around them. Nothing came out from the door "the door must have just swung open by itself" said Jumper. As they moved around the garage they looked around to see if there was anything they could use or even eat. The

Created and written by I C Henderson

Adventure of the Mouhumes
Jack and Annie's new
Visitors

noise from the cage was getting louder and louder, so they decided to be brave and go and see what was behind the carpet.

Jumper leaped onto the top of the cage, Scallop and Ruddy helped each other up then Woozy and Ruddy helped Mousey up. When they where all on top of the cage they pulled the carpet up; it was a hard task especially as they were just young Mouhumes.

The thing inside the cage was now more excited; it was pacing around the cage. They now had the carpet pulled all the way on top of the cage. Claws were now coming out from the wire mesh door. The smell was nothing they had ever smelled before. So they were unsure what to expect. It started to head butt the door and scratch under the gap at the door, it was determined to get out.

Woozy was standing on the edge of the cage when all of a sudden something grabbed hold of him and pulled him onto the floor; the rest of them looked over the side towards Woozy. Woozy lay lifeless on the floor.

The cat picked him up and started to walk away when Ruddy jumped from the cage onto it's back and pulled hard on it's whiskers as if she was riding a bull, just like a cowboy. The cat held on to Woozy with its jaws. Ruddy then punched the cat in the side of its eye, the cat give a loud growl and dropped Woozy onto the floor. Ruddy held on for her life as the cat ran, jumped and rolled over trying to get her off.

Scallop and Jumper went to Woozy and pulled him away to safety, Mousey and Linden without thinking pulled the catch on the cage door and opened it, thinking that the thing inside would attack the cat. The polecat jumped out of the cage and ran towards the cat. Linden called out to Ruddy. Ruddy turned her head to see the polecat running towards them. She jumped off and ran towards the hole in the wall.

Adventure of the Mouhumes
Jack and Annie's new
Visitors

Linden and Jumper ran to help Scallop and Mousey with Woozy. The polecat leaped onto Jumper and bit into his neck. The others knew he was gone, they scampered away knowing that they would have to recover his body.

Outside Ruddy was gasping trying to get her breath back, when the others came out holding onto Woozy, she asked where Jumper was, they shook there heads. Ruddy with an all mighty scream, ran back inside, and with a sharp pointed stick she ran it into the side of the polecat. It dropped Jumper and ran a short distance away. Ruddy picked up Jumper's body, carried him over her shoulder and out the hole they had came in.

The others had gone back onto the riverside and hid under the shrubbery for cover. Woozy had starting to come around now. When the cat got hold of him he had passed out and this may have saved him. The cat probably thought he was dead so the cat would not go any further than hold onto its prey.

Ruddy was heading towards them carrying Jumper, all of a sudden Mousy saw the polecat coming out of the hole and heading towards Ruddy. Mousy also had a sharp pointed stick and ran towards the polecat. The polecat saw this and pounced towards Mousy; Mousy quickly moved to the left side ran up and hid in a nearby bush. Mousy needed time to help Ruddy as she was exhausted. The polecat ran in to the bush looking for Mousy, giving them valuable time to escape.

The rest quickly moved under the undergrowth for protection; the rain came down even harder as they moved along heading back to the camp. They came along a clearing when suddenly an owl swooped down and took hold of Jumper and flew away. It was often the case when a Mouhume had died, another animal would often devour the body. This was the Mouhumes way; this was how they never got discovered.

Created and written by I C Henderson

Adventure of the Mouhumes
Jack and Annie's new
Visitors

They started to head back to the warren knowing that Jumper's family would be devastated with the news that he had been taken from them. All of them were exhausted from the struggle they had just encountered. They now had to move quietly with speed but still be aware the polecat was on the prowl. They had to be cautious, not only the polecat but other hunters too would be out and about; the smell of a kill would attract all types of killers.

They heard a sound from the side of them, but luckily it was still some distance away. They stopped and listened to see what direction it was coming from. They still held the sharp sticks they first took out with them, these were ready to use, if needed. Whatever it was had also stopped. After standing for some time they moved slowly and quietly. Ruddy, the first to do so, she was upset and thought whatever it was, if it came to attack her she was ready and willing for a fight. Her eyes were full of tears, she found it hard to concentrate on what she was meant to be doing, all she could think was how Jumper, had been taken away from her.

The sound came closer, then suddenly a nose poked out of the foliage. Still with tears in her eyes and without any focus, she jumped onto the head of the polecat and started to scream and pierce its neck, it rolled around trying to get her off but she hung on then stuck the stick into its eye. The stick broke and she fell off, it ran away bumping into everything in its way. The others came but Ruddy continued to run after the polecat with what was left of the broken stick in her hand.

Linden called for her … but nothing came back; Linden tried to smell the air to see what was around them. The damp air was full of strange aromas that he had never smelled before; he just knew that danger was all around. Just then a noise came from the direction that Ruddy and the polecat had gone, a scuffle and screams and then a deadly silence. Mousey's heart sank.

13

Adventure of the Mouhumes
Jack and Annie's new
Visitors

The others came back to join him but he insisted they should carry on back to camp to warn the others. Then the sound of crackling from broken sticks and things on the wet ground could be heard and suddenly out from the shrubbery came Ruddy, blood dripping from her. Her fur clothes ripped and chunks of fur missing, she fell to the ground, Scallop and Woozy ran to her aid.

They picked her up and ran, they hid under a large prickly bush for protection. By now they were all worn out physically and mentally through fear, they could not see how they could get back and if they did, they might take danger back to the camp.

What could they do? Mousey said they needed to catch their breath and get anything they could use to protect themselves. Scallop's head stretched up, he could hear something, so he signalled for them all to lie down, which they did. Under the fallen leaves and in the wet earth, they lay still, whatever it was, looked into a bush not that far away from them. Luckily, the wind was blowing towards them and away from whatever it was. For now the danger had passed.

They still had a long way to go to get back to the camp. They could still encounter all sorts of danger but they knew if they did not at least try they would also lose Ruddy. Her body was now limp; she was not in a good way. Once full of fight, Ruddy was now lifeless. They started out with six, now there was only five and they all thought they might end up losing her. Jumper, who had been the leader that night, was now dead. Ruddy, who was their strength, was now all but dead herself. Could they make it back?

As they lay under a well established blackberry bush, with thorns and prickles, they had plenty to help protect them from any attack that might come from the sky and also from the ground.

Mousey was upset; after all he did persuade them to go into the building and now they were all at risk. Not that they had never been in this situation before but because now they did not have

Created and written by I C Henderson

Adventure of the Mouhumes
Jack and Annie's new
Visitors

anyone who could help. None of them had the experience to take command; it was as if they had lost all hope when Scallop spoke up, "look we cannot stay here all night we must move and move soon".

"What about Ruddy? What can we do with her, she's heavy and when we are in the open we are in more danger," voiced Linden. Woozy's head was buried in Scallop's chest, he was crying. The thought of leaving Ruddy; it was Ruddy who helped save his life. "No, no", then "NO" with an almighty scream "you cannot, no she saved me, please don't, don't".

"Quiet, quiet do you want us all killed?" Mousey said in a calm but persuasive voice. He knew that if they carried her they would be putting themselves at risk. Two of them would have to carry her and then take turns; none were strong enough to bear her weight, not like her. She would have picked anyone of them up and carried them and still have the strength to protect them. They knew they had to decide what to do with her: not an easy decision and one that could put them all in more danger. Any hunting trip always had that danger and there would be times there would be those who would not make it back.

Mousey then came up with the proposal: "We have two things that we can do, one leave her and hope that she, that she ..." he stopped, the words would not come out, "... and the other is taking turns and carry her".

"We could stay here and one of us could go back to camp and get help," Scallop said with confidence in his voice.

"What happens if the one that goes for help gets hurt or worse, then what?" Linden asked. Feeling very worried that no one would make it back to camp at all. They all knew at this time of night every predator would be out hunting.

Created and written by I C Henderson

Adventure of the Mouhumes
Jack and Annie's new
Visitors

After what seemed a long discussion they decided that Woozy, Scallop and Mousey would go back to camp and leave Linden with Ruddy. This was the best thing to do. Woozy would be too afraid to stay by himself and Mousey could defend himself better than Linden could.

The rain had now stopped, the clouds had parted and the moon was almost full. This gave a good light to see and be seen. They would keep in the cover of the foliage that had been crushed by the rain. What once stood tall was now half the size but this would give them better protection. The density from some plants would make it harder for predators to spot them.

Linden being left alone was fearful, not just for himself but also for the other three who had a great distance to travel before they would be back at the new camp. He went to check on Ruddy. They had covered her with leaves to try and keep her dry and warm, she was so cold. Linden had no idea what to do; he had not been on many hunting expeditions. He tried to think about what they had experienced.

Now the rain had stopped all he could hear was the odd raindrop falling from the trees and branches. Suddenly there was a noise, a distinctive sound; something else was hunting, walking slowly and gently over the ground. What could it be? Linden stood up and moved closer to the external covering from the thorns that helped keep him secure from anything bigger than a Mouhume. Looking out from a clearing, he could see across the river. The hillside met the skyline. His eyes had to adjust to the difference in light and the sound of the night.

There were different animals in the distance: cows mooing in a field and sheep making the odd noise. It all sounded normal he thought but then suddenly a muzzle with big teeth was at his chest. He froze with fear. The teeth were now very close to his head, only the thorny bush stopping it getting any closer. This is it he thought,

Created and written by I C Henderson

Adventure of the Mouhumes
Jack and Annie's new
Visitors

then suddenly a yelp from the animal, Ruddy stabbed the thing in its nose with a long thorn.

She then ran after it with a number of thorns. She was on a death mission, the animal yelped again, she must have stabbed it again and again, it made off yelping as it ran away.

Linden stood in the same position with fear; Ruddy came back and tapped him on the shoulder. "Hurry up", she said "we best be off before he comes back and eats us", she laughed. Linden could hardly believe his eyes, she was all but dead moments before and now she was back as if nothing had been wrong! She went out of sight for a moment and then back again in a flash. Her fur was ripped from earlier and it had bits missing. She looked tattered and yet she was full of spirit, what had got into her?

Linden was unsure but he knew if he had any hope to get back to the rabbit warren it was with her. She always had strength but now she had something else. This night she had taken on animals, in their own right were killers, this was not something you would want to encounter even with numbers on your side but she took them on by herself and won.

A hand grabbed hold of Linden's arm, "hurry up" she whispered then she was off. Linden did not waste anytime; he

Created and written by I C Henderson

Adventure of the Mouhumes
Jack and Annie's new
Visitors

hurried trying to keep up with her. Side by side they were moving in the undergrowth. Where did she get this energy from? Linden could barely keep up with her. She had to slow down so the distance would not grow too great from her.

A sound from up ahead alerted Ruddy, she stopped suddenly as she had been running. Linden who also had been running fast trying to keep up with her when she stopped promptly he carried on running into her, knocking her over.

She jumped to her feet then up the bush from one stem to the next. Linden had no idea what was happening. Why had she stopped? Why? What had she seen? She was back down on the ground as quick as she had scaled the bush. Then she ran into the open space and onto the grass verge. She picked up a half eaten apple that a human had dropped; it was as big as she was. Linden ran over to help her. They started to eat into it.

After a short time they carried it between them heading back to the camp, moving quietly but with urgency, they headed back the same way that they had come.

Now that it was only two of them, Linden wondered if the others got back safely. Only time would tell. All Linden knew was that whatever they would encounter Ruddy would give them the edge. Linden realised why Ratty would always let her go on hunting expeditions, she was better than the male Mouhumes. He also knew that he would have to keep an eye on her; it was as if she was on a death mission.

Linden had heard Ratty talking about Ruddy once and now he knew what he had overheard was true, why she needed one of them to try and calm her down.

Ruddy was always being talked about by the other Mouhumes. She was almost a living legend. Mouhumes often

Created and written by I C Henderson

Adventure of the Mouhumes
Jack and Annie's new
Visitors

would speak about how Ruddy had taken on creatures twice the size of her and always won. Now Linden had seen this for himself.

Suddenly, Ruddy dropped the apple and was off. A thud and a squeal, Linden's thoughts were interrupted. Ruddy was on top of some creature. Linden ran to help, when he got to Ruddy, he realised she was on top of Ratty.

Ratty had came looking for them with a number of other Mouhumes, when they had came across Mousy and the others. They had told him what had happened. Ratty would have normally left an injured Mouhume to other creatures but he could not with Ruddy. She had saved many other Mouhumes without a second thought. He knew he would have lost his own skin a number of times had it not been for Ruddy and not just the one time the Mouhumes had talked about.

Ruddy jumped to her feet laughing, Ratty was covered in the wet earth. He cursed her and those around as they were all laughing. Some were holding onto their stomachs and some were rolling on the damp ground. It had looked ever so funny for them. Ruddy often made them laugh with her antics. Ratty wiped some of the mud from his side and plonked it on Ruddy's head. With mud rolling down her face, this made them laugh even more. Being little creatures, they could laugh quite loud.

It was time for them to head back to the rabbit burrow. Some of them were tucking into the apple. Before long it was all gone. The Mouhumes had seen some food on the way to find Ruddy so they would pick that up on the way back. As they approached the food they could sense that something was not right. They spread around, all in sight of each other. What could it be? A strange smell, a smell that they had never came across before. They were anxious more so than any other time. Even Ruddy was fearful, Ratty at this time, decided they should leave the food and beckoned to the others.

Created and written by I C Henderson

Adventure of the Mouhumes
Jack and Annie's new
Visitors

They all moved away silently, but one whose greed and curiosity had the better of him returned and went towards the food, not making any noise he grabbed a handful of food and ate it, he was just about to take hold of another handful when he fell to the ground dead. The food had been poisoned. A human must have placed the food there to kill creatures in that area. They had not known that it had been poisoned but Ratty's instinct had put them off trying the food.

The young Mouhume was now dead; his little body was left on the ground not seen by the others. The poison might already have been amongst the junk that had already been there or even the park assistant might have put it there, as some of the waste had been attracting rats. The fact is the Mouhumes had not come across this before. Now this would be an added danger. Not just the day-to-day wildlife that often got in the way but also this group of humans. They would have new experience in a world that they never knew existed.

They still had some distance to go before they would reach the warren and nothing to take back. It had been a disappointing hunting expedition and a poor hunting party: nothing but tragedy and failure from start to finish. A lesson had been learned about this part of world they had come across. They would have to learn and learn fast if they were to survive. Those who were lucky enough to escape and find others had more chance of survival than those who were now by themselves. This small group was getting smaller day-by-day with the new surroundings and new dangers they had never encountered before.

They had tools and weapons. They used thorns from the thorn bushes: they would snap them off the bush whilst they were still growing at the beginning of the year then dry them off in the hot sun to harden them. There was also a gooseberry bush with thorns that were long and sharp. It did not just supply them with food but also the tools and weapons that they needed to survive. Mouhumes learned from an early age.

Created and written by I C Henderson

Adventure of the Mouhumes
Jack and Annie's new
Visitors
Chapter 3
Back at the warren

TUBE CAME TO see them, he was not happy that they had gone without permission. This small group that went out hunting had lost lives, not just from those who had gone but also from those who had went looking for them.

Tube asked to see Ruddy, she was now in the lower part of the warren. She had gone to a little hole that she had scraped out from the soft sand, a small hole just big enough for her to squeeze into.

Ruddy's energy was low due to the fighting that night and lack of food. She had no idea if, when she fell asleep. would she wake up, part of her hoped that she would not. She had lost the love of her life. Just as she was going into a deep sleep she heard a voice. "Ruddy…Ruddy…are you awake…wake up Ruddy, you're needed...hurry" With her eyes squinting she looked towards the voice, once again the voice asked if she was awake

Ruddy jumped to her feet and got hold of the arms of the young Mouhume and pinned him to the ground. "Please let go…Tube asked me to come and see if you were ok and if you would come to the meeting area." The young Mouhume had heard stories about Ruddy, but when seeing her lying all helpless and almost dead, he thought that's all they must have been…stories. But when she jumped up and held his arms and had him on the ground before he knew what was going on, he then knew that the tales were true

Unknown to Ruddy, she had been asleep for almost a day and a half, Tube needed to see her. She had been the topic of conversation not all good. Some of those who had been talking about her, were afraid of her and wanted her out of the colony by any means. Even if it meant kill her but Tube knew they needed her more than she needed them.

Created and written by I C Henderson

Adventure of the Mouhumes
Jack and Annie's new
Visitors

He was defending her against some more of the younger and stronger Mouhumes. Ratty was telling them she had saved more lives than any other, if she was to go he would go too. She had also saved his life and there would be a great number of Mouhumes who would probably go as well.

The Mouhumes who had wanted her to go said that she would have to go quietly, as they could not lose any more Mouhumes from the colony. They new the colony would become weak if any other Mouhumes left with Ruddy.

Ruddy entered the large room with the young Mouhume at her side. The young Mouhume was asked if she had come willingly. "Yes" the young Mouhume replied "Ruddy put up no resistance"

Ruddy started to wonder what was going on. The young Mouhume stood back, just at the side of Ruddy. His hand went into his fur cover. Ruddy could see that his hand was on a sharp thorn similar to what she had often used herself. She could see the council talking quietly. The only two she knew were Tube and Ratty. The others had taken charge when they had found the rabbit warren, purely through numbers and aggression.

Tube was the leader but these young Mouhumes were now taking over. It was clear to see, Rug, dressed in bits of old bits of fabric, came forward. He was a big strong Mouhume he had a number of other Mouhumes at his side. He spoke out loud.

"Ruddy we have all decided that you should go. You are not welcome here anymore you have made too much trouble; we have lost too many Mouhumes with your actions. Collect your things and go without telling any of the others"

Ruddy looked around the room there must have been thirty Mouhumes if not more, all against her, she knew some would do

Created and written by I C Henderson

Adventure of the Mouhumes
Jack and Annie's new
Visitors

this but others she never thought they would do any harm towards the colony, even Tube and Ratty stood without saying anything. They must be standing down from the position, they had held as leaders. She had never known this to happen in the history of Mouhumes

"Do you not hear me go now or you will be put to death" Rug's voice filled with anger it was as if he wanted Ruddy to rise to the bait. He could see that she was worn out, she was as thin as a twig and she had little if any strength left. Ruddy started to walk away, back towards her area where she had left all her things. She could hear them laugh at her and then came a voice.

"You go now we need what ever you have, you go as you are" then more laughter

Ruddy stopped in her tracks. Just for a moment the young Mouhume, who had woken her, stood with a worried look on his face, Ruddy smiled at him then walked on heading towards the way out. The young Mouhume walked towards her his hand moved inside his over coat, towards the weapon Ruddy had seen him place there

As Ruddy got out of sight from the others the young Mouhume pulled the weapon out Ruddy jumped back giving herself some distance, there was a look of surprise on both their faces. He was handing it to her with the handle towards her. He told Ruddy he had been told what might happen and that he should give her something to help her, he then handed her some food.

"There had been talk for some time that the Mouhumes who had told you to leave were trying to take over. They knew that Tube wanted to move out of the warren. They thought that they should stay and they also knew you would protect Tube and Ratty. They decided to tell you now because you are at your weakest"

Adventure of the Mouhumes
Jack and Annie's new
Visitors

Ruddy took the weapon and the food from the young Mouhume. Then off she knew that she would not be safe. As she went around the next bend in the warren she was met by a number of Mouhumes, all with there own belongings

Must have been twenty or more, Tube and Ratty were there, they said that they would have to hurry as if those left in the warren knew what they were doing they would try to stop them leaving.

Ratty and some of the others took food supplies and some of the weapons that they would need. They had not taken a lot of food; just enough that they could carry. Each one had a little pouch not much bigger than a fist attached to a piece of string holding together what ever over coat that each Mouhume was wearing. Ruddy was then told that the other Mouhumes had sneaked out from some of the holes away from the others, after all it was a big warren.

The larder in the warren was away from the area that held the meeting. They had left enough food for those who were too afraid to leave with them, but those who had left knew it was the right thing to do.

Created and written by I C Henderson

Adventure of the Mouhumes
Jack and Annie's new
Visitors
Chapter 4
Departure

NOW THEY HAD to decide which way to go: over the river or up the steep hill? On the other side of the river they could see woodland and up the hill houses. The river was running fast from all the rain so that would be out of the question.

Up the hill there would also be danger, but between the two, the hill would really be the only way to go. They could not go back to the warren as the Mouhumes now in charge would most likely kill Ruddy and one or two of the others.

It was still light so they would have to keep under cover. There were trees and a hedge running up towards the top of the hill and there were areas where they had some ground cover, but parts with no cover at all.

They decided the hedge would be the better way to go. At least they could stay out of sight from humans and any prying eyes, such as wild birds of prey.

It was a long way to the top of the hill. Once they got to the top there was a road: cars were running in both directions. The Mouhumes had only seen cars a few times before in the car park but they had always been parked or moving slow. These cars where moving fast, how could they get to the other side?

Just then they heard a noise. Humans, they were jumping around with each other. There was also a strange smell. What could it be? The humans were carrying paper; putting their hands in, then pulling something out and eating whatever was in the paper.

The Mouhumes watched in amazement. It must be food! As the humans got near, things were dropping out of their hands and onto the ground. The smell was the same as what was in the air. All of a sudden one of them ran towards one of the others and threw his

Adventure of the Mouhumes
Jack and Annie's new
Visitors

package towards the other humans head, laughing as he did so; the contents fell to the ground. The humans all ran off. This was not that much different to how the Mouhumes sometimes carried on, apart from, they would never waste food.

Some of the Mouhumes had been so hungry as soon as the humans were out of sight they ran towards the food. They picked it up, dropping it just as quickly as it was hot. What was this food?

Suddenly a crow swooped down. Then others came. The Mouhumes quickly ran under a prickly bush. The crows, now around eight or ten, were eating the chips on the ground. Some were ripping the chip paper open to get the chips that were still wrapped up. The Mouhumes remained hidden.

Darkness was creeping in. The car lights were now turned on. This was strange for the Mouhumes. The crows were eating the last few scraps. The Mouhumes had a sinking feeling there would be no food left the crows had eaten all the chips.

26

Adventure of the Mouhumes
Jack and Annie's new
Visitors

The Mouhumes who were still on the other side of the road could not cross over. The road seemed to be getting more and more cars coming from both directions. They had to stay separated for longer than they wanted. The coming and going of the cars slowed down, then for a short time stopped. The rest of the Mouhumes finally crossed the road. They ran as fast as they could, straight into the shrubbery. There were a number of houses on that side of the road with fences around the gardens. Some had sheds. The Mouhumes knew they had to find shelter before it was completely dark.

The nearest houses were over a grass hill which was in the open. They would have to go now if they were going to go there. There were semi-detached houses with trees around the back and small front gardens.

The shrubbery was not large enough to hide them all so they would have to be quick to decide what to do. They made a dash in small numbers to the first house. It had a fence around it but had gaps big enough for any small animal to go through; even a full grown rabbit would not find it difficult to go through the fence.

In the yard at the back of the house there was a coal bunker. The Mouhumes had never seen a coal bunker. The hatch was open and lucky for them not a lot of coal inside. It was now dark. The bungalow had its lights on, giving a glow outside. Not that the Mouhumes needed any lighting to see, they had good eyes, even in the dark.

The coal bunker was not big enough for all the Mouhumes to be safe and sound and out of sight. Some of them ran to the tree that had some of its roots raised above the ground. They hid under the roots. There was more than enough room as there had been some earth dug away. Others hid under a shed in another garden. At this stage they had no idea of gardens, homes or anything else that belonged to those who lived in the houses but they would soon

Created and written by I C Henderson

Adventure of the Mouhumes
Jack and Annie's new
Visitors

find out the benefits of hedges and fences that ran around the different properties.

They needed to rest. They all carried little bits of food they had been given or had taken from the rabbit warren. Some would have to share as others had not had time, or the opportunity to collect anything.

Some came for the adventure; others knew they could not stay at the warren because they knew the Mouhumes had been split. They also knew the leadership was being questioned by a reckless young Mouhume who would never want anyone in his group who might have an opinion or those who might have high regards for Tube, Ruddy and any of the others that were highly respected or had any status. Now they were just trying to survive and find somewhere that they could settle down, not just for the night, but for the future.

After a while, Tube called for the elder Mouhumes, those who once held some sort of rank. He was aware that some had stayed at the warren. There were still a strong few who had proven themselves again and again, one more than most, Ruddy. She was something special. She hardly ever questioned his commands. She had the intelligence only to question when she thought she needed to and she could fight with speed and agility to get out of almost any danger.

Ratty was one of the first to come along with a number of others. Tube looked around, one was missing. He took a deep breath which was almost a sigh. What was she up to now? It was not the time to worry he had to tell the others his thoughts. Tube knew it was not safe, a rest would be ok but he himself had never been in such close contact with humans before or the buildings that they lived in. Tube explained that he thought it was best to move on. They had rested for a while, longer than he intended. Now it was time to decide which way they would go.

Created and written by I C Henderson

Adventure of the Mouhumes
Jack and Annie's new
Visitors

It was dark. Some of the lights that had been lighting the homes had now gone out. One or two in the distance still had a glow from up above on big poles. The Mouhumes had never seen such things. It was a lot to take in. These were new dangers.

After a short discussion they decided to go up towards the hill. Unknown to them, they were going deeper into a housing estate but from where they were they had little choice. Rug and the other Mouhumes were down that hill, along with other dangers.

It had been an unwritten rule: that Mouhumes did not kill another Mouhume unless other Mouhumes lives were in danger. Yet Rug seemed like he would kill anyone who got in his way. So Tube did not want to go back, he did not want Mouhumes fighting with each other.

They collected what things they had and what might be useful later. Then suddenly Ruddy was back with a bag full of food. She had been on a bird table and taken little bits of allsorts that were there. She had picked up a small bit of cloth rolled it out and filled it with as much as she could carry. It was shared around. Ratty gave her a smile but he knew Tube would be slightly angered as he did not want any of them wandering around this new world without help, or another Mouhume to at least warn the others.

They decided now might be the best time to move on again. The streets were almost empty apart from the odd car. Some of the Mouhumes had been covered in coal dust from the bunker. They were as black as night. Ratty saw this as good camouflage. They could go in and out of the hedges and not be seen by any humans or any other potential danger; but not all the Mouhumes wanted to be covered in this dust. SO they stayed as they were with whatever they had on.

They moved in groups of six or eight depending on age and ability. They all went the same way leaving a little distance between them. Some were as fast as lightning and others hesitated

29

Adventure of the Mouhumes
Jack and Annie's new
Visitors

so were just a little slower, some were just reckless, like Ruddy, but it all worked because no doubt, as things happen no matter how fast or even hesitating; only experience might get them out of a life or death situation.

They started to move further up the hill not knowing where it would take them. Ruddy was in front followed by Ratty who was finding it hard to keep up with her. He wondered what was driving her. It had not been that long since she was at death's door and now, as always, she was determined.

Tube had put together the teams, knowledge, strength, then speed – the first troop had been mostly strength to overcome any danger and deal with it and fast enough to go back to help any other group that may need a helping hand. The middle group was mixed with young and old, experience and youth. The two groups either side were strength and again age but would be able to help the old and young Mouhumes, if needed.

Those who had been in the coal bunker were as black as coal. The damp dust clung to the clothing they had on which in turn made them harder to see. They were like shadows, creeping in and out of the shrubs. They had never seen coal but soon found out the benefits of the dust.

They had to go over another road. This would be the second road they had ever crossed. Unlike before, it was now quiet. There was no traffic but they still went with uncertainty.

The sky was dark. The half moon was behind clouds. Street lights were giving off light. This was not something the Mouhumes wanted so they went quickly into gardens where they could hide in flower beds and other shrubbery.

They had no idea what they were looking for but they would know when they got there or found it. Ideally no houses, just

Adventure of the Mouhumes
Jack and Annie's new
Visitors

woodland would be the best place for them: a place that would cover and feed them and protect them from danger.

They had travelled through many gardens and were getting tired. They needed to find cover. Morning was coming it was starting to get light and they would have to get out of sight.

In the distance they could hear running water. This was never a bad thing as they would need a drink. They would often just go under a plant, depending on the type. It might be a flower that might hold water. Therefore, they would tip it and let the water pour into their mouths. Sometimes they even got washed this way whether it was intentional or not.

Ruddy was with Ratty. Ratty was not going to let her run off into what might be danger. He was not holding her back by her arms, but it was emotionally exhausting having to watch her. It was like trying to hold a wild bull back. She was ready to run off into the distance, wanting to see what was there. She always wanted to see what was around the next corner or what was over the hill. Just as he thought he had her under control they heard a noise in the distant. She was off as fast as ever. Her energy had been building up and now it was being released. Ratty and the rest try as they might; to keep up with her were left behind.

As Ruddy approached the noise, she hid behind the vegetation, looking out to see what it was. A white dog with a black patch over its eye was barking and rolling around a hedgehog. This was not something the Mouhumes liked. Hedgehogs could kill a Mouhume with their sharp prickly spines. The Mouhumes could do nothing with a hedgehog so they kept away when possible.

The dog was rolling the hedgehog around the grass, hitting it with his paw and yelping as he did so, one or two spikes were in his face. The dog moved the hedgehog near to the hedge then the hedgehog unrolled and went on its way. The dog, covered in blood

Adventure of the Mouhumes
Jack and Annie's new
Visitors

from his paw and face, was lying on the grass rubbing his face trying to get the quills out but each time pushing them in deeper.

Ruddy was memorized by this. The dog was as round as a barrel a strong looking muscular beast. It was whining. She crept towards the dog from behind, the only experience the Mouhumes had with dogs had not been pleasant.

She jumped onto the back of his neck. The dog froze. Then Ruddy, holding on to the dog's fur, bent down towards the side of the dog's face and started to pull out the spines. The dog was still not moving as she pulled out another one. She then leant towards the other side and pulled the last one from his face. The dog then rolled over onto his side and lifted his paw up as if to show that he had a quill in his pad. Ruddy looked at his pad then pulled hard to get it out.

Ruddy had no sooner done this, when she heard a noise from the top of the garden. Another dog, similar to this one, but with different colours was barking. This was a female dog; she came running down the garden towards Ruddy with bad intentions on her face.

Created and written by I C Henderson

Adventure of the Mouhumes
Jack and Annie's new
Visitors

The white dog jumped up head butting the other dog, knocking the wind out of her, knocking her over. Then he stood over her as if he was telling her something. The dark colour dog got to her feet then ran towards Ruddy. Her expression now changed. She had mischief but not in a bad way, more playful.

Her head went down and her front legs pouncing on the ground. She began jumping from side to side. Her rear end was up and her tail was wagging. She wanted to play. Ruddy walked towards the dog, rubbing the dog's face. Then the dog licked Ruddy: its wet slavery tongue was licking Ruddy from her feet to the top of her head, covering her with saliva. She was soaking wet

Ratty and the others were now hiding in the vegetation. They had not seen everything that had happened but made up their minds that she was something of a marvel. No other Mouhume had ever made contact with any type of creature, yet to be licked with affection was an achievement. They were amazed and amused by what they were seeing but they needed to move on. Suddenly, a voice from the house was calling the dogs.

"Buster, Tilly come in."

The dogs stopped what they were doing and ran up towards the house, wagging their tails with affection for the voice calling for them. As they got nearer to the house the white dog, Buster

Adventure of the Mouhumes
Jack and Annie's new
Visitors

turned and looked down the garden. His body language and the look in his eye, was full of appreciation as if to say thank you.

Tilly, as always, was playful with her owner. She barked and jumped around with fondness and with misbehaviour in her eyes. If you never knew the dog you would be a bit apprehensive, but her owner knew it was just Tilly's way for attention. Buster was bigger in build but just the same as Tilly with his playful ways. When his owner came in from work he would take her shoes and run off with them just for a chase.

The two dogs were of similar age. Buster was a year older. Not that you could tell. They would walk for hours and when they got back they would still run around the house. Kez lived with her father who was away most of the time with her brother. They worked all over the world. Her father was the owner of Buster and her brother the owner of Tilly. The dogs were both English bull terriers. Kez liked the company of the dogs and often had Tilly when her brother was away but when he was back he would take Tilly back. It was always just a short time that he was back so that was not too bad and he would be around most Sundays for lunch. Kez was okay with this as she had as much energy as them so they were well matched.

Once again the Mouhumes had to move on. They moved as it turned out, about two gardens higher. It was a big garden with a large shed, a large greenhouse and another smaller shed just behind them.

Created and written by I C Henderson

Adventure of the Mouhumes
Jack and Annie's new
Visitors
Chapter 5
Out of Sight

IT WAS GETTING lighter now so they would be better off hiding with some sort of shelter over them. They could hear running water from the top of the garden. One of the Mouhumes scaled up the side of the shed, high enough to see where the sound of running water was coming from he told the others that it was at the top of the garden. The pond was nearly as big and as wide as the garden with a bridge over it.

But now they would have to hide as they could hear the cars starting up, doors being shut, humans talking and plates being scraped in gardens nearby. It was as if all the humans woke up at the same time. The Mouhumes could now be in danger of being seen so they would have to move in and around the shrubbery. This was something they could do easily. They hurried. There was plenty of room under the two sheds, plenty of buckets and plant pots lying around that would give them cover if needed.

There were around ten or so under the smaller shed and the rest under the larger shed which was nearly twice the size as the smaller shed. One or two of the Mouhumes under the smaller shed noticed a hole in the floor, so they climbed up to see what was in the shed.

It was a right mess. There were tables, chairs and even an old lawn mower. There were also tools of all types: some for the garden and some for other things. None of the tools looked as if they had been used for a long time and everything seemed like it had been put away in a hurry. Things were piled on top of each other but for a Mouhume it was okay as there were plenty of hiding places.

It turned out to be a sunny day. There was not a lot of cloud, like it had been over the last few weeks. Now they were in a human region: a dangerous place they had no idea about so they would

Created and written by I C Henderson

Adventure of the Mouhumes
Jack and Annie's new
Visitors

have to make do with where they were until darkness came and then they could move on.

The leaders, who had gathered under the larger shed, were talking about what they should do. Should they send two or three teams out in different directions to save time later in order to see which way they should go and which place would be better? Or should they wait until all the others had returned as a number had gone out looking for food after they had decided they would stay under the shed during daylight.

A group of Mouhumes who had went in search of food, once things had gone quiet, after a short time the noise returned. The humans were back but this time from what they could see they had some that were younger and smaller.

The Mouhumes watched as some of the younger humans went into a big motor vehicle, this had lots of windows. They could hardly believe what they were seeing. Humans were going into these things. The Mouhumes could see them sitting: some quiet, some clearly finding it unsettling and some were laughing and were jumping from one place to another. The older humans were waving their hands, then walked off as the motor vehicle drove away. It was a strange place to say the least.

Once again it went quiet, hardly a human to be seen. The Mouhumes, who had been watching, could now go back and report what they had seen.

The Mouhumes leaders wondered if this was a daily ritual but one thing they had no doubt about, was they must leave as soon as possible. They would send small teams out to find a way out and to find food. They knew the pond near the house would provide them with water.

They got five sets of two to go and explore the area. It might be the right time in daylight and smaller groups would hardly be

Created and written by I C Henderson

Adventure of the Mouhumes
Jack and Annie's new
Visitors

seen by any potential enemies. At night time other dangers would show themselves. At least in daylight they could see a good distance ahead this would help avoid any possible danger.

So five groups of two Mouhumes went on their way, they knew what they had to do and the areas they had to go. Tube, the leader, simply spread his fingers out onto the dry ground under the shed and the groups had to go in that direction. Those left behind knew which group went in which direction: the small finger was two experienced Mouhumes, those who went in the direction of the thumb were also experienced Mouhumes, the ones that went in direction of the index finger would also be experienced, those who went in the direction of the middle finger were likely to be the least experienced and those on the ring finger were there to help, if and when needed.

Off they went, spread out and hidden away. It was a journey they needed to do, they left with their little bags of food, water and a time they had been given to go as far as they could, taking in everything they possibly could then to return and report back.

They went through gardens and open fields that the humans had used, the Mouhumes knew this by the tell tale signs. If there were any obstacles in their way they would have to change direction slightly, so the Mouhumes would often leave a sign, a broken twig, a scuff on the ground, not always the best sign, however, it was still a sign of sorts, it was better than none at all. Especially if they ever got lost and a rescue party would be needed to come look for them,

When they reached the end of their time, they found themselves still in the large housing estate, it was never ending. Some gardens were better than others. Some just had a lawn: that was no good for the Mouhumes an open space like that would be fatal.

Created and written by I C Henderson

Adventure of the Mouhumes
Jack and Annie's new
Visitors

It had been quiet but for some reason the humans started to appear again. Cars were pulling up with children and parents coming home. It was not as busy as the morning time but there were still too many humans arriving. It was lunchtime; some children were coming back home for lunch as well as some of the adults. It was nothing like it had been in the morning and nothing like it would be later that evening.

Time was up they headed back too the others, back towards the two large sheds. Back to where they realised was the most secure place they had found as most the other gardens had little, if anything, to hide under. In the distance all they could see were more and more houses.

When they arrived back to the sheds they reported what they had seen while on their journey both the good and the bad. They explained that they had taken a little longer to return than expected but that was due to the fact that it was now lunchtime and humans were back around the houses and they had to hide and keep out of sight, they reported everything back.

Tube trusted the judgment of those he had sent out. He had kept Ruddy back, as she, more than any needed to rest. Tube knew if they were to stand any chance, he needed her at full strength. He was right to do so; she slept most of the time the trackers had been out.

Outside it had gone quiet again. They knew they would be safer staying another night, they would all rest and tomorrow they would send another team out in other directions to see what if any way they could go. In no time at all, in the smaller shed, they had all the space cleared and hiding areas created to keep them safe. Under the big shed they noticed pieces of wood and all sorts of other things that they would be able to make use of.

This was only going to be a short stop. This was not going to be a permanent place. They knew what they had in their old home

Created and written by I C Henderson

Adventure of the Mouhumes
Jack and Annie's new
Visitors

and that's what they wanted back. A place away from humans and any danger humans brought with them. They wanted a place on top of a hill with woodland around them so they could see from the tree tops as far away as possible. They wanted to be able to see if human machines were heading towards them to give them a chance to escape, not like what had happened to them before. It was sudden and it wiped most of them out, killing some and those who had been lucky enough to flee were now spilt into areas that they had never visited before.

The Mouhumes were in a world they had no idea about. It seemed that they might be stuck. If they went back the way they came, the dangers could be even greater so they needed to find a way out of this human pack and move on. They started to settle down and rest.

Soon they knew they would have to go out gathering food. What kind of food would they find? They had seen humans putting food out on, what they could only call high platforms, for the birds. Did the humans worship the birds? A large number of houses had these raised areas. Birds and Mouhumes did not get on that well. Equally wanting the same food and often ended up in a fight. Depending on which type of bird, the Mouhumes often had to take a step back.

It was nothing they had not encountered before. There were one or two Mouhumes who were good climbers but even they had problems with most of these bird tables because the platform was normally over a post. They might have been able to climb the post, but at the top they had no way of getting onto the platform.

During the night before they settled down, one or two of the Mouhumes had a look around the area. The garden next to them had lots of little houses, almost if not better, than the human houses around them. There were different in styles, and each one looked as if they had been constructed for some creature not much different

39

Adventure of the Mouhumes
Jack and Annie's new
Visitors

in size to the Mouhumes. They mentioned this to one of the older Mouhumes but received no response.

The elder Mouhume had then reported this to the Mouhumes leaders. They all agreed that they would have to be on their guard, so that night they had more than the normal number of guards on watch. The night passed without any misfortune. Different types of animals had come their way but nothing amiss. Even one or two creatures they had not seen before had passed through and some they were only too aware of. On the whole, it was a quiet night.

The next day came. There was a lot of noise again and it lasted for a good while. The dry ground under the shed where Tube, the day earlier, had pressed his hand to create the directions for them to go, could still be seen. Tube now wiped it clear with his foot so he could use it for today's directions, even though they knew which way they had already gone the day before.

They had a number of ways to show other Mouhumes which way they had gone, that only a Mouhume would know, something as simple as putting or turning a leaf: even better if there were a large number of leaves lying on the ground. A Mouhume would see the difference almost straight away and know which way to go.

The Mouhumes had experience along with great fighting skills. The younger Mouhumes would have to learn from the older ones and learn quickly. They knew that with these strange times and new experiences, they would always have to be quick thinking and have fast reflexes. Normally there would always be at least a third of the community resting, enabling these skills to remain sharp.

The noise started to dim. The humans just like the day before thinned out; they were going about their way and just like the day before they would return later that evening. This was the time the Mouhumes would have to be out of sight.

Created and written by I C Henderson

Adventure of the Mouhumes
Jack and Annie's new
Visitors

The next squad, who were going out to find a new and hopefully a safe area so that they could make a new home, as those the day before were given their directions, food and whatever else they needed. A small pouch was tied around each of their waists: a bladder, no bigger than a Mouhume's fist that once belonged to some poor creature that had met their misfortune, was now used as a water carrier.

This time Tube only sent four pairs of scouts. The time came for him to place his hand in the dry earth to direct them. His fingers were closer than the day before and they were told how far they must go and the time they had to do it in. The time was a little longer than the day before.

As always they had to make a decision after reporting back, whether it was going to be worth the journey for the others? A heavy burden for any to make, that was why Tube would listen to each and every Mouhume individually who made it back.

It was like a military operation with speed and agility. They had gone in and out of hedges and undergrowth. In no time at all they had gone through a number of gardens then they came to the beginning of woodland.

First they had to get through the fence that was separating the last garden to the woodland. It was easy enough: a wired fence with holes in it as big as tennis balls. They had not got far when a smell of rotten flesh was in the air. They would have to go and inspect what it was.

The sight that greeted them was breathtaking. They were shocked this was something they had never seen before. Black bin bags were ripped open: parts of birds in one and the other had parts of rabbits. Rats were ripping into the bags taking out the rotten bodies.

Adventure of the Mouhumes
Jack and Annie's new
Visitors

Suddenly another bag was thrown over from one of the gardens. They heard a human laughing; another bag was thrown over, ripping open as it landed on to the thorn bush. No sooner had the human gone when hundreds of rats came out from the undergrowth. It was a terrible sight to see and no way could they go that way. The Mouhumes would be killed!

The scouts had the sense to remain far enough away when this feeding frenzy that was going on; the dead animals had caused a distraction. Quickly they turned and hurried back, leaving no trace that they had been there. If the rats had not been so intense with what they were doing then the Mouhumes would have been slaughtered, there was no doubt about that.

They headed back, taking a different route so that if they had been seen they would not lead any enemy straight back to where they were based.

This took them back in the direction they had first come days earlier. The same direction but to a different area, it was five or so gardens apart, a big enough area for it to be new and undiscovered. They gathered back together. They were all shaken, shocked and bewildered about the events they had just seen. None of the group had the experience to deal with what they had seen.

They had forgotten to leave signals for any Mouhume that might come looking for them, but under the circumstances they could be forgiven. Each of them held on to their weapons, one had a nail and one or two had the spines from the hedgehog that they encountered days before. They split up again so they would be harder to detect, but they kept in sight of each other.

They moved in and out of the gardens with speed and agility but not the same mindset as they had only a short time before. This time it was a matter of life or death and the determination each one had, it was going to be life first before death.

Created and written by I C Henderson

Adventure of the Mouhumes
Jack and Annie's new
Visitors

The scouts had recovered their directions. They were back on the track they had came through days earlier, there were still one or two directions that had been left days earlier by those who had been in front. A little mark here and a twig there, only a Mouhume would know the signs. This put them at rest to a certain degree, at least now they knew they were not that far from the shed.

As they approached the garden they were greeted by those who were on the lookout. One or two led them to Tube; he was in the smaller shed with the hole in the floor. They were working on defences so that if they had an attack they could prevent anything getting into the shed of a similar size.

They knew the drill: not to talk to anyone about what they had seen, good or bad. Tube had to be the first to know and sometimes one or two of the Mouhumes that were high up in the leadership, but that was only when Tube needed another opinion, only when he was unsure what they should do for the best.

Tube came as they sat down eating and drinking. Tube knew by the expression on each of their faces that things had not gone too well. Tube called some of the other Mouhumes over to listen. Carefully they listened as they got the reports back from each Mouhume who had been on that expedition.

By the time they listened to the last one they knew that danger was not far away and in great numbers. Ratty who had sat listening knew by the numbers they had the Mouhumes would not stand a chance. They would be killed and eaten.

The talks went on late into the early hours of the next day. What should they do? Try somewhere else? Go back to the warren and join forces with Rug?

The decision was too much for any of them. It would have to be a vote and if split, it would make one side even more vulnerable. As they were talking about the possibilities, some of the

Adventure of the Mouhumes
Jack and Annie's new
Visitors

Mouhumes continued digging under the large shed; they were getting a good way down. In their minds it was going to be for a short time. But for now they needed somewhere for safety, at least until they knew what they were going to do.

Created and written by I C Henderson

Adventure of the Mouhumes
Jack and Annie's new
Visitors

Chapter 6

ONE MORNING AS dawn was breaking, Jack was sitting in his chair looking out of the window down towards the waterfall, when he noticed something scurrying across the bridge- "looks like we have mice" he thought to himself.

Upstairs Annie had woken up and was getting up to see where Jack was. Annie knew that he was getting depressed, since the accident sleep was something they did not get a lot of.

Jack just could not get comfortable for very long, because of this Jack was getting fed-up with this and the pain.

Annie often awoke through the night when Jack was in pain and would get up to see if she could help.

Jack could hear Annie coming down the staircase, the floorboards often squeaked near the bottom of the stairs.

"Annie come look at this" he called "Quick see this"

"What's the matter?" Annie asked as she came through the living room.

"We must have mice running around the pond, after our breakfast will you get two or three mouse traps, when you go out?" Asked Jack

Annie agreed as she did not want the garden overrun with mice and she knew the mouse traps would keep Jack occupied for some time, so she would go along with it. Jack told Annie that they could put one in the greenhouse and some in the flowerbeds around the fishpond.

Created and written by I C Henderson

Adventure of the Mouhumes
Jack and Annie's new
Visitors

All at once he had his day worked out; this was the best Annie had seen him in months. He was making plans and had a day to fill.

"Are you coming with me to the shops?" Annie asked Jack. "You could see what things you may need"

Annie knew that there were a lot of different types of traps. It was also a chance to get Jack out of the house.

"Yes I better come as there are a number of different types of mouse trap's available so when do you think you will be ready?" Jack said all ready and wanting to go.

"Jack you have not been this keen for a long time, give me a chance" replied Annie as she started to get herself ready "I've just got up let me at least get a cup of coffee"

Jack was full of enthusiasm, he had not been like this for some time; Annie was pleased to see him full of excitement.

Annie got her drink and took it back to the bedroom so that she could get dressed, when she was ready off they went to the local DIY store; while there they looked around, and then decided to buy two rat traps and two mousetraps.

Jack as eager as ever, paid for them, and then wanted to get straight back and sort out what he was going to do in the garden. "This will sort them out, I'll get started when I get back, do you think we could go back now?" he asked Annie.

Annie smiled to herself, not saying anything she thought to herself he's like a young boy wanting to play with his new toys.

"Yes we will not be long now" Annie replied.

Created and written by I C Henderson

Adventure of the Mouhumes
Jack and Annie's new
Visitors

When they got back home Jack looked around the garden to see the best place to put the traps.

Then Annie came out "Jack don't put them out just now, just the birds might get hurt in them" Jack agreed "I'll just look to see the best place, I'll put them out tonight"

Jack had not thought about the birds, he was glad that Annie had realized, and that he was just going to put them out. So he went back into to the house so that he could draw a diagram, so he could remember where he had put the traps

That night Jack placed the traps, one under the bridge, one near the waterfall, the other two he placed in the greenhouse, well, he thought to himself, this should help clear up the mouse problem.

Adventure of the Mouhumes
Jack and Annie's new
Visitors
Chapter 7
Indecisive Tactics

TUBE AND RATTY sent the word around for all the Mouhumes to gather under the larger of the two sheds. There was far more of them than Tube had first thought so some ended up under the other shed as well.

They were told what the scouts had seen the day before, Tube told them all about the human and the dead animal remains, then they were told about the number of rats that arrived to eat the remains.

There was a lot of talking, then suddenly a voice from the middle of the crowd, Joy, spoke up and asked why they could not stay here: food was ample and some had already started to make living accommodation under the sheds.

Others were still talking amongst themselves; no-one could clearly hear what was being said, some were agreeing and others wanted to move on to find a place out of sight from the humans who seemed to murder creatures on mass numbers then feed them to rats. Who were even more dangerous in large numbers.

Rats had always been around, never too far away from any food source but the Mouhumes had never seen this amount. The discussions lasted a long time, in the end they all agreed they had to make it as safe as possible while they were there.

Everyone left and went back to whatever they were doing before their meeting; those who had been hunting for food went on their way whilst other Mouhumes went to rest or continue making their accommodation comfortable and secure.

Meanwhile Tube and Ratty were discussing the next group of scouts who might be going this time. Tube and Ratty were also going too.

Created and written by I C Henderson

Adventure of the Mouhumes
Jack and Annie's new
Visitors

Ratty started to pick those who he wanted. They only needed six more to make eight in total. Happy with those he picked, he knew they were strong, fast, had agility and between them they could cover a large area in little time. As there was only one more area they had not explored they needed to be experienced Mouhumes.

It would be later that night when the streets went silent. It still had danger but no different to what they were used to in the field they had moved from.

As the rest of the Mouhumes went about their business Tube and Ratty and the others went on their way to discover what ever lay ahead, wonderful lands, they hoped.

Back in camp, Woozy was looking around the next door's garden at the magnificent model houses they were big enough for a Mouhume to go in. He had seen nothing like it, he wondered if the human who lived in the house built these and if so why?

Inside were rooms, these were not just models these were homes for something small like a Mouhume, but what? Woozy looked around, he sensed something was watching him, he turned around quickly, nothing was there feeling uneasy he left in a hurry.

Back under the shed some of the Mouhumes had started to dig into the dry earth. In no time at all they reached clay. This was met with mixed feelings. It was hard for them to dig through clay. They had gone through a lot in a short time and digging clay used up a lot of energy. They had never worked so hard but they needed it to be safe and underground would be the best place to be. Linden was helping to dig out the earth under the shed. They had done a lot. Most of the Mouhumes could live there for now. This was good practise, if and when they moved on because no matter where they moved. Underground was nearly all the same and they could shape it as they needed it to be.

Created and written by I C Henderson

Adventure of the Mouhumes
Jack and Annie's new
Visitors

Ruddy was out and about. She had not been asked to go on the scouting expedition. She was doing her own exploring, five gardens up. Next to a big grassed area with a path leading down. She hid in amongst some plants, watching humans walking up and down. She was trying to understand them: how they talked, what they were doing, where they were going, what was in the bags? There was so much going on in her head, she needed to know.

The garden she was in had beetroot growing. She had never had beetroot before and she was feeling a little hungry so she bit into the beetroot, still in the ground. It was firm but not what she had expected, it was not dry or juicy but just right. In no time at all she had eaten nearly all of what was shown above the soil.

She had never felt so good. The beetroot made her feel different. The nutrients in the beetroot were something the Mouhumes had never had before. She would have to go and tell the rest of the Mouhumes how good she felt and they would have to dig up this wonderful plant. As she approached the camp the look on some of the Mouhumes faces was of shock, one or two even ran away.

What was going on? She turned around quickly to see if there was something behind her. Why were some of the Mouhumes running away? Then she was surrounded by a number of Mouhumes.

All they could see was that Ruddy was covered in a red and purple colouring; it was all over her mouth and her hands. They wondered if she had she been attacked but by what? This was not blood from a Mouhume, What had she done?

She pulled a chunk of beetroot out from her pouch and bit into it. To those watching it was as if she was biting into a lump of flesh. She then passed it onto a younger Mouhume who then took a bite.

Created and written by I C Henderson

Adventure of the Mouhumes
Jack and Annie's new
Visitors

It was as if the goodness from the plant was absorbed almost straight away by the Mouhumes body. It was something the Mouhumes had been missing and needed.

They all had a taste. The goodness from the beetroot worked: helping to feed them and gave them the nutrition that they needed to help with healing. The only downside was that they were covered in the purple juice making them look frightening because they had a reddish purple colouring around their mouths.

The next thing they did was to collect as many beetroots as they could. The gardener lost half of his crop.

Once back, they had to get cleaned up, luckily for them there was plenty of water at the back of the shed. There were three water barrels and one had a tap, the Mouhumes worked out how to turn it on and off, ideal to help get them clean.

***

Meanwhile Tube and Ratty had reached as far as they would go. They had travelled fast and now it was time to rest. They sat under a bush that had grown out of control, but provided good cover for them. There they took out their little bags of food.

Looking around while sitting, the Mouhumes took in the surrounding area. It was nowhere a Mouhume could or would want to live. It had been a place where humans had once lived but now it was rubble. Houses were half pulled down, machines pushed and pulled at the bricks and there was a dusty smell in the air from the machines.

Tube realised that all the areas had been checked, they had travelled as far as they could go without having to stay in a makeshift shelter. Tube thought about doing that but as always that would have to be a decision made by all the Mouhumes.

Adventure of the Mouhumes
Jack and Annie's new
Visitors

After they rested for a short time they were ready to go back. Ratty said that they should go back a slightly different way. Tube was unsure. But as usual Ratty persuaded Tube. He could put up a good argument: the path they would go back along Ratty would be on right side. He convinced Tube to go on the left side but still in sight of each other, there would be four in each group.

This would give them a better idea of what was around the area and if it looked promising they could quickly look it over. It made sense; a wider area was being explored. But Tube's worry was that if they got into danger would the others see and be able to help?

In no time at all they were back in the gardens belonging to humans. Some gardens they had not been in so this might be beneficial to them discovering more about the surrounding area. Tube did not want to stay any longer than needed. He had plans to move on once they all had a day or two of resting and collecting food.

They finally approached the path they had previously come on. It had been a disappointing mission. There was nothing at all to show for it. So when Tube and Ratty and the other explorers came back in just a short time, the change was astonishing. As they approached the camp, to there surprise it had altered, the work that had been done was amazing.

The goodness from the beetroot had given the Mouhumes energy as it released its nourishment into their little bodies.

Something they had needed but never had. Some who had been under the weather had also tried it and seemed better in no time.

Tube and Ratty went around the new camp. It was almost finished. If they had not been intending to move on, it would be as

Created and written by I C Henderson

Adventure of the Mouhumes
Jack and Annie's new
Visitors

good as they could possibly want but they felt that they must still go and find a safer place. But this would be a good place. Safety and defensive devices had been put in place so as a short term solution it would do.

Tube and Ratty were given some beetroot and almost immediately they felt the benefits. The beetroot had worked like nothing they had before, it was like magic. The nourishment they had been missing was in this one plant.

It was getting dark now and they needed to sort a few things out. They needed to arrange who was doing what tasks the next day? What they needed to do and how far would the next group of scouts go? All of these things would have to be discussed.

Created and written by I C Henderson

Adventure of the Mouhumes
Jack and Annie's new
Visitors

Chapter 8

THE NEXT MORNING Jack was first up as always, he looked out of the window he could not see the trap under the bridge, looking confused Annie was up and half-asleep.

"What's happening Jack?" She asked as she rubbed her face trying to wake up properly.

"The trap, it's gone!" Jack replied in a disappointed tone.

Looking and feeling confused Jack could not work out what had happened to the trap .He got his crutches and went outside.

"I'm going to see if it has fallen into the pond"

Annie shook her head as if he was an old fool.

"I'll stick the kettle on for a cup of tea, do you want one Jack"?

Jack gave no answer as his head was all over the place; he was determined to find his trap.

"Don't answer you old daft…" muttered Annie

Just then Jack put his head back in the door with a smile on his face.

"I'm not old, and yes I will have a cup, hurry up, just put it on the table I'll not be long"

Annie having been caught out laughed, and got on with the breakfast.

Jack went out into the garden; he looked around the pond, but could not see the trap he had placed under the bridge.

Created and written by I C Henderson

Adventure of the Mouhumes
Jack and Annie's new
Visitors

The one near the waterfall was still there.

He then walked over to the greenhouse to see if the traps had been sprung, he noticed one of the traps in the greenhouse had something in it. Whatever it was looked bigger than a mouse but smaller than a Rat it was like nothing he had ever seen before, so Jack buried it at the bottom of the garden.

He wondered if he needed a rat trap near the pond, as he only had small mouse traps around there, so he decided to move a larger trap from the greenhouse, closer to the fishpond.

Created and written by I C Henderson

Adventure of the Mouhumes
Jack and Annie's new
Visitors

Chapter 9
Next Door

EARLY THE NEXT morning Ruddy was doing what she did best and that was exploring and getting herself into trouble. She thought that something in the next garden had been watching her but she could not see what it was. Every time she turned around, no matter how fast, there was nothing there.

She was determined to find out what it was. Some of the other Mouhumes were waking up as she went out with her hunting weapons. One of the younger Mouhumes saw this and sneaked behind her, following her from a distance.

Ruddy was fast and almost in stealth mode. She was through the hedge that parted the two gardens in a flash. She looked around at the different plants and the life-like ornaments of animals and houses. She thought the houses looked as real as the human houses. Yes, she thought, they were small enough for something similar to her size to live in.

She had been in one of the houses a day earlier but now she was on the hunt to see what might live in there. Ruddy would find out one way or another. She drew out her sharp thorn and she held it in her mouth so that her hands were still free. If needed, she could scale up or down the plants.

As she entered the little house she was astonished how big it seemed inside. It was hollow but the ground went down some 12 inches or so. She jumped to the bottom to see if there were any holes or tunnels leading off underground.

Nothing, empty, all she could see was a deep hole with a model house above it. She looked up at the roof of the house. A little light was coming in through the doorway she had entered. One or two cracks in the sides and roof were also letting in light.

Created and written by I C Henderson

Adventure of the Mouhumes
Jack and Annie's new
Visitors

It took a little time for her eyes to adjust to the difference in light from outside. She stood in the middle turning around and looking from side to side. Nothing seemed out of place. She could not sense anything that might be harmful.

Then, suddenly, she knew she was not alone. She jumped up the side of the hole, heading towards the doorway and reached out, grabbing a hold of whatever it was hiding at the side of the outside wall. She then flung it on the floor and jumped onto it, with her thorn just stopping at the side of the Young Mouhumes neck.

The young Mouhume had followed her. He had almost lost his life. There were not many Mouhumes who could have stopped in that situation. It would be kill or be killed. A split moment, a slight hesitation has cost many a Mouhume their life.

Fortunately for the young Mouhume it was Ruddy. She was the fastest and most skilful of the Mouhumes. That was exactly what all the young Mouhumes had talked about. Not the leaders, like Ratty or Tube but Ruddy.

Ruddy picked up the young Mouhume and slapped his head with the back of her hand. No words were said as Ruddy had already realised that something else was close by and she knew this time it was not a Mouhume.

She pulled the young Mouhume up by the scruff of his neck and put him in the ornamental house she had just come out of.

He hid behind the doorway knowing that something was going to happen, scared for his life and for Ruddy he kept still. In the meantime, Ruddy was climbing up one of the tall plants. Where she would get a better view of what was around her.

Nothing seemed to be obviously wrong. The birds were still on different plants picking insects off. They would normally be the

Created and written by I C Henderson

Adventure of the Mouhumes
Jack and Annie's new
Visitors

first to be off if danger was around. So what could it be? Even she could not understand, but her senses were never wrong.

She jumped back to the ground and headed back to where the young Mouhume was so she could get him out of the way. This was not somewhere she wanted to be, especially with a young inexperienced Mouhume.

As she approached the little house she suddenly turned around and jumped on whatever it was. She held on to it and was just about to strike it when she was lifted up into the air. Whatever they were she had two holding onto her, one was still on the ground as she looked down to see what she was up against.

It was something she had never seen before. Its body was similar size to hers but it had wings like a dragonfly. That was it, it was a giant dragonfly. By now she was high in the sky then suddenly she felt herself being let go. She spun towards the earth knowing that she would die. There was nothing she could do.

The young Mouhume on the ground, with fear in his eyes saw what was happening. This was Ruddy, the bravest Mouhume ever! Now he was going to see her end, not in any battle they had encountered before. Yes she had fought birds that had tried similar things, picking up and dropping the enemy from the sky.

Ruddy was heading towards the earth with speed. Now her back would smash onto the ground. She could not turn around. She stopped trying and accepted her fate. Allsorts was going through her head. It seemed to last forever.

There was not a thud as you would expect but a gentle landing. The thing that she had attacked earlier had now swooped up and with precision timing saved Ruddy. Ruddy's weight knocked the wind out of this thing and they crashed landed onto the earth, both rolling into a heap.

Created and written by I C Henderson

Adventure of the Mouhumes
Jack and Annie's new
Visitors

Ruddy was first up, dazed and unsteady on her feet. The two others who had dropped her landed beside them then jumped onto Ruddy pinning her down and knocking her weapon out of reach.

The young Mouhume saw this so he started to run towards them, he ran straight into a fist, knocking him head over heels. He rolled then jumped to his feet as he had seen Ruddy do. His legs were trembling with fear and his head was still in a daze from the blow to his head. Before he knew it he was also taken to the ground with one of these creatures on top of him, who was laughing at the same time at how easy it was to take them down.

Ruddy, trying hard to get up, was unable to do so. She had never felt so useless in all her conflicts. She closed her eyes knowing that she had met her match and now she believed she was going to meet her end just like she had taken so many lives before.

But instead she was picked up. It was not that different to how she had picked up the young Mouhume not that long before. The creature that broke her fall had picked himself up. The two who had took Ruddy for a flight stood in close proximity watching for anymore violent behaviour.

Ruddy looked at this creature and tried to work out what it was. Then it started to talk to Ruddy. To Ruddy's surprise she could understand what was being said.

It turned out he had been watching the Mouhumes from a distance and had seen how Ruddy was fearless. Her speed and her agility was something he had not seen before in any other living thing and curiosity had got the better of him.

They had been watching all the time but not letting themselves be seen. They could blend into any surroundings. Ruddy had the ability and skill to know that something was nearby and grab hold of one. That in itself was something they had rarely come across.

59

Adventure of the Mouhumes
Jack and Annie's new
Visitors

Their ability was better than any Mouhume could ever be. They were not as aggressive as the Mouhumes but they could defend themselves.

They told Ruddy the humans call them fairies and they could understand all living creatures, not that they got on with them all. They had their enemies, just as all living things did. As much as they tried to get along with everyone, sometimes this was mistaken for weakness.

As this was being explained to Ruddy the young Mouhume had gotten away to get help for Ruddy. In no time at all there was a number of Mouhumes ready to fight for Ruddy. This would not happen for just any Mouhume. But Ruddy had saved so many, now they needed to try and save her.

They got themselves into position ready to attack. After all there was only three they could see and they didn't look very strong. Before anyone could say anything the young Mouhume went to attack the fairy who had punched him in the face earlier.

In no time at all Ruddy was back on her feet. She stood between the fairy and the Mouhume and the other Mouhumes stopped in their tracks. Ruddy called for them to stop. This was something she had never experienced before.

Dropping from a great height she was certainly at death's door and there was nothing she could have done to avoid her end but for this fairy. Without doing what he had done for her, her fortune would have been sealed.

She also knew the Mouhumes were at a disadvantage. The fairies had speed, wing power and strength, and maybe more skills, and even more in hiding, ready to come out and attack or defend.

Adventure of the Mouhumes
Jack and Annie's new
Visitors

Her knowledge and instinct knew they would be better friends than enemies. The Mouhumes stood down but would be ready for a full attack if needed, watching for any sudden or aggressive movements.

Ratty stood near Ruddy and looked at her in a way as if to say was she all right? Without saying a word Ruddy knew what he wanted to know.

Her eyes told him what he needed to know but even behind her assurance, her eyes, when Ratty looked deeper, not even Ruddy could conceal her fear.

After a short time the fairy who had been attacked by Ruddy came forward and told Ratty they had unfortunately met during a moment of madness and all they wanted was to make acquaintances.

The Fairy told them that he had not intended to startle Ruddy, who in turn had attacked him, knocking him to the ground. His friends had to save him and the only way they knew was to get her into the air. They had seen her fight and knew this was their only chance.

Saying this took nothing away from Ruddy's fighting skill. Her reputation was still intact, but to her she knew that she had no chance. She was as weak as a baby and would have been easy killed if not for the mercy of the fairy.

Her confidence had been dented. She had faced death many times and never thought anything of it, but what had just happened, had her self-esteem at an all time low. She could hear the younger Mouhumes talking about it and how she had, once again, escaped death.

Created and written by I C Henderson

Adventure of the Mouhumes
Jack and Annie's new
Visitors

They headed back to camp. There was going to be a big discussion and the heads of the Mouhumes would have to seriously consider if they should move now.

Ruddy went to a part of the camp to be by herself. She had to get her head around this. This was something she found hard. Some other creature saving her, never in all her days had this been done.

Mousey came to talk to her, she told him her concerns. He listened then asked her if she had ever shown mercy. She looked up at him and shook her head. He asked again, once again she shook her head. Mousey asked Ruddy about the dog that had thorns in his face and pads, she looked at him without any expression on her face.

"Was that not kindness? Pity, you could have left it be, you had no idea what it would do if it had bad intentions. I must admit it doesn't happen often, more so when it had just been attacked."

Ruddy jumped to her feet and agreed, the meeting was about to start and she needed to talk to Tube and the other elders before it was opened up to all the Mouhumes after all the meeting was about whether they would go or stay.

The talks, once again, lasted almost all night. Would the fairies be friends or would they take advantage when they found out if they had any weakness?

Created and written by I C Henderson

Adventure of the Mouhumes
Jack and Annie's new
Visitors

Chapter 10
Next Day

EARLY THAT MORNING one or two of the Mouhumes were already up and going about their business: some were on food mission whilst others were scouting the area.

Tube was with Mousey. Mousey was explaining to him that Ruddy was concerned about what had happened to her and her confidence was knocked.

Ratty walked into the area where they were talking. It was part of a chamber some of the Mouhumes had made the day before. It was not very big, five or six Mouhumes would be comfortable in there.

It was not that long into their conversation when word got to them that Ruddy was up and about. Tube sent Mousey to go and ask her to come he needed to talk to her in the light of day.

Mousey went to find her, she was sitting near the rhubarb plant at the back of the shed. The rhubarb was just starting to ripen. The big leaves were hiding her from any danger that might come from the sky.

She was still looking sad. She could not work out why she was feeling like this. Mousey tried to comfort her but she was having none of it.

She decided to go and see Tube and Ratty, to see if they could help her with their wisdom, but even they could not work it out. After another long talk it was Mousey who came up with the idea that Ruddy should go and find the fairy who had saved her and ask why?

She was ever so confused. As she went into the garden next door she had a good look around and took notice. It was like a

Created and written by I C Henderson

Adventure of the Mouhumes
Jack and Annie's new
Visitors

smaller version of a human village. There was an odd house here, a bungalow there and at least three in the garden near the main house.

Suddenly something took hold of her arm; it was the fairy from the day before. She jumped but held back her normal instinct which would be to attack. The fairy beckoned her to follow him. There was a large hedge that Ruddy had not taken any notice of before. It blended in with the rest of the garden, there was no reason to take notice of it; it was nothing out of the ordinary.

But as she was taken through the hedge she became fully aware of what she was being shown: at least a quarter of that garden was a small village. How did none of the Mouhumes see this when they were exploring the area and how did she miss this?

There were about twenty miniature houses. They were big enough for the fairies or even the Mouhumes. So how had she missed seeing this? Something this big! She was now being led down what could only be described as a street. Houses on both sides made to look like what humans lived in.

Her head now was full of questions. How did the human of this garden not see this? How did they not interfere? How could they be next to humans and never be discovered.

She was then taken into a doorway that led down a passageway and then taken out into a clearing. This was nothing like what she had just seen; this was far more than what she had ever seen before. This was nothing that she could have prepared herself for. Her head, already doing overtime was now about to be blown away. It was too much to take in that she passed out.

Mousey was going to follow her just to make sure that she was alright but got distracted by something. So when he picked up her trail, or what he thought was her trail, it did not take him long to work out that it was from the day before.

Created and written by I C Henderson

Adventure of the Mouhumes
Jack and Annie's new
Visitors

Ruddy had not left a trail today for some reason. Not that this was unusual. A Mouhume did not have to leave a trail so near where they had a camp but really should when they were entering some strange area.

Mousey took some time looking around the garden next door but could not find anything to tell him where she might be.

She maybe changed her mind and went off somewhere else to clear her mind. After all she had been under a lot of strain. Yes that would be it Mousy thought but he would still have to go and report back to the leaders Tube and Ratty just so they knew what was happening.

As Mousey approached, Tube and Ratty were in the distance talking to another Mouhume or telling him off. They were round the back of the two sheds in a little clearing. All sorts of plants were growing so there was plenty of overhead cover.

Mousey approached Tube but was silent as Tube's hand was raised in away that Mousey knew that he had to wait and stand quietly, which he did by the corner of the greenhouse.

There was nothing worse than being reprimanded and knowing others were watching. He knew he might also be getting the same in a short time for losing sight of Ruddy.

If she was in danger he would be in the deepest trouble, as he was the one who said that he was more than capable to look out for her, and he had also talked Ruddy into going to see the fairy who had saved her.

Ratty came towards Tube, looking very angry he started to talk to him just out of earshot of Mousey. This was so Mousey could not hear what was being said. Ratty might have looked angry

Created and written by I C Henderson

Adventure of the Mouhumes
Jack and Annie's new
Visitors

but Tube looked at ease. Mousey tried to get closer to hear what had upset Ratty but dared not get in eyesight of either one of them.

Ratty had now finished talking to Tube and saw Mousey wandering closer towards them, he called Mousey over with a kind of a growl in his voice.

This made Mousey jump, he had thought that he had not been seen but Tube knew that he would try to get near to hear what was said. Tube knew Mousey so well that he always wanted to know what and who were saying what.

This was not a bad thing as he was a walking knowledge of information on just about anything. If he did not know, Tube knew that just by asking Mousey it would be enough for him to find a way to find out what was needed.

This was one of Mousey strengths. Finding out things was something that he had done from an early age. Being inquisitive was second nature to him.

But this did puzzle him. How could Ruddy disappear? Not even a trail, which was second nature to all the Mouhumes. Mousey reported what he had found, or in this case not found. He also explained what his next actions would be.

Mousey's was going to talk to the young Mouhume who had seen the fight. He wanted to know from start to finish just what happened. This would or might help him to find Ruddy …

Created and written by I C Henderson

Adventure of the Mouhumes
Jack and Annie's new
Visitors

Chapter 11

THE NEXT TWO weeks were the strangest, the traps were set off, but there was always a stick near them or even in them.

Jack picked the sticks up then put them into the compost bin, but the next day there would be more sticks beside the traps.

This went on for weeks. A little bit confused Jack was now set on finding out what was happening.

"Annie can you get some of those solar power lights?" Asked Jack with a smile on his face.

"What do you want with them Jack?" Annie asked, as if she did not know.

"Well when I'm sitting late at night and early in the morning, I'll be able to see what's there, and it would make your garden look nice" Jack told Annie trying to make it sound as if he was doing her a good deed.

Annie thought, he is going mad, but it would keep him occupied, and give him something to do, plus it will make the garden look nice at night. So she soon came around to the idea.

"Are you coming then, to get those lights? And who's paying for them!"

Annie knowing that she would have to pay still liked to ask, to see what Jack might come up with.

"Well Annie I'm not working and you are, so if you can I'll not mind," He said with a smile.

"Well come on then, I don't have a lot of time, so hurry up. As I have to be at work, so it's straight there and straight back ok?"

Created and written by I C Henderson

Adventure of the Mouhumes
Jack and Annie's new
Visitors

Annie replied not too happy with having to rush around, before she had to go to work.

"How about that store at the end of town, they have a special offer on?" Annie asked. Jack knew Annie did not have a lot of time, so he thought the store was the quickest to get to. And then he could get on quickly when he got back home, so he nodded.

"Yes let's go are you ready?" Asked Annie as she put her jacket on

Jack nodded again and off they went. Jack was determined to find out, what was going on in his garden, and he would not settle until he found out.

When they got back home, Annie had to go straight to work so she left Jack to do what he needed to do. Jack put the lights straight outside so that the solar panels could charge up the batteries

That night he put the lights where he thought he might be able to see well.

Annie was due to come in from work; he wanted to have something ready for her. What can I do? I know I'll have a cup of coffee ready for her.

It had been a sunny day but the weather was now cold and wet; the dark nights were cutting in. He thought a warm drink would be nice…Just then, he heard the car pull up, he switched the kettle on, as the door opened in came Annie, her arms full of shopping, dripping wet as the rain was coming down hard.

Annie squeezed past Jack saying, "Come on. Get out of my way; you can see these bags are heavy."

"I've put the kettle on for you. Do you need a hand?"

Created and written by I C Henderson

Adventure of the Mouhumes
Jack and Annie's new
Visitors

"You spoil me!" Annie said in a sarcastic but fun way,

"No, you will just get in the way and end up hurting yourself"

Annie knew that Jack liked to help, but at this time when he did anything active (bending lifting) he would suffer the next day, his injuries were not healing as quickly as he wanted, and at times he pushed himself too much.

Annie did not like to leave him too long by himself, she knew he would try to do things, then he would disturb her because he would be in pain during the night.

"I'll put this away and start the tea. I've got a nice bit of lamb and some roast potatoes." Annie told Jack.

"Have your drink first, as I have gone to the trouble to make it for you" Jack said in a concerned way.

"That will be nice." Annie said, as she looked into the conservatory from the kitchen window, picking up her drink.

Jack put his hand up, as if to say be quiet, he beckoned her to come and see, what could be so interesting?

Annie whispered "what's wrong?" She left the shopping and went to see.

"Look over there… can you see"

Jack pointed to the waterfall. At the side was a rockery. In the flowers was something moving. You could just make it out… but this was nothing they had ever have thought of.

They looked at each other in amazement; their eyes were as big as the biggest apples,

Created and written by I C Henderson

Adventure of the Mouhumes
Jack and Annie's new
Visitors

Jack asked in the quietest way he could.

"Can you see that… can you"?

Annie nodded and got hold of Jack's hand. This was the most, not to say unbelievably best thing they had ever seen. They sat down, not knowing what to say. What could this be?

That night the tea was not made, they just looked out all night. In that one night they learned a lot about their own garden. The little creatures were so clever; Annie and Jack could only sit and watch in amazement.

That night went by so quickly; the food for the freezer just went to waste.

In no time at all it was early morning. Annie was meant to go to work it was her early start.

Jack asked her not to go, not only because she would be tired, but also because they had to find out what it was that they had actually seen.

Annie had not had a day off work sick or otherwise. They were both tired and looked exhausted and felt it!

"Let's go to bed as I'm worn out" suggested Annie.

Jack nodded, not knowing what to say.

As they came out of the conservatory, Jack looked into the kitchen, and in his fun way told Annie.

"Looks like you have some clearing up to do"

Annie thumped his arm and told him off.

Created and written by I C Henderson

Adventure of the Mouhumes
Jack and Annie's new
Visitors

Off to bed they went. Neither one could sleep. After some time, Annie jumped up in a panic.

"Jack! I forgot to ring work." Annie said in a right old panic.

Just then, the phone rang.

"I bet that's work, what can I say?" Annie asked Jack

Annie never told lies; she had no idea what to say. She could not tell them what she thought she had seen. Jack told her that he would answer the phone; he knew that if Annie answered and told them what they had seen; both of them would be in line for the loony farm.

Jack picked up the phone Annie stood close by, looking as if she had just robbed the bank.

"Hello" Said Jack,

"Hello… it's Ted. I'm wondering if Annie is coming in today"

Ted was one of the mangers, he was a jumped up young so and so, Jack had no time for him,

"No she's not! I'll get her to ring when she's ready to come back, ok?" Then he hung up.

Annie not happy with what Jack had done told him off for hanging up, and the tone he had used to speak to Ted.

"There was no need to speak like that to poor Ted!"

"Never mind him, what about last night?" Jack was not bothered about how he spoke to Ted, as he was more concerned about what they had seen the night before.

Created and written by I C Henderson

Adventure of the Mouhumes
Jack and Annie's new
Visitors

Annie was feeling confused and not sure what to make of what she had seen,

"I don't know, what do you think? Was it real or what?"

"You hear and see things in films and nursery rhymes, gnomes, elves, goblins… do we have them in our garden! Are they something else?" Jack asked.

"None of those… were they?" Annie said with a concerned look on her face.

"Who knows what we have seen. We will have to get some books, find out if they have any information about them."

"Where do we look and what do we ask?" Annie did not know where to start.

Jack asked her what she had bought the night before, and if it was all right to eat, as he had had no tea or supper.

"You're always thinking of your stomach, you are never full," Annie said shaking her head, she then thought to herself what could I do with that food? Just then she saw Jack looking through the bags, she knew that he would not like to put anything into the bin, as he did not like to see anything wasted. He would try to salvage everything.

Just then he came up with an idea.

"See this ice cream, it's melted, you could make one of those smoothies's, you just have to whisk it up and add fruit. You can do that can't you? The sooner we get fed and sort this mess out we can find out what's in the garden so come on woman lets get to work" Jack clapped his hands as if to start the work then he sat down.

72

Adventure of the Mouhumes
Jack and Annie's new
Visitors

Annie looked across towards Jack and told him that he's good at telling her what to do but not too keen on helping. Jack just smiled and told her to stop complaining.

"How way pet you know I cannot do things right, not as good as you anyway" Jack knew that Annie did not like being called a pet so he knew what was coming next.

"Don't call me pet! I'm nobody's pet! Who the devil! Do you think you are? Calling me pet…!"

Off she went mumbling under her breath, stomping around in the kitchen. Banging and thumping .to say that she was not happy would be an under statement.

Annie put the Lamb in the fridge and put all the food away that needed putting away. Some had to be put in the bin. Then she made the smoothie's. She knew that it would keep Jack happy, and when he was finished, they could go and try to find out what they saw in the garden.

"Here you are, Jack, your strawberry smoothie, and your cup of tea will be ready after you eat this, is that ok?" off Annie went to get ready upstairs, she knew what they had seen was not gnomes or elves; in fact it was not any of those things. But she did wonder what on earth they could be?

Meantime Jack was filling his face, he had a good appetite and he needed building up as at this stage he was still under weight, his appetite had not taken any hurt, so it would not take long to get back to normal.

Annie never had breakfast, so all she had to do was get cleaned up and ready to go.

Created and written by I C Henderson

Adventure of the Mouhumes
Jack and Annie's new
Visitors

"Will we try the library first as it has lots of books I am sure that we can find out what we need to know there?" Annie asked Jack.

Jack nodded as he was enjoying his breakfast.

"How long do you think you will be? they have computers, and if needed we can ask someone" Jack had it all worked out, when looking for things on the computer he often found it harder than first thought, and had no one to ask .

"I'm ready; I'm waiting for you so hurry up!" Annie snapped, getting cross due to the lack of sleep.

Jack got himself up and got ready he knew from past experience that she got snappy when she had not had a good sleep, the sooner he got himself ready the better for him. In no time at all he was ready for the off.

"Come on lass are you not wanting to go?" Jack teased Annie

By then Annie just wanted to get there and get back as she was really tired.

As it happened the library was just a short drive away. They had a canteen there. Annie loved the coffee they had; you could not buy it anywhere else. On the way there Jack asked what they would do when they got there, Annie looked at Jack confused

"What do you mean?"

"Well Annie do we ask about elves and gnomes and things or do we?" he shrugged his shoulders. "Or what?"

"We'll just see when we get there, and get all the books we can and see if any make sense". Annie as always saw things in black and white, straight to the point not wasting anytime.

Created and written by I C Henderson

Adventure of the Mouhumes
Jack and Annie's new
Visitors
Chapter 12
The library

WHEN THEY ARRIVED they went straight to the Garden section and the small animal books. Jack spent some time in that section but could not find out what they needed to know.

Annie in the meantime was on the computer, not far from Jack.

Jack rubbed his mouth and spoke quietly.

"You know what we need now don't you? The fairytales and elves section"

Annie nodded; they looked for them in the children's section.

Jack had a brainwave and asked the Librarian.

"Hello I'm looking for any old books on elves and gnomes do you have any" And without thinking he asked "Do you think that they are true you know… real?"

The librarian looked at him in the most unusual way and told him he must behave or leave the building. She must have thought of him a bit foolish, asking if she thinks they are real, and if she believed in them.

Annie came over and got hold of Jack's hand and sat him down.

"Stay there and don't move!" she insisted. She whispered in his ear and told him (which was clear to see, that they thought he was insane) Jack put his head in his hands trying to hide.

Just then an old man came over and asked what they wanted to know about elves and things, and told them that if they were

Created and written by I C Henderson

Adventure of the Mouhumes
Jack and Annie's new
Visitors

really interested they should go to the museum and ask to see professor B L Glass. He might be able to help, and then off he went; as quickly and strangely as he came.

"What was that? And who was he?" Jack asked… And, what do you mean? They think I'm mad, I just asked about gnomes!"

Annie put her finger over Jack's lips, and told him to be quiet.

"Let's look at these books, and see if anything matches whatever is or was in our garden"

They looked, but couldn't find anything, its just stories and make believe none are real not even in the oldest books.

Jack pointed out, that there were two little girls who had taken photos of fairies.

Just then Annie jumped up and told Jack that they (the little girls) had not, that they had just pretended, and owned up to it years later, that they had faked the photos.

"That's me told, but what if it was true? And they did not want anyone to know? And they wished that they had not told anyone, maybe they did not want the world to know"

"Yes they are going to say that they just pretended, give over Jack" Annie snapped

Then Jack got up and shook his head

"Let's go to the museum" he beckoned to Annie

Annie not sure if going to the museum would be the answer hesitated.

Created and written by I C Henderson

Adventure of the Mouhumes
Jack and Annie's new
Visitors

"Look Jack, I think we should go back home and talk about what we have seen"

Just then Jack stumbled and fell over the chair; the Liberian and some of the other members came and helped Jack to his feet.

Annie could not thank them enough, and went for the car.

They helped to get Jack into the car, by this time Jack was in terrible pain.

"There you have had more than enough for one day, I need to get you home, we can ring the museum from home ok!" Annie had had her fill for one day.

Jack sitting in the car, could not get comfortable, in desperate need for his painkillers; he nodded and put his head down on his chest.

"Look Jack you know that you have done too much, you're meant to be taking it easy; I don't know you are your own worst enemy. It's me who has to pick the mess up that you make, if you don't stop, and start doing what you are meant to do I swear…!"

Then off Annie went in an unthinkable mood.

When they arrive back home, Jack tried to get out of the car, Annie by this time due to the fact she has had no sleep, and Jack trying to do things for himself. Is in the shortest temper, and really snappy.

"Jack stop being a silly old fool and wait till I come around please!"

Jack put a half smile on his face and said, "I'm not old" and nipped her bum. Which did not go down too well, the fact was she had had too much for one day.

Adventure of the Mouhumes
Jack and Annie's new
Visitors

The day just seemed that it's not going right at all, Annie needed her sleep, just wanting to get to bed and lie down.

When they got into the house she told Jack that they must think what they were going to do, that they both needed some rest before they do anything else. They both went to lie down, and in no time they were both fast asleep.

,

Created and written by I C Henderson

Adventure of the Mouhumes
Jack and Annie's new
Visitors

Chapter 13
Unrest at the Warren

HE WAS THE only one that would be the hero. Only he could lead the Mouhumes to safety and now it was his time. He had driven all those out who had once been leaders. He would now have to do more than drive out the one time leaders he would have to destroy them to put fear into any other Mouhumes who might think the role was up for the taking.

With the role he would have to have advisers and strong leadership. They might advise him but he would have the last say.

He had some big shoes to fill. Tube had been the leader for a long time and had some good followers and some fearless fighters at his side, one being Ruddy, Ruddy the living legend….

He should have killed her when she was weak and worn out he thought, he had heard the stories about her being almost dead then attacking and killing her enemies, therefore he dared not underestimate her.

If he had ordered her death and she was to take out one or more of those who tried to carry out her demise, even in her weak state. The rest of the Mouhumes would have killed those without hesitation.

He had done the right thing. He had tainted her reputation at a time she had little fight left in her, but he had no idea that she would still have a number of followers.

Now they were divided and open to allsorts of danger. What was the way forward? In numbers they had fighters, strength and wisdom. Now their numbers had more than halved. This was a new world, new danger's none of them had faced before. So not even Tube, with his experience and knowledge, would be any help.

Created and written by I C Henderson

Adventure of the Mouhumes
Jack and Annie's new
Visitors

Rug was standing with his followers looking out into the night sky wondering what his next move should be. He was feeling a bit fearful. If he had kept quiet he could have learned more from his elders.

It might have been new to all of them but their experience would have been useful. All he had around him was weakness and inexperience. Even his own fighting skills were no match for what lay ahead. He knew he had to find a way to get back with those who had left but not to show any weakness by doing so.

The weather was improving; the humans were starting to use the park area again. Sometimes they dropped bits of food around the car park and on the grassed areas after they had their picnic. It was not a safe place, he could sense this. As the weather got better more and more humans came around the area and it would be only a matter of time before they the Mouhumes were found out.

The nights were getting lighter; the protection of darkness was disappearing. If they were to make a move it would have to be now and hopefully they would find some sort of trail, even after the weeks that had past. The likelihood of that would be almost impossible but the unrest in the warren was reaching danger point. The lack of food and the wildlife around that would kill them, if they were found, was more than Rug had ever known.

He summoned those who he had ordered to follow Ruddy when she left so that he could find the start of the trail. There were only around fifty of this group left. Some had died by poison left on food to kill vermin and others had met their end through a variety of wildlife.

Some in the warren would not be strong enough to leave; their health had taken a turn for the worse. Rug had taken the decision now was the time to leave and hopefully, if they were lucky enough to find Tube and any of others, they might join and it might be as it used to.

Created and written by I C Henderson

Adventure of the Mouhumes
Jack and Annie's new
Visitors

Those who had followed Tube and Ruddy came to see Rug. Rug had learned to question them separately. Rug listened to what they told him, he went deeper into certain parts so that he could get a picture of what danger lay ahead, what obstacles they would encounter.

It would appear that they had both lost sight of those who had left around the same time as there was a steep hill that they had to travel up. It was so steep that the two Mouhumes following them had given up near the top but they did climb half way up a tree, near the top of the hill so that they could see what was beyond. It had been a dark night but what they had seen in the distance was nothing but more danger.

Rug had asked what sort of danger there might be. They both told the same tale, lights in the sky (street lights) lights that were moving (cars) noise in the distance nothing that they had heard before, (humans having fun).

They equally believed that they would meet their death heading that way. They waited a long time before they came back to the warren, so that they knew for certain that Ruddy and the others were not coming back that way.

Rug had asked why they had not reported back to him. They said that when they had returned there was mayhem. Some of those who went with Ruddy had taken food and had left little. They had no sooner returned to report what they had seen but were told by some of the others to go and find food.

Rug nodded and admitted that there had been panic. When they discovered that food had been taken, fear, confusion and a number of other worries set in. The food supply was still no better. This was the main reason why they would have to move as soon as they could. They still needed to work out the best way forward.

Created and written by I C Henderson

Adventure of the Mouhumes
Jack and Annie's new
Visitors

Illness was taking its toll, numbers were dwindling, Tube had always said that the burrow was only going to be a short stop until they had rested and had enough food to take with them.

Tube and those who had been forced to go had to take some of the food supply. Not as much as they would have taken if not for the speedy exit but enough to keep them going until they found more. They had left what they considered to be sufficient for those left behind. After all they had been a community of friends and family for as long as they could remember.

Rug's thoughts drifted to those, who he had not seen after that morning when the earth had been dug and ripped apart in that moment. Many fled in different directions; some were even swallowed up by the earth as it turned.

He had seen, in that short time, so much death that he found it hard to rest or sleep. He was always on edge and always waiting for the next disaster. That's why he needed to be the leader. He did not want to be told what to do but the one telling the other Mouhumes as he had done on the morning with his quick thinking. He had saved a number of Mouhumes. Some had been killed by being told misleading things.

The fact of it was, it was either good fortune or bad luck. What had happened that day was awful for the Mouhumes community; big machines tore the earth apart. Some building development company had decided to build on the land. It had been undeveloped land that was no good for farming. Just land that no one wanted until now.

That's how the Mouhumes had never been disturbed. Once in a while they had encountered a human that was when someone had walked out of their way as it was not somewhere people would want to walk to. There was nothing there. The wildlife could go about their lives as normal.

Created and written by I C Henderson

Adventure of the Mouhumes
Jack and Annie's new
Visitors

Now Rug had to decide when they were leaving. He could see that it was pointless waiting any longer. Those who were poorly were not going to get any better. It was up to them if they wanted to attempt the next journey.

They waited until nightfall. It was not as dark as they would have liked but it was as dark as it was going to get. The food was shared out; each Mouhume would carry their own. Those who were staying would have food left for them.

There was around twenty or more Mouhumes going with Rug. At least another fifteen left in the warren who were old or injured and poorly. These and another twenty or so who wanted to stay to help those who were ill.

Rug felt bad about leaving them but over the past few weeks he had seen a number of deaths and illness due to the lack of food. So he decided he could not risk the rest of the Mouhumes in a place that was only going to kill them one way or another. It was going to be a try or die journey and he decided to try the way that Tube had tried. If Tube and his followers had met their ends then there would be some sort of sign.

The hill was as steep as the scouts had said it was. That in itself was a hard task for some of the weaker Mouhumes, but slowly they managed it. It took a lot longer than they thought it would. A number of trees up the hill give them cover so that they could rest awhile.

When they got to the top the road was empty. The street lights were on, giving them some idea what was in the distance. There were buildings, more than they had seen in the bottom of the park, lots more, Rug's thoughts were going crazy, more humans meant more danger but if Tube could make it through this then he could.

Created and written by I C Henderson

Adventure of the Mouhumes
Jack and Annie's new
Visitors

They went through a number of gardens, not knowing they had missed the garden that Tube and the others had stopped at to rest the first night.

It was only two or three gardens away but far enough to miss the evidence that a Mouhume had stayed in that area. Rug had no idea how near he was to being on the same track as Tube. His heart and determination was starting to sink.

Rug was hoping that he could help those who were now with him and also hopeful that those who had left had found safety. He realised that he had been wrong trying to get rid of Ruddy, Rug should have known that she had a strong following.

It was not much longer when he decided that they should stop for a rest. He had pushed them harder than any other leader would have. They stopped just outside a garden in amongst some trees that ran alongside the gardens.

There was lots of undergrowth as well as dead bramble bushes. There was also a lot of new shoots just starting to grow. The thorns from the dead bushes would help to protect them from any overhead danger.

The morning sunrise was just starting to light the sky. Now would be the time to establish what was around them, and plan how to deal with it. It would also be a good time to try and find some food, but they had to keep out of the way from any danger that might be around.

Quickly they had made a little camp. It gave them protection from up above and from the sides unless it was big and strong and could break through the thorns

They started to eat the little food they had brought with them; they rested but only for a short time. Rug wanted to know what was around them and whether they could make use from anything. So

Created and written by I C Henderson

Adventure of the Mouhumes
Jack and Annie's new
Visitors

he and two others went out into the woods to see what they could find.

They may have been undernourished and some in poor health but Rug had pushed them hard and fast. He had covered twice the distance that Tube had done. He had left the rest to eat what they had and so that they could recover their energy to be ready for the next move. Rug wanted to see which way they might go. He took two strong Mouhumes with him, both young and full of energy

In a little distance they came across a dead rat, then another then more than he had ever seen before. It was like a battle field and then he came to the source. Black bin bags torn apart, dead pigeon's half eaten. The smell was more than they could take, the three of them moved away as quickly as they could.

No matter how far they moved away from the devastation they still came across a dead rat, even other animals that had eaten the contaminated bodies.

Rug and his two companions settled down out of the way. One had recognised the smell, not the dead rotten corpse smell but something else in the air. He started to tell Rug that when they went to find Ruddy that they had came across something similar but Tube, in his wisdom, had said not to eat the food that was lying around no matter how hungry they were. Tube would not let anyone go near the food.

The Mouhume, telling the account, sunk his head. He told Rug how one Mouhume had gone back as they were all hungry, got a handful and ate it as he himself was going to do, but the Mouhume who had eaten the food fell to the ground dead. His eyes filled up. He could still see it, as if it was happening in front of him now. If it had been him, a moment earlier he also would be dead.

Rug could see that he was upset so he jumped to his feet. It was no good getting down in the dumps. He needed to lift morale.

85

Adventure of the Mouhumes
Jack and Annie's new
Visitors

As the leader he believed himself to be and as he had seen so many times from Tube and Ratty, how they lifted the moral. Rug said without hesitation that they had learned something important and they should share this with the rest of their group.

He nodded to them and off he went to explore. They still, had not found any trace that Tube or any other Mouhume might have been in that area. It was frustrating for him; he had hoped so much that he would have found something by now.

They had not travelled very far when they came to the gardens of humans. He scratched his head. They would not have gone anywhere near humans. He shook his head No what a silly idea!

It was time to head back to the others but first he wanted to find some food, then suddenly something took his attention. Birds were flying to the ground eating something left on the lawn; it looked like big lumps of food had been thrown out for the birds.

They all looked healthy enough. None were falling down dead. Would he risk it and take some food? As he considered this the other two Mouhumes ran towards the birds shouting and screaming, arms waving in the air so that the birds flew away.

Rug was not far behind the other two, all of them grabbing handfuls of food then, just as fast they ran back into the woods and under the undergrowth their hearts beating so fast with excitement.

Now was the test! Would they dare eat it after seeing the mass of dead animals not that far away? They sniffed the food, nothing out of the ordinary. Not that they knew how bread would smell. Rug looked at the Mouhume, who had told him about the poison food… was the smell the same?

As they sat they watched the birds going back for the remains of the food that was on the lawn. They continued to watch

Created and written by I C Henderson

Adventure of the Mouhumes
Jack and Annie's new
Visitors

the birds again. The birds ate every scrap of food that was on the lawn and still none fell down dead.

Rug tried a bit of bread, the other two started to eat theirs as well. It was nothing that they had tried before so they had no idea what it should taste like. It seemed to fill the spot. That's all they wanted, to get rid of that hunger.

Lucky for them they were big chunks of bread, so they did not have to try to find anymore food. The bread was not that heavy to carry. All they had to do now was to go back and find the Mouhumes they had left behind.

With each one of them carrying two bits of food each it took them longer than they wanted. When they arrived back to the others, it was worth it, seeing the expression on their faces, joy and hopefulness. With what had seemed to be a death sentence back at the warren, there was now hope.

They stayed there the best part of that day. Only now and again they popped out in the nearby area to see what was around them. Plenty of birds and rabbits were around, now and again the odd human with dogs some off their leads.

There was plenty undergrowth for them to hide in. There was also the smells from the plants and the dampness in the air this all helped to hide their aroma.

One of the Mouhumes who had been with Rug was wearing an old crisp packet. When he was running across the garden lawn he must have just looked like an empty packet blowing in the wind.

Rug with his bits of cloth would also have looked like something blowing in the wind. The only one that might have looked like an animal was the third one. He was wearing bits of mouse skins put together to keep him warm. Now was the time they had to blend in with the human's world and use anything to

Created and written by I C Henderson

Adventure of the Mouhumes
Jack and Annie's new
Visitors

help them, even things they may never have normally come into contact with, things like the crisp packet.

Rug once again sat with his thoughts. Tube was right to want to move away from the warren. There was not enough food around there. There might not be enough food here either but at least they had some to put away for the next day. They had eaten their fill for that day.

The daylight had seemed to last longer than normal, or it might have just been because they did not know the area and did not want to venture out of their camp.

Rug knew that they could not stay there for a long time. They would have to take it in turns to make trips out to discover what was around them.

Rug went out most times, only having a rest after every third outing. He was kept up to date with what they had seen on each occasion he had not gone with them.

Rug told them every time to look out for any sign that another Mouhume might have been there. He was desperate to find Tube and Ratty, Ruddy and all the others. He felt sick and upset that he had forced them to leave. Rug regretted it even more now that he too had made the decision to leave, especially after telling everyone that Tube was wrong when he had said that they would have to move on

The only difference was that he had told those he had left behind at the warren that he would be back with food and hopefully somewhere they could all be together and secure again.

Created and written by I C Henderson

Adventure of the Mouhumes
Jack and Annie's new
Visitors

Chapter 14
Alone at the Burrow

NOT ALL THOSE left at the burrow were sick and weak. Some had stayed to try and help the weak and ill to recover.

The weather was getting warmer. The sunlight was longer in the sky giving light for most of the day. The park area was getting fuller with more and more humans each day. This was not always a bad thing, as some would drop food anywhere. Later that day, if the birds or other animals had not eaten it, the Mouhumes would scurry out of hiding holes and get it.

Food now was not becoming the issue as it was starting to mount up. They were storing it in the deepest part of the burrow in the darkest coolest part to help keep it fresh for as long as they could. For now, those who were left had more than a sufficient amount of food. It would seem, those who had left due to there not being sufficient food was not a bad thing.

Those who had been too ill to travel were now getting stronger. Some had lost their lives but most had made it through. Numbers were picking up with new baby Mouhumes arriving.

Their health started to get better and they got to know their surroundings better. Some days the park would have more humans than other days but they worked out when would be the best times to leave the warren.

The main competitors for the food left by the humans were the birds. The rats and mice were also getting food but the Mouhumes often would chase them away or kill them if they were in small numbers.

They made devices that would kill the rats as they were bigger than Mouhumes. Those left at the warren had little fighting skills; the main fighters had left along with Ratty and Tube. These

Created and written by I C Henderson

Adventure of the Mouhumes
Jack and Annie's new
Visitors

Mouhumes had to depend on outwitting everything in their way. They learned fast, they had to for their own survival.

Weeks had passed since Rug and others had moved away. If only they had stayed, they could have had more than enough food. The community was now growing fast and they were all healthy young Mouhumes. Not one Mouhume was what you would call a leader but they worked as a group. Each one was known for his or hers own abilities.

What had been a small proportion of the Mouhume community was now split into three groups. What ever became of any other group was unknown to them. Those who had gone with Tube would not know about the split at the warren, so as far as they knew they would still be there.

Those who had gone with Rug would not know about how well they were doing now. They had split up into different parts of the area; to them it might have been different worlds. The only similar thing was humans had a part in their survival.

Now, unknown to them, they were starting to depend on humans, much more than they should or would have if they had noticed.

Some days were quiet but two days a week, one particular, was always full of humans especially if it was a sunny day. The grass area was full of humans sitting, eating and running around. Some Mouhumes would hide in the long grass or on the embankment watching.

Some humans would be kicking and chasing a round thing. The Mouhumes could not understand why they would kick something then run after it. Then more humans would join in, doing the same thing. It was very strange.

Created and written by I C Henderson

Adventure of the Mouhumes
Jack and Annie's new
Visitors

They would then sit down, eat their food, dropping little bits or even throwing it at each other, laughing as they did so. Not all humans did this. Some would put the food waste in the large circular containers. The Mouhumes found those hard to get into but they had worked out a way of getting into them and retrieving food.

As always birds would be their main competitors as they did not show any concern for the humans being there. The Mouhumes did not want anyone seeing them so they had to wait until it was safe to collect the food.

In the burrow, they had dug deeper into the soft sand to store what food they could. It was cooler the deeper they went. So this worked out well for them, the food would last longer. They had worked out that during bad weather humans did not go to the park so food was harder to find. There were fewer berries growing here, nothing like the amount growing where they used to live.

Other wild animals were mostly in packs so it was sometimes dangerous to hunt them. But then it was a risk if they had eaten the poisonous food sometimes put out by the human who lived in the bungalow in the car park.

That was a great risk, more than they had ever known before. Not just finding the food but the danger of eating contaminated food. Contaminated food was infecting whatever was eating it then it was being passed onto whatever was eating that. They still had to take the risk sometimes but not as much as they might have had to do if the park had not been so busy.

They soon discovered or recognised the odour of the food that had been poisoned and that of what had eaten it. The odour had often been on the breath of an enemy so they would avoid killing that animal for food.

Some food was found in parts of the woodland: wood nuts, elderberries and even some raspberries growing wild, but it was not

Adventure of the Mouhumes
Jack and Annie's new
Visitors

enough to sustain a growing community of Mouhumes. Some of the food supply could be preserved, but some had to be eaten straightaway.

Everything had grown now. When they arrived it was near the end of winter so food was on low supply but now this was summer and things were starting to grow. It was a good spot to stay at this time.

They learned to keep food supplies in the deepest part of the burrow, not just for the coolness but also to keep the smell away from other predators who might stumble upon their food.

No other creature they knew kept food for a later date. When winter came other creature numbers decreased due to the lack of food. Some became aggressive and would raid almost anything due to desperation. The Mouhumes knew this. It was something they had always known, even at their last home, so they had precautions in place.

Something new to them was the river and what was in and around the river. Such as fish, frogs and other reptiles' even newts lived near the river. They often caught a newt or a frog. The first time they tried to eat a frog they all stuck out their tongues trying to rub the taste off on something. But most would often be sick.

Frogs had a taste on the skin to help protect them and the Mouhumes did not like this at all. Having once tried them they knew not to try them again. The newts, on the other hand, they liked but they were too fast for them to catch, until they found ways of doing so.

The fish were something else they had never eaten before and there were allsorts in the river. Some were far too big for them to catch. Such as eels. They had seen the eels take hold of a rat and swallow. Some were only small but they were very aggressive so they kept away from them as well.

Created and written by I C Henderson

Adventure of the Mouhumes
Jack and Annie's new
Visitors

These were all new things that they would have to learn to understand or try to work around or even kill them. Whatever way, they would have to make the most of it. They were now content and with numbers growing, they had little ones to feed and take care of.

Created and written by I C Henderson

Adventure of the Mouhumes
Jack and Annie's new
Visitors

Chapter 15
The *poacher*

THE SOUND OF a telephone ringing woke Jack; he jumped up. Looked at the clock as he made his way to the top of the landing to answer the telephone, He thought to himself it's half past nine, we've been asleep since half past two. It had not seemed five minutes since they went to bed the time had passed so quickly.

He turned around and looked back into the bedroom Annie was still fast asleep.

The phone was still ringing his head was pounding. He felt as if he had been drunk, and had a hang over, He picked the phone up and said hello.

"Hello Jack, this is Sharon one of the managers from the store we rang earlier but got no answer, we thought that you might be out?"

Jack rubbed his head, and tried to wake up properly.

"No, we were in bed, we never heard the phone, Annie is still in there now"

Sharon asked if they were both all right.

"Yes we are, but poor Annie, I think she's run herself into the ground, I think it's just that she has done too much. What with me and work"

Sharon was a good friend of Annie's. She knew that she was working as hard at home as she was at work.

"Look Jack, tell her that we will put her down for days we owe her, and to take it easy, I'll tell them not to put her down for any shifts for the next two days, and she "must ring" the day before

Created and written by I C Henderson

Adventure of the Mouhumes
Jack and Annie's new
Visitors

she is ready to come back. She knows all that anyway, I must go, see you later and hope you are both better soon"

Jack put the phone down, put his dressing gown on. Then hobbled down the stairs, he went straight into the kitchen, he looked at the clock it was nine forty five in the morning they had slept from two o'clock the after noon before; his first thought was to turn the kettle on, and get the teapot ready, he liked to have a mug of tea first thing in the morning.

He heard Annie on the squeaky floorboards in the bedroom, she must be getting up, he got her a cup out and got a chocolate biscuit and put it on a plate. He knew she liked to be pampered. And he would be pleased to see a smile on her face.

"Jack who was that on the phone?" Annie asked as she was coming down the stairs wrapping her dressing gown around her.

Jack told her that it had been work and they said that she had to give them a call when she was ready to go back.

Annie was in two minds to ring them up, but Jack persuaded Annie that she needed at least this day to help her rest, and that they could have a lazy day, after all Jack needed to make some phone calls to see who this B L Glass was from the Museum, so that morning Jack made his calls, later that afternoon they both fell asleep in the sitting room on the big soft sofa.

Jack was first awake as he got himself up he picked up the blanket and placed it over Annie, to help keep her warm, he then went to put the kettle on, and get something to eat, as he was waiting for the kettle to boil he went into the conservatory, Annie started to wake up, and called for Jack.

Jack did not hear her; he was in the conservatory looking to see if he could see those little things that they had seen the night before.

Created and written by I C Henderson

Adventure of the Mouhumes
Jack and Annie's new
Visitors

"Jack can't you answer?" Annie asked with displeasure in her voice. Still no answer, that just made things worse. She stomped through the living room, as she passed the conservatory she saw Jack.

"Oh no not again…!"Annie sighed.

"No not another night please!" Annie not wanting another late night asked Jack to come and help make the drinks. Jack nodded and put his hand up as if to say just a moment. Annie shook her head knowing that he must have seen something again. Not wanting to have a look herself, she knew that nothing would be done, (the supper and drinks) Annie just got on with it, and made the drinks and some sandwiches.

By which time Jack was sitting on the chair, looking across towards the pond.

Annie crept in put the drinks and the plate of sandwiches on the small table. Sat down quietly, nudged Jack and pointed towards the supper.

Jack pointed to where he wanted Annie to look, and whispered that there seemed to be more than the night before.

Annie put her hand over her mouth and gasped.

The creatures seemed to have doubled, there were a lot more than the night before, what they were doing was unbelievable. Annie picked up her cup and sandwich and sat and ate while watching.

She ate hers then picked Jacks up and gave him his. Annie whispered to Jack and told him to eat his supper.

"Look can you see that? That one it's trying to turn that small bit of wood over." Jack asked Annie.

Created and written by I C Henderson

Adventure of the Mouhumes
Jack and Annie's new
Visitors

"It's not any small bit of wood it's your rat trap" Annie replied.

"What do you think it's going to do?"

Just then more came to help the one trying to turn the wood over; they had already sprung the trap but seemed to be trying to turn it over Jack could not work out why .The reason would soon become clear. They finally turned it over and pushed it into the pond, Annie and Jack looked at each other with confused looks on their faces, still not sure what might be happening but not wanting to take there eyes off them.

Two of the things got onto the wood, which became a raft, and drifted out onto the pond. It was still not clear what was going to happen but one thing for sure, this would get Jack jumping out of his chair.

The creatures seemed to be trying to get something out of the pond; it was hard to see what it might be.

The night was a lot clearer than the night before; there was no rain and little cloud. The moon was not full but it was still bright.

Just then all became clear, a fish came out of the water, not a big one, but one of the ones that had just been bought.

Jack jumped up, Annie grabbed him by his hand, and told him to calm down and sit down. Jack stuttered and blurted and was in a right state.

Annie finally thought it better to take him out into the living room, so that they didn't frighten the creatures.

When they got into the living room Jack was in a right temper.

Created and written by I C Henderson

Adventure of the Mouhumes
Jack and Annie's new
Visitors

"Did you see what they have done? They've pinched my fish! What are they going to do with my fish?"

Annie laughed and told him the obvious.

"They are going to eat it you silly man" Annie told him hardly keeping her laugh in.

"What? They're not are they? Oh No what the…!"

Jack did not want to believe what Annie had told him, he put his hands on top of his head, shook his head and paced the floor.

Annie told him to stop being silly, they have to eat don't they?

"Yes but my fish? Not my fish!" Jack loved his fish he had not long bought some young ones, there were lots of big ones but they seemed to be hunting the little ones. Or that was what he thought.

"Look at the time Jack its half past one already, lets go to bed I am tired and have to be at work in the morning." Annie Said, she was feeling tired and irritated.

Jack thought that he had forgotten to tell her, that Sharon had been on the phone.

"By the way Annie, Sharon rang and said that it's all right to take the day off tomorrow"

"And you're just telling me now! That's typical, what time did she ring? And what did you say?" Annie not happy with being told this late at night got herself in a right temper.

Created and written by I C Henderson

Adventure of the Mouhumes
Jack and Annie's new
Visitors

"If you give me a chance I'll tell you!" Jack jumped in with a little shyness in his voice.

"Look its late I'm tired and these late nights have to stop!" Annie snapped, not wanting to listen, she put a stop to whatever excuse that Jack might try and pull out of the top of his head.

Jack new he had told her, About Sharon ringing earlier he then realized that Annie must be worn-out so he knew it would be best if he said nothing more.

They went to bed with nothing being said between them. As they got ready for bed Annie began to laugh, the thought of Jacks face when he saw the fish being pulled from the pond!

"What are you laughing at? What's funny?" Jack asked.

"The look on your face when the fish was pulled out of the pond" Annie couldn't stop herself laughing. The thought was too much for her and she was giggling all night.

Created and written by I C Henderson

Adventure of the Mouhumes
Jack and Annie's new
Visitors
Chapter 16

THE NEXT MORNING Jack was up early as always. He went straight to the conservatory window, to see if there was any sight of the fish, as he was really concerned.

There was no sign but he knew deep down there wouldn't be.

Then suddenly he saw one of the little creatures, this was the first time in daylight he had seen one. Was it that they were getting more confident? Or was it the first time he really had looked in daylight?

As he watched he began to realise what they were doing, it was so obvious now, he could understand them better.

It was so clear; he could make out what they looked like, as he watched he heard Annie getting up, he could still hear her giggling she was not going to stop.

"Hello are you up?"Annie asked, with big a smile on her face.

Jack turned his head towards her and nodded, then came out of the conservatory into the kitchen.

"Look I think we need to go to see that Professor from the museum. They are in the garden now, right now" Jack told Annie.

"Ok after we have had something to eat, how many do you think we have?"

Annie not understanding that Jack meant they were in the garden (now) in daylight.

She was not sure how they would tell someone, as they might not have seen or heard anything like this, so she was not paying attention to what Jack was saying.

Adventure of the Mouhumes
Jack and Annie's new
Visitors

"Look they are there, right now!" Jack told her.

The look on Annie's face was that of amazement. She was not going to look; she knew that once they did the time would just disappear.

"Jack, we have discovered something fantastic, do we really want the world to know?"

"But Annie, we have to find out what they are doing, don't we? And that old man in the library told us to see the professor"

"But was he not just having a bit of fun? I bet there is no Professor, and what's more how do you tell someone, what will they think?"

Annie was getting herself really worried. She thought if the people where she worked heard, they would think she was having a nervous break down.

"Look Annie I know you're probably worried, but you don't have to say a word, I'll do the talking ok?" Jack was aware that Annie was unsure about telling anyone.

Jack rang the university to see if Professor Glass would be in, and what time would be best to go along to see him.

The receptionist told Jack that Mr Glass would be doing a speech that day, but it was going to be at the museum and that would be the only time they would be able to see him, as he was a busy man doing work all over the country, she was unsure when he would be back, she also told Jack the times he would be available, for that day.

Jack told Annie that they had to go that day, he told her what the receptionist had told him "Annie it has to be today, don't you

Adventure of the Mouhumes
Jack and Annie's new
Visitors

see it's fate, destiny what ever else, today is the only time we can get to see him, these are the time's he is obtainable"

"Have you been hit over the head"? Annie asked with a grin on her face.

"What do you mean" Jack asked rubbing his head, "I don't think so"

"Obtainable you must have swallowed a dictionary or something, I've never heard you talk like that" they both started to laugh.

Jack asked Annie if she was ready and if they could go, Annie agreed and off they went.

Created and written by I C Henderson

Adventure of the Mouhumes
Jack and Annie's new
Visitors
Chapter 17
Mousey

AT LEAST TWO days had passed since Ruddy had been seen. Tube and Ratty were concerned and it was now beginning to show. This was not like Ruddy to disappear. She might go and do her own thing but she would always be back or at the least leave some sort of clue. All they knew was that she had left the garden, she had gone to where the fairies were and she had not returned, had the fairies killed her?

Mousey was standing with Ratty. Ratty was now on the war path and his temper was short. Mousey knew this so he had to be careful with anything he said and how he said it, after all he was the one who had persuaded Tube and Ratty that he should talk to Ruddy and help her.

In Ratty's mind, it was Mousey who was to blame him and only him. He told Mousey it was up to him to find Ruddy before this day was over. Mousey told Ratty that he had no idea where to start looking because he had already looked. But Ratty was having none of this. Mousey could find out anything Ratty replied with sarcasm and anger in his voice, he then gave Mousey a look that turned him cold with fear.

Mousey knew what he had to do. This time it would be different, not like what he had done just days before, a quick look! This time it had to be done properly. So Mousey left the shed then he went into next door's garden.

Where had he lost sight of Ruddy and why had she not left him any signs? Once again Mousey looked into the house that had the deep hole. There was nothing there. He looked around the plants, some tall and some not so tall. Mousey climbed up on to one of the tallest plant so that he could observe what was around from a higher view. Nothing seemed to be out of place.

Adventure of the Mouhumes
Jack and Annie's new
Visitors

He looked to see if he could find any fairies: there were none that he could see so he called out for them. There was a little panic in his voice as he had no idea what to expect. Still nothing! Had these fairies harmed Ruddy? Were they in hiding, ready to pick off any straying Mouhume? Mousey thought to himself, after all they could hide better than Mouhumes. It was as if they just appeared from out of nowhere.

Fear started to take over his thoughts. He was alone in a place where the fairies had made their home. What could he do? He had called for them to come out and face him. What if they did? He knew that he would not be able to hide and the fact that he was scared meant that he was not thinking right!

He started to think that this was a bad idea and started to go back down the plant with the idea of going back altogether. Then the thought of Ratty and the look he gave him just before he left. He gave a little sigh. He was doomed in every way. Half way down the plant he stopped suddenly, his head was almost ready to explode with all the thoughts going through it.

He knew he would have to go back with an answer of some sort. More importantly maybe evidence of one kind or another. He called again for the fairy that saved Ruddy. He did not know its' name, or even if that one would come but he thought if he shouted fairy it would get some sort of attention.

Still nothing, he finally got back to the ground and stood thinking. He decided he should use his senses and his awareness. He stood with his eyes shut and let his mind become one with what was around him: he could hear the birds, not just because they were singing but the sound of their wings flapping; insects were landing near him, and the slight breeze blowing leaves on the plants. He could sense all of this and more, so why could he not sense the fairies?

Created and written by I C Henderson

Adventure of the Mouhumes
Jack and Annie's new
Visitors

He started to look around the garden. It had a number of model houses. They were all different in shape and style. He went into each one some had rooms and other ones were covering a hole. In the hole there was nothing, no passageways, nothing, why?

He started to doubt his own ability and how he always found answers (somehow) He searched almost every inch of that garden, except near the human house. He went as near as he dare but in his heart he knew Ruddy would never get that close to a human home.

Time was getting on. He was feeling a little hungry and he had not brought anything with him. He did not dare go back without something to tell the elders so he started to look for something to eat in the next garden.

Halfway up in the garden he made his way through the garden hedge. He knew there was a possibility of food lying on the ground. He was right. The birds had brought it but not eaten it yet but he would have to be quick. He ran across the lawn and took a handful of old broken biscuits.

He never stopped running until he was on the other side of the garden under a large area covered with shrubbery. He started to eat his food: the biscuits had currents, raisins and other fruit mixed in. It was ideal to give him some energy. As Mousey sat looking around for potential danger he saw the human from the garden where they had made their home. He was looking around the pond area. Mousey wondered what could he be looking for?

Mousey decided to go somewhere better for a look. The birds were still eating the remaining food on the grass. He stuffed what he had left into his fur jacket so that he could have it later. Once again he hid among the plants in between the hedge. It was a good spot to hide and see what the human was up to.

The human had a long stick. He was poking it into the plants around the pond, and then he came down the garden a little way.

Created and written by I C Henderson

Adventure of the Mouhumes
Jack and Annie's new
Visitors

He seemed to be looking for something. What was it? Mousey knew he would have to find out. His curiosity was taking hold of him.

Then from the corner of his eye, he saw Ratty hiding on the other side of the garden looking at him. Then suddenly Mousey remembered his task was to find Ruddy. His brain was now in overdrive. What if the human could lead him to Ruddy?

Suddenly there was a tap on his shoulder. He almost jumped out of the shrubbery onto the lawn but a hand held him back, it pulled him to the ground with a thud quickly putting a hand over his mouth to keep him quiet.

It was Ratty. As Mousey had been daydreaming about what he should and should not do, Ratty had come around the edge of the garden in between the bushes. Ratty when he had spotted Mousey had seen this look on his face before and knew that he needed waking up.

The human had not noticed this happening and was still looking around; he stood for a little longer then went back into his house.

The birds had not been disturbed; they just carried on eating the last little bits of food. Ratty looked down at Mousey as he got up, he then asked him if he had forgotten what he was meant to be doing? Mousey did not say a word, he just shook his head.

Ratty gave Mousey a hard slap around his head knocking him back onto the ground. Mousey stayed there for a moment until Ratty had gone away. Now he had understood the desperation in everyone's mind to find Ruddy. Off he went back to where he had left off. In his mind he was going to find Ruddy one way or another.

Created and written by I C Henderson

Adventure of the Mouhumes
Jack and Annie's new
Visitors

He went back near the plant he had climbed up earlier. Near the top he had to stop to have a bit of his food again and a little drink from the flower that had been holding a little rainwater. Now he was ready to do what he was known best for, better than any other Mouhume … and that was finding things out.

He was more determined now and focused on the job in hand. He had already called for the fairy and not had any response so they must be behind the disappearance of Ruddy.

His razor-sharp thorn from a bush nearby was going to get the evidence as to what and where Ruddy might be. He had not seen everything that had happened to Ruddy when she had been thrown down from the sky but he had seen her on the ground and what other Mouhumes had said about what they had seen.

So he was going to strike first, wound it, then ask questions later. He went in the direction he had last seen Ruddy go. It was towards a big dense hedge. He stopped. Why would she head towards that? Not even a tiny mouse would be able to go through that without difficulty?

But he was determined to find out. There had to be a way into it and he was going to find out. As he got near the hedge the difference in the daylight made him stop so that his eyes could adjust. Something was not right, as he stood near the hedge. He looked at it but his eyes were still not adjusting, he could not focus properly.

He took a few steps back. Stood a while then he heard a noise from up the garden. It was the old man who lived in this house. He was calling for something or someone; the old man had a tray with something on it that he thought looked like food.

Mousey stepped back and back again, watching the human all the time. The human was still up the garden, at a table and placing whatever was on the tray onto the table. He carried on watching as

107

Adventure of the Mouhumes
Jack and Annie's new
Visitors

he took another step backwards, but before he knew it he was in the hedge that had made his eyes blurry. He went backwards into it. The strange thing was, it was as if he could see through it and it was around him but not touching him? He could move around and nothing was stopping him. It was as if the branches from the hedge were there but not, there appeared to be no restriction.

At this time he had taken his eyes off what was going on up the garden. He was too engrossed with his new surroundings. This was magic. Had he discovered some magical power that enabled him to go through and into plants without any restriction?

He stood for longer than he should have in his new surroundings, making only slight movements with his hands. This was great he thought. Nothing was stopping him, he could move through solid objects.

The aroma was not of anything he had come across before. It was not something he wanted to be around any longer than he needed to be. Mousey looked up the garden once again. The human was still up there. But to his surprise he could see a number of fairies: one on the shoulder of the human and others eating from the table the human had put the food on.

But the human was still there. Suddenly he was flying in the air, two fairies had him by a shoulder each, heading towards the human. He had no time to do anything before he was dropped onto the table where some of the fairies were eating.

Those who were eating turned around sharply almost snarling at Mousey and ready to attack him. The human picked Mousey up by the scruff of the neck. (Mousey being dressed in a fur skin from a mouse looked like a mouse at first glance)

Looking straight into the human's eye, Mousey could see what was going to happen next. The expression on the human's face told him that he was going to kill him.

Created and written by I C Henderson

Adventure of the Mouhumes
Jack and Annie's new
Visitors

Mousey never took his eyes off him. Then the human pulled back his arm ready to throw Mousey as far as he could. Mousey felt sick in his stomach. It was like nothing he had ever experienced before. He was hoping to pass out, but no, in no time at all he was flying in the air, spinning around with no idea in which direction he was going. The whole world, sky and ground was twirling and twisting into one but still he never passed out. He was expecting a thud, unbearable pain and then everything to go black.

Created and written by I C Henderson

Adventure of the Mouhumes
Jack and Annie's new
Visitors

Chapter 18
The Museum

NOT MUCH WAS said in the car on the way to the museum. They had never been there for years; no doubt it would have changed.

They decided that they would just look around first.

That would be better than just jumping in with two feet. And asking anyone, this way they could find out whom to ask, and not mention anything about it. More so if they thought the professor was not going to believe them, or take them seriously.

When they arrived they could hardly believe the change; they held each other's hand s as they stood outside the main entrance. Jack told Annie how nervous he was.

"Annie pet, I feel like a little lad starting school for the first time, the butterflies in my stomach are having a party and a disco, God …I feel sick"

Annie gave his hand a squeeze, she told him he would be all right and she will be with him all the way.

When they got inside they looked at the notice board to see what was on, and what time. There was nothing for Professor Glass, so they went to the receptionist and asked if Professor Glass was doing any talks today?

The receptionist told them that it was his day off, the sinking feeling the two of them must have had. Was clear to see on their faces,

"But he's doing a class for Mr Jones; he's been brought down with flu or something. Isn't that funny, Professor Glass doing a class, doesn't it sound ever so funny" The receptionist went on.

Created and written by I C Henderson

Adventure of the Mouhumes
Jack and Annie's new
Visitors

Just then Annie interrupted and asked what time was the class starting?

"Its all ready started its down the corridor first left then the second door on your right" The receptionist went on to tell them.

"He's doing a talk about wild life in the countryside"

"Thanks" Annie and Jack both interrupted at the same time. And off they went as quickly as they could.

Just as they arrived outside the classroom door they held their breath, just then they could hear that someone was getting a right telling off. This had done nothing to help their confidence. (The classroom door) the top half was frosted, the bottom half was wood, so you could see a silhouette through the glass, As Annie and Jack were deciding whether they should go into the classroom.

Suddenly the door flew open. And there was a sudden sharp Question. "Who are you? And are you going to stand there all day?"

Professor Glass was not one for any mix-ups, or any misunderstanding he was straight to the point. And his tone was sharp, but that was the way he was with everyone, he was tall and of a medium build.

Jack and Annie both began stuttering and both trying to speak at the same time. Sounded and no doubt felt silly, even more so when Professor Glass asked for just one to talk

"Can just one talk?" there was a silence. Then the professor asked again, but this time even more sharply.

"I'll make it easy for you I'll point to one of you and that one speaks ok?"

Created and written by I C Henderson

Adventure of the Mouhumes
Jack and Annie's new
Visitors

By this time Annie and Jack were getting cross with themselves as well as the Professor, Jack asked if it was all right for them to come in and listen to the lecture that the Professor was giving.

The Professor in a loud and cross voice told them who he was, if they came into the room, he did not want them to disturb the rest of the students.

"You must be silent; I would like it if you did not disturb the class any more!"

They both agreed and went to the back of the class. The talk was interesting and Professor Glass was not at all bad with the speech. However, the only complaint they had, was that his people skills left a lot to be desired!

After the class was finished, Professor Glass was just about to go when Annie stuck up her hand. The people who were in there were on the way out. It would be hard for the Professor to see her as she was at the back of the class and still sitting. When suddenly, Jack shouted which got the attention of those who where still in the class.

"Hey you, Mr Glass my wife would like a word with you!" That got him noticed all right but not in the way Annie wanted. Professor Glass came up to the back of the class like a whippet

"For one thing I am a Professor, and another thing I do not like being shouted at like that, what is so important? That you disrupted my class from start to finish!" The Professor asked angrily.

Jack had rubbed him up the wrong way, and felt a little silly. He tried to put a bit of fun in his answer.

"I got your attention I'm sorry that you did not find it fun…"

Created and written by I C Henderson

Adventure of the Mouhumes
Jack and Annie's new
Visitors

Just then Annie jumped into the conversation.

"It's just that we have something in the garden and not sure what they might be?" Annie said in a shy and shaky voice.

The Professor told them to look in the library. There are plenty books there.

Jack not wanting to upset the Professor anymore than he already had. Told him that they had already looked at the library and they were told to come to see him, as he might be able to help.

"As you have a good reputation concerning, strange creatures".

This went down well, the Professor seemed to grow six inches taller, Annie standing at one side saw this and smiled to Jack. They both thought this had gone down well.

"So what kind of animal do you think you have?" the Professor asked in a better tone.

"Well we are not sure as they seem to look like a mouse" Jack trying to explain. But just then Annie finished off the tale, as she knew that Jack would get it all mixed up.

"Well they're like a mouse to look at, at first. But when you watch them after some time you see that they are different, in all sorts of ways"

"What sort of ways?" asked the Professor.

Annie went on to tell him some of the things they had done.

"Well there was last night. A mouse would not do this, one of the thing's set a mousetrap off, (sprung it) then tried to turn it over. But when it could not do it by itself three others came to help."

113

Adventure of the Mouhumes
Jack and Annie's new
Visitors

Just then the Professor interrupted and asked, "Why were the things trying to turn it over?"

"Well I'm just about to tell you why" Annie carried on and told him!

"Two of them got on after pushing it into the pond, they were fishing! And even got a fish hooked and pulled it out"

At this stage Jack was shaking his head not at all happy that these creatures were poaching his fish.

"I think they're more like poachers in my garden" Jack said in a disapproving way.

Annie interrupted and said in a fun way. "I don't think they would have poached them. Maybe fried them"

The look on Jacks face was a picture. That made Annie and the Professor laugh, if nothing else this broke down any barriers that the Professor might have had. They laughed for some time, the thought of Jack's little poachers.

After they had stopped laughing, The Professor asked them if it would be at all possible for him to come and see them some time. They agreed and arranged for him to come that night.

"Would seven be all right?" Annie asked

The Professor just wanted to see the things, and probably would have agreed to anytime. He got their address. And off they went home, Annie wanted to get back to tidy the house.

Adventure of the Mouhumes
Jack and Annie's new
Visitors
Chapter 19
Woodlands

BACK IN THE woods. Rug and others made camp. They had found some trees with passageways under the roots so they did not have a lot to do, just a little modifying here and there. They decided this would be the best place for now. It was not that far away from the humans so they could go and raid the gardens for food when they were struggling with the resources in the woodland. There was plenty of wildlife which meant they could feed on plenty. There were new plants they could make use of.

Rug always said that once they had set up somewhere to live he would go back and get those left in the park area. He knew he would have to go back sooner rather than later to help them as they had little food. He would have to take food supplies with him but first he would have to make sure they had enough in his new camp.

This would take a day or two as they had to find out what was around them and how they would take advantage of the new area. They knew food was put out for the birds at certain times in the day. The only downside was that the birds could be aggressive and sometimes the humans would stand at a distance to watch the birds feeding. Some humans put the food out and walked away. That was the time not to hesitate and go for it. The idea was to run and grab as much as possible and get back to safety.

This area was not all that different to where they had once lived; the only difference was being so close to the humans. They would adapt soon and make the best out of the situation.

The passageways they had from one tree to another were already there, so this saved them a lot of work. They only needed to dig out chambers for their own space. The sandy ground under the trees had clay in parts but they could find use for it and make things they would need from the clay.

Created and written by I C Henderson

Adventure of the Mouhumes
Jack and Annie's new
Visitors

It did not take them long to make their new home. It was as safe as they could make it using knowledge they had gained though the different experiences they had encountered in their lives. Safety and defensive areas were made to keep them safe if they were ever attacked underground.

The main concern was all of those dead rats. Had the rest of them moved on or were they still in the area? Rats were strong and fearless fighters and came in large numbers which made them almost impossible to defeat. Even though a large number were dead and it would have made a big hole in the numbers, rats multiplied quickly so their numbers would increase in no time.

One thing the Mouhumes had though was intelligence and skills that might help outwit any enemies that were large in numbers. They had encountered rats a number of times. Rats ran all over the place scurrying and killing almost everything in front of them. They were an enemy to all creatures.

Rug had been told this from a young age and from what he had seen nothing was going to change his mind. They plagued the land, leaving behind them death and famine. They would eat everything in their path then move on and then another pack would follow.

The food that had been poisoned would put off any other Rats from coming, but no doubt they would be back at some stage. The others must have moved on but Rug knew they needed defence weapons in and around the area they lived in.

Rug was now a leader and not a bad one at all but he still wanted to find Tube, Ratty and the others. He would not rest until he found some sort of trail. He still had no idea where they would be or even if they were still alive. Rug knew they had a strong chance as Tube had taken some of the strongest warriors.

Created and written by I C Henderson

Adventure of the Mouhumes
Jack and Annie's new
Visitors

Rug knew he had some young up and coming fearless fighters but they still lacked the experience of those who had left. This was his main fear. He now knew he had made a mistake, his own lack of knowledge had been his error for demanding Ruddy to go. He had no idea that she had a lot of followers, more than he had ever thought. He believed they would all be too frightened to leave with her and that he would be the new conqueror.

Now he was frightened. He told those who had come with him that he would be the leader and take them to safety but now doing it was far harder than he had ever thought it would be. They depended on him and already he had left those who were too weak in the park.

He started to doubt his own ability but those around him seemed more than happy to go along with most of his decisions. This gave him some comfort. He would still be in charge for now but when he thought of Tube he began to think how happy he would be if he could pass the leadership back to him without question.

His group soon developed their own habits they all had there own roles. Some would be out during the day gathering food; others would be out during the early hours of the morning, still in darkness, collecting food and setting traps, The Mouhumes knew they would put defences and traps up that would slow down if not kill a potential enemy and all those in their camp knew what to do, when and how to do it.

They had it as secure as they possibly could. Not a lot could come and attack them without been hurt or killed and to help prevent attacks from large numbers they made a lot of harmful hidden traps with lots of sharp bits sticking up. The traps were set all around the camp, thorns were placed under the fallen leaves, sharp end pointing up so if a dog was to wander near their home it would get a thorn in its pad and head back to where it came from. They also had traps to kill smaller animals such as rats, mice, moles

Created and written by I C Henderson

Adventure of the Mouhumes
Jack and Annie's new
Visitors

and rabbits. They might be smaller than most things but they were just as dangerous.

It would take at least six of them with experience to kill a rabbit. Then there were squirrels, they were as fast as any Mouhume but three times bigger. The Mouhumes were no match for them. They could move around trees and the ground at ease with speed and suppleness. As for rabbits they were pretty much grounded so a Mouhume could get extra height by going up a tree or a bush if and when they needed to.

They picked an area with trees that had good long strong roots so they could have a warren between a number of trees with plenty of space and places they could go and hide in, if the need arose.

The next thing Rug had to do, was to return to the park area and bring those he left behind back to their new home just as he promised;

Created and written by I C Henderson

Adventure of the Mouhumes
Jack and Annie's new
Visitors

Chapter 20
Tube's Action

TUBE WAS TALKING to some of the Mouhumes when he was interrupted. Scallop had run in all flustered. He ran straight to Tube who was taken by surprise but had reacted quickly and took Scallop's feet away straight from underneath him... Scallop fell to the floor.

Scallop quickly jumped to his feet, two Mouhumes got hold of him restraining him. Tube quietly asked what the matter was. Why was he out of control? This was not like Scallop. This was not how Scallop behaved!

Scallop broke free from the hold of the two Mouhumes and got a firm hold of Tube's arm and whispered something in his ear. The colour from Tube's face drained almost grey. His legs weakened slightly but Scallop held on to him.

Tube knew he had to show strength in front of the others. He demanded that everyone leave and sent for Ratty to come straight away as it was a matter of great urgency. Everyone left as they were told, leaving Scallop and Tube alone.

Tube told Scallop they would discuss what he had just been told but he had to wait for Ratty. Not another word could be spoken until Ratty arrived.

Once Ratty arrived Scallop started telling them from start to finish. Starting from when he had seen Mousey in the garden next door doing his detective work.His story was something unbelievable it was hard to understand what they were now being told; it was something they could hardly get their heads around as he explained it.

He told them that he had stayed hidden and out of sight. As he was always amazed at how Mousey could find out things so he

Created and written by I C Henderson

Adventure of the Mouhumes
Jack and Annie's new
Visitors

thought he would keep an eye on him to learn how he did it so well. He explained that Mousey was going into the small houses: in and out looking around them and going from one area to another. He was also going up tall plants then down and then up another.

Then the human from the house next door came out. He was making some sort of sound and putting food on the table. Scallop had thought the food was for the birds but to his surprise the fairies came from out of nowhere.

Scallop carried on with his story. Tube and Ratty did not say a word. The fairies had been on plants or hidden around the plants? It was hard to say but they just appeared.

Mousey had seemed to disappear as much as Scallop could see from his hiding place. He looked around he could not see Mousey but there were one or two plants and objects in his way so he could not get a clear view at all.

However he did see one of the fairies who had picked up Ruddy. He recognised her by her torn wings. She was clearly a fairy who had been in more than her fair share of conflicts. Her battle scars were clear to see.

She had a stern look about her. She once would have been beautiful but instead she was full of scars, she looked disappointed, stressed and worried.

Scallop said that she reminded him of Ruddy but had a different pursuit. That much became clear in the strange circumstances. The story began to unfold.

"Mousey was unseen then suddenly, like Ruddy, he was pulled out from somewhere. Two fairies had him and dropped him on the table where the others were feeding around the human. The fairy with the damaged wings was on the table when Mousey was dropped."

Created and written by I C Henderson

Adventure of the Mouhumes
Jack and Annie's new
Visitors

"She must have gotten a fright. She turned quickly and was ready to attack but the human picked Mousey up and pulled his arm back to stop them from hurting him. There was some movement but then they settled down."

"That's when I saw that Mousey must have passed out. His body was lame and floppy. The human put him on the table. Some of the fairies crowded around. I could not see what happened next. The human walked away and Mousey was gone."

"The next thing was that young fairy at my side. I thought that I was going to be the next one. One by one they were picking us off. So I pulled my thorn out and was ready to attack when that fairy with the damaged wings came. She told me to calm down but in a way that I knew was … right and true."

"She asked me to follow her up the garden which I did. The human had gone into the house but I was still unsure what was going to happen. I still held on to my thorn ready to kill or be killed. She led me into a building *(The outhouse)*"

Tube and Ratty sat listening with amazement. All would become clear as they sat without interruption.

"As I went into the outhouse it was Mousey that I saw first. He was still unconscious. They said that he would be alright. It was the shock of being picked up by the human. Ted that's what he's called, Ted. Anyway he passed out. Ted had put him in the outhouse away from any harm,"

"That's when I saw Ruddy lying in a box with some sort of bedding. She was nursing a baby. She had been carrying a baby. She had been pregnant. That's why she had not been herself these last few days. The fall had brought it on faster than it should have."

Created and written by I C Henderson

Adventure of the Mouhumes
Jack and Annie's new
Visitors

The gasp Tube and Ratty made was of relief. She was ok. Well as ok as a mother could be. She was now with the fairies and they were looking after her until she felt able to come back.

Scallop carried on with what he had seen and what he'd been told. The fairy that was going to attack Mousey was also the mother of Capheus. Once again Ratty and Tube looked on with confused expressions.

Scallop told them as if they should have known who Capheus was; Capheus was the one who Ruddy had thrown on the ground. It was his mother. Just like Ruddy she was a fighter. He said that with superiority.

Ratty asked Scallop what it was about this particular fairy? Why was he so taken with her? It was clear to Ratty and Tube, his head was turned. Rightly or wrongly it was too soon to tell so they let him tell the rest of his story.

As they had found out the days before, the fairies could talk and understand most living creatures and they get along with just about everything.

Scallop wanted to tell them everything that he had seen and been told. It was something he could hardly understand, so telling Tube and Ratty with their knowledge of most things they might be able to help him to understand. After all, it might not be all that wonderful.

Some of the fairies had two wings and some had four wings. Some had so many colours they looked like flowers. Some were big and some were tiny.

There were not many older males, just young males. You could tell that some female fairies were a lot older and yet it seemed they done most things such as defending, hunting for food and talking to the human.

Created and written by I C Henderson

Adventure of the Mouhumes
Jack and Annie's new
Visitors

As he told Tube and Ratty about what he knew it seemed that the fairy world had a lot going for it. Tube asked about Mousey, when would he be back to give his account?

Scallop told them that someone would have to go to see them as he was still shaky. They did not want him to get hurt by any predators such as birds, cats and any other danger that might be around.

Now they had to decide who and when they would go to collect Mousey and see what help they could be to Ruddy.

Tube was thinking why had they not told anyone about Ruddy? They would have seen us. He sat for a while going over a few things in his head and looking at it in different ways but still could not justify why they had not made contact.

Tube sent Scallop away so he could talk with Ratty. He told Ratty his thoughts. Ratty also had similar thoughts. Was it a trap? It was a hard thing to decide but Tube said that he would go and collect Mousey and more importantly, see how Ruddy was.

Tube had a way of working out what actions they might take from the way they held their bodies, just little signals. It was something in the eyes that made him react without hesitation.

He might not be as young as most but he had more experience than any. He would go with only Scallop. That way they would see that they went in peace. Ratty stayed back but gathered all those he could, without making it obvious to any hidden eyes.

Scallop took Tube straight to the outhouse where Ruddy and Mousey were. Two fairies' came, none of whom Scallop had seen earlier. These two were smaller and both were bright in colour: red, green and yellow. Both were beautiful. They could hardly stay in the same place for more than a second or two.

Created and written by I C Henderson

Adventure of the Mouhumes
Jack and Annie's new
Visitors

Tube could not get anything from this action. It was not aggression or anything else, more than their behaviour. Tube thought because of their size, being less than half of a Mouhume, they might be fearful of being swooped up from a bird. After all they were a lot smaller than some of the fairies they had already seen.

This was all new for the Mouhumes. They had never had anything to do with other creatures, apart from fighting or killing. Now they seemed to be receiving help, help they never asked for or had ever been given before. So why were the fairies so keen to give them help? This was going to be something Tube would have to find out. He had a suspicious mind and rightfully so.

He was led into the washhouse. Scallop stayed at the doorway. Tube was led up on to one of the benches. Ruddy was in a shoebox with a hole cut out. As soon as she heard Tube she was out the box with her little baby in her arms. Her face was full of smiles and pride.

Tube walked to her. This must have been the first time he let his emotions be seen. A smile from ear to ear and a tear ran down his face. Ruddy put her arm around him and cuddled him. There were countless things he wanted to ask her but this was not the time.

Mousey emerged from behind another box, full of smiles that were short lived. Tube gave him a glance and Mousey knew that he had let him down. Now was not the time, this moment was for Ruddy.

Was she ready to go back to camp? Was she in good health? Was she getting everything she needed? Tube fired question after question at her. Ruddy smiled as she did not get time to reply to the first question when another was asked.

Created and written by I C Henderson

Adventure of the Mouhumes
Jack and Annie's new
Visitors

Then to the side of Ruddy appeared a fairy. It was the one who had saved Ruddy. His wings were still a bit tattered from the fall but otherwise he was ok and still full of high spirits. Then his mother came. She was as big as Tube in height. Her wings were torn from previous fights. Scallop was right, she had a beautiful face but one of worry. Tube looked at her looking at her son. It was the worry on her face, a parent's worry for a child who was now almost fully grown. The adventures he would now want to do not knowing all the danger out there, but still wanting to find out all new things and learn like his parents had too.

His mother wanted to hold onto him as long as she could. A male fairy could only mate once and then the male died. So having a male was a mother's heartache. A male would be protected by all the adults but being a male he would find mischief and that's why he needed watching.

He had been watching Ruddy for a number of days but got too close to her and that was why she attacked him. He might have been hard to see but her instinct told her something was near. He thought with his hard-to-see camouflage. He would be ok getting near other living things even though he never thought they could see him.

His mother started to talk to Tube. She told him her name and her son's name. She was called Glow and he was called Capheus. She explained why he was protected so much. There were two other males of similar age and they would be moving to other fairy communities in the near future. The males from other communities would move to theirs and so on. That would be the last time they would see their son. It was both a joyful and sad time. This would happen only once a year.

They stood chatting for a while. Tube was keen to know as much about these wonderful creatures. He would learn so much from them but now was the time to go back to his own with Ruddy, the baby, Mousey and Scallop.

Created and written by I C Henderson

Adventure of the Mouhumes
Jack and Annie's new
Visitors

As they left the outhouse a number of fairies came and said their goodbyes. It was only the next garden but they said they would not interfere in that garden anymore so the Mouhumes could have their own space.

Tube was told a little about those who lived in the house. Jack was the man who sat in the early hours looking out of the window and the woman who comes and goes they did not know her name. It was Jack who spent most his time in the garden but not so much recently, he was walking badly so he just sat looking out the window.

The fairies had never shown themselves to anyone else but Ted. They could talk to most living things but humans could not understand them. They could understand humans. They needed to know a lot more.

Tube went back and the welcome Ruddy got was amazing. The legend was back and had a baby. Word spread quickly around the camp so all day she had visitors wishing her well. In the meantime Ratty and Tube had to talk to Mousey about his experience. This would be a long and detailed discussion, one that Mousey was not looking forward to.

Created and written by I C Henderson

Adventure of the Mouhumes
Jack and Annie's new
Visitors

Chapter 21
The visit

WHEN THEY GOT home, Annie not wanting anyone in, until she had made it spotless, got straight to work and did the dusting, and cleaning.

Jack not being able to do much just went down to the greenhouse. Just to stay out of Annie's way. The time passed quickly and in no time at all Annie was coming down the garden.

"Are you coming in for your tea? We are having it early so that I can get cleaned up for the Professor coming" Annie said.

Jack ready for his tea. Took no time in going up to the kitchen, to get washed and cleaned up. He was first to the table rubbing his hands

"How way lass hurry up I'm starving!"

Annie brought the dinner in; in no time at all they were eating. It didn't take them long to finish.

"What did you think of the Professor? I tell you what, I thought he looked like that man out of (faulty towers), you know the mad man running about all the time" Jack could never remember his name.

Sighing, Annie told him.

"You mean Basil Faulty .I thought more like Mr Bean."

Then Annie picked up the plates and washed them. Not long after she was all cleaned up. Someone knocked on the front door.

"That will be the Professor quick Jack get that paper and move it"Annie pointed to the newspaper on the chair.

Created and written by I C Henderson

Adventure of the Mouhumes
Jack and Annie's new
Visitors

Jack picked it up then put it down on the table; Annie brought in the Professor. She asked him not to mind the mess but they had not had time to clean up. She looked on the table and saw the newspaper. She picked it up rolled it up and slapped Jack across the ear. Then put it in the newspaper rack.

Jack looked at Annie, and shook his head in a disapproving way.

Jack whispered to Annie "you've been cleaning up since we got back"

"Come in to the conservatory and I will get you a drink" Annie asked the Professor what he would like to drink.

"A glass of milk please if you have enough"Replied the Professor.

Annie looked in the fridge. "Just enough" she replied.

Jack sat down near the Professor and told him the best place to look to see the little poachers. Annie was not long getting the drinks and then they turned the lights off in the house.

It was a bright night so they could see all right. The moon was just about full. It wasn't long before Jack pointed to the flowers near the edge of the pond; the Professor looked but couldn't make out what he was supposed to be looking at.

He shook his head not saying a word. Jack put his finger up as if to say just one minute. Just then he saw them the Professor's mouth wide open. You could tell that he'd seen them.

He looked like a jabbering fool. No words coming. Just finger movements, his whole body was shaking.

Created and written by I C Henderson

Adventure of the Mouhumes
Jack and Annie's new
Visitors

"Are you all right? You haven't stood on a pin have you?" Asked Jack in his daft way.

Annie gripped The Professor by his wrists and took him into the living room. So they wouldn't frighten the little things.

"What do you think of that?" Jack asked with a big smile on his face as he came through the dinning room.

The Professor still not right and all excited took a bit of time to get himself back to normal. When Annie thought that he was ok, she told him that they should all go back in to the conservatory, to watch and later they could talk about what they had seen, Jack and she had not had time to talk.

In no time at all they were ready to go back into the conservatory. They watched for best part of the night and early hours in the morning. The time just disappeared. When they came out the Professor told them what they have. They are called Mouhumes.

"What!" Jack and Annie asked at the same time.

"Mou-humes" the Professor said again

"They are a rare and unusual animal, I have not seen one until now, I heard about them when I was a child, my Grandfather would tell me about them but I never saw one. Not one person apart from my grandfather, I know of has ever heard or seen one. This is amazing!" The Professor was in his glory and wanted to tell Jack and Annie more about the Mou-humes.

"But first can we watch them a little longer. Later we can converse and tell each other about these wonderful creatures… if that's ok?" asked The Professor, he was keen to get back to see the things, which he had been told about as a young boy.

Created and written by I C Henderson

Adventure of the Mouhumes
Jack and Annie's new
Visitors

The time went quickly when watching these creatures. The morning light came, and they could still see what the Mouhumes were doing. When they realized the time, it had not seemed possible that the time had disappeared. Jack was first to notice the time that was only because he was hungry.

"Look at the time it's nine thirty all ready! Annie can you put the kettle on as I'm sure the Professor and you would like a cup of tea or some thing"

"Would you like a drink of anything Professor? I suppose you would like one as well Jack" Then Annie went into the kitchen and turned the kettle on.

"You don't have to keep calling me Professor, my name is Brian, yes I would love a cup of coffee please" Brian got up and went into the dinning room. He sat down on one of the chairs. He was smiling from ear to ear, Jack was still in the conservatory, and Annie was in the kitchen making the breakfast.

Jack came into the dinning room. And asked Brian what did he think and what plans did he have. Would he keep it to himself? As he would not like the Mouhumes to come to any harm!

Brian agreed, then went on to tell them, what he was told as a young boy.

"Can you hear me Annie he asked? Annie was still in the kitchen.

"Yes the door is open and I'm just getting the drinks ready and I'll be in, in a minute. I can still hear you so just carry on"

"My grandfather described them as small, furry; at first glance you would think they were a large mouse. But when you look at the face they are totally different. Round not long like a

Adventure of the Mouhumes
Jack and Annie's new
Visitors

mouse, they didn't have a long tail, and they stood like a small man, they can and did overcome anything. "

Just then Jack interrupted "what do you mean overcome things?"

"Well they can work things out, my grandfather was a doctor, and he would set tasks for them"

Jack interrupted again "What kind of tasks and what happened?"

Brian didn't know all the tasks, but he did remember one that his grandfather had told him.

"They have a keen interest in learning. I remember my grandfather telling me one of the experiments he had done. What got him started was an old clock .He had an old wind up clock that never worked, he had put it around the back of the outside shed, it had been there for the scrap man, rag and bone man I think they where called in them days, but he'd never got round to putting it around the front for him. Anyway one day when he remembered, he went and got it. All the insides were out; they had been taken completely out"

Jack asked, "Why did they take the insides of a clock out?"

"Well at first he had no idea, but when he found out he was surprised. After he found out what they used the clock mechanism for. That was when he started his experiments. He spent the best part of his life studying them. And trying to learn all about them, well they put the mechanism to good use. They used it as a wind up drawbridge. To stop rats and predators getting into their living area"

Adventure of the Mouhumes
Jack and Annie's new
Visitors

Annie and Jack were flabbergasted. Jack when watching the day before had seen what they were doing, or looked like what they might be doing.

"Yesterday when I was watching it looked like they were… "Jack stopped for a short time then carried on. "I feel a bit daft but anyway I'll just carry on and tell you. It seemed that they were trying to make a hole in the rocks around the pond. Where the waterfall is, let me explain! When we made the waterfall I built the walls and although it's hollow in the middle, there is no way anything can get in. There are paving stones on the bottom, then bricks build the rest up. I was watching a program on the television, and it said ponds and waterfalls could sometimes attract mice and rats. So anyway, there is no way anything can get in there. It's rodent proof…"

Then Brian asked if he could go out and have a look to see close at hand.

"But first you will have your breakfast, I'll get cleaned up, these late nights will be the death off me"Annie said in a tired and low way.

"Never mind get the food, we will see what the little Mou-Humes- is that right? Brian" Jack still not sure if he has pronounced it right.

"Yes that's right Mouhumes we will have to be careful when we go out so that we do not disturb them" Brian just wanted to get a closer look, all his life wanted to see what he had been told when he was a young boy. And now it was real.

Just then his mobile phone rang it was his wife. He went into the living room; Jack could still hear but not make out what was being said. By the sound of the noise coming out of the receiver she was not at all happy. Brian was trying to explain but it was a one way dispute, no way could he get a word in.

Created and written by I C Henderson

Adventure of the Mouhumes
Jack and Annie's new
Visitors

All embarrassed, Brian went back in to the dinning room and said that he would not have anything to eat as he had to go. He then explained that he was meant to be picking his wife up from the airport early that morning.

"She was at a lecture the day before. I've some explaining to do when I get back. When she got home and there was no one in. she was concerned and worried. Would it be possible to have your phone numbers? I'll get back to you some time today"

Just then Annie came back into the room and the look on Brian's face she could tell that something was not right.

"What's wrong? Brian you look worried, has some thing happened" Annie was upstairs when Brian received his phone call. So she had no idea what had happened.

Brian not wanting to explain, as it might take too long, (*more like if he took too long he would be in more trouble then he already was*) told them (*Jack and Annie*) that he did not have time, but he would be back. And thanked them for letting him into this wonderful experience. Then off he went

Jack still sitting at the table with a big smile on his face said to Annie. "He seemed a bit wound up; a bit worried I would say. And maybe a little bit under the thumb. ."

"Don't be silly he is a gentleman and felt silly that he left his wife at the airport. Not like you. In fact you would probably just laugh" Then Annie hit Jack with the rolled up newspaper. The one Jack was meant to put away.

Annie feeling tired asked if they could go to bed. Jack agreed and they went to bed. In no time at all they were asleep.

Created and written by I C Henderson

Adventure of the Mouhumes
Jack and Annie's new
Visitors

Chapter 22
Return to the Park

RUG AND FOUR others headed back to the park. It was early evening but they still had the cover of the trees. Rug had thought if they left now by the time they had to cross over the roads it would be quiet and there was less likelihood of them being seen from any harmful eyes. As it worked out he was right. They scurried in and out of shrubbery, not coming across many dangers. They were fast and now they were near the top of the hill above the park.

The nightlight was dull but it was still light enough to see the bottom of the hill. Cars were still in the car park and noises were coming from the grass area. Humans were still running around.

Rug pointed out the area that he wanted to go to. They all nodded but now it was time to take a break. They had travelled a great distance without stopping. Rug had picked the fastest and strongest for this journey. They were fearless and proved themselves many times before.

After they stopped and had a short rest they decided it was now time to go forward with the last part of the journey. They would need all the energy they had as with the humans still around, they would have to move with speed and agility.

Running alongside the green area, there were trees and blackberry bushes that were good for them as they knew they would have cover, especially from an overhead threat.   As soon as they got to the end of the bushes they stopped to assess what they would do next. The humans were now thinning out but some were still near the area they wanted to be.

Rug wanted to be back at his new burrow before morning but at the same time he did not want to be seen by humans. And at this moment he could not make out how many humans were still there. He could see six but there were also noises coming from places out

Created and written by I C Henderson

Adventure of the Mouhumes
Jack and Annie's new
Visitors

of his sight. They sounded close to the area where they were heading. After a short consideration of what to do or not to do they made a run for it. They criss-crossed each other in and out of the clearing and into some sheltered areas. They may have been spread out but they were still in sight of each other.

With only a few yards to go, they would be in one of the burrows entrance. Rug was, at this point, a bit worried. He was wondering if they would still be there, or more importantly, still alive. He had left food for them but some had been so poorly, he knew that it would take more than what he had left behind.

It was getting dark outside; the warren would be in total darkness. There would be no light at all deep inside. Mouhume eyes took a little time to adjust to different lights and darkness but once they did they could see reasonably well. The danger was that if they ran straight into the burrow they would not see anything for a short time, so they could be in an unsafe, even fragile state for a moment. Rug was sure that those who were with him would be ready for any attack.

The humans were now in the distance. He gave the signal and they ran into the burrow stopping a little way in so that their eyes could adjust. They pulled out their weapons all made from thorns and bones from small animals they had killed for food.

As they went deeper into the burrow they could hear sounds coming from below. The sound was muffled from the sandy walls. They headed down with caution. They were unsure what it was. Then they could smell something. It was a strange odour, not one that Rug had come across before. It was not unpleasant but nothing that he knew.

Rug suddenly stopped. One of the Mouhumes behind him almost went into his back. They were at the end of that tunnel. The sound was just around the corner. Rug listened to see if he could work out what it was.

Created and written by I C Henderson

Adventure of the Mouhumes
Jack and Annie's new
Visitors

There was still a lot of noise and still muffled. He thought he would just go for it and round the corner which he did. The other four went with him. The sound of a twig snapping; a cry for help, then the sound of thudding, bodies being hit then it was over. Silence nothing was moving.

Then there was the sound of bodies dropping to the ground with a thud and then laughter and shrieks of surprise.

The Mouhumes left in the old rabbit warren had made a net from roots and hid it under the sandy ground so when they had a surprise visit it would tangle up who or what ever had stepped onto it. With two Mouhumes pulling up the ends it gave them time to attack those in the net.

It was only sheer luck they were not run through with a thorn on the end of a long shaft. Something they had not finished yet so they had to bash the enemy with clubs first then with anything sharp they had, at least until the trap was ready. This had saved them.

Rug and the others were let loose with hugs and laughter from those in the warren. A lot was needed to be said from both sides and it would be, but it had not turned out how Rug had thought it would. Rug had thought this was going to be a rescue mission, there and back taking home those who were still alive, if any.

Rug knew the warren as well as those who now had made it their home. They went to the biggest part so they could talk. Rug was told after he had left, there were a number of those who were so ill that they had died because of the time of year, poor weather and the food supplies were almost none.

Then when the weather started to get better and humans came with picnics. They began dropping food and putting food in bins. It was collected as soon as they could get it. Now they had a good

Created and written by I C Henderson

Adventure of the Mouhumes
Jack and Annie's new
Visitors

storage and had more than enough food. Not all the food was from humans, some came from plants that were growing around the woodland area.

Rug was taken to the storage area. He was astonished at how much they had and how well they all looked. There were young Mouhumes on the way. It had become a strong group and they seemed to have worked out what they needed to survive. It was done so quickly.

Rug told them about his journey and his new home. He was asked about Tube and Ratty and the others. He sank his head, told them that he could not find them and that there was no sign of them.

He was reminded about the way they left and how they would not want to leave a trail. He agreed time was getting on. Then he was asked if he would like to stay for the night. He sat for a while and agreed that it would be for the best. This gave him an opportunity to see how they managed and get to know their way of doing things whilst being so close to the humans.

He could not help himself but he had to find out what the smell was. They showed him it was cooked meat that kept longer than other food stuff. It came from the top of the hill. They had no name for it but the other food stuff came from the same place.

They told him how humans eat it a lot but throw a lot away too. He was then told more Mouhumes came back into the burrow with more food from humans. Things like part eaten sandwiches, kebabs, chips, broken biscuits, crisps and just about anything a human would take on a picnic. Some of the Mouhumes made the empty crisp packets into clothing to help them keep dry when it was raining.

Adventure of the Mouhumes
Jack and Annie's new
Visitors

Rug was surprised how well they had come on. He wanted to know about the trap that he was held up in, how it worked and so on …

He stayed the night and early hours of the morning. He was to go back home with a small party from the warren so that if they needed to know where his camp was they could come. That way they could keep in touch and help out each other when needing extra help with food or anything.

As they headed home to the woodland the Mouhumes had already been as far as the chip shop but not much further. Now they were in new land and going in and out of gardens then finally into the woodland area were Rug had his camp.

There were more trees than at the park so they had more cover. The Mouhumes from the park made little symbols so they could find their way back. They also saw some that were already made from Rug when he first explored that area.

In the park the Mouhumes asked if there were any signs from Tube and the others when they left, he told them none that they could see.

Daylight was now upon them so the parkland Mouhumes would have to stay until later that night. This would give them time to discover the area. They had brought food supplies with them, more than they would need. They gave Rug's camp some to try. The kebab meat took a bit of getting used to. It was edible but only as a last resort.

The parkland Mouhumes were shown around the area. None of them knew how near they were to Tube's camp. In truth they were only across the road and five gardens down. If they knew they might have found each other.

Created and written by I C Henderson

Adventure of the Mouhumes
Jack and Annie's new
Visitors

Chapter 23
Awkward Reunion

RUG HAD MADE his mind up. He was going to spend the next few days looking for Tube and the others. He was a little more experienced now. Rug had realised that he was wrong for trying to take over the leadership and also for making demands about Ruddy.

He had convinced himself that she had brought danger to the rabbit warren but now he knew that it was not as he had thought, before they had known the dangers around them. Now the danger was all new, not just from predators but the real danger came from having very little food.

He had to find them, he just had to. No-one in his tree stump had any idea how to store food. He realized this when he went back to the parkland warren. They had worked it out: they knew what food and the best way to do it and it worked well.

He had done the right thing going back to the warren. From the short time he was there he learnt all about how to store food and also how to make netting from thin roots to trap enemies. He knew there was so much more that he needed to learn.

He had already looked around the area on a number occasions so what they would now have to do was one of two things: they could go higher up into the woods or go over the road to the other side and look around the houses there. This was not something Rug wanted to do but, he had considered it a number of times. Still a little unsure as he always thought that Tube would never go near humans unless, something made them cross paths.

Rug and some of his camp had already been as far up into the woodland area as they dared so this meant there was only one option left and that was to go over the road to see what was there.

Created and written by I C Henderson

Adventure of the Mouhumes
Jack and Annie's new
Visitors

At least they would know and then they could get on with looking somewhere else if they didn't find them.

Rug with his companions went into the nearest garden. It was early in the morning; there were no lights on in the houses. They crept along the side of the house into the front garden, stopping just outside the hedge.

They looked up and down the road to see if anyone or anything might be there. The streets looked empty. Higher up the road a house light had just been turned on so Rug knew the humans were starting to wake up. It was now or never to cross the road.

They took no time crossing the road: slightly splitting up due to the fact that straight over the road was a garden with a wall around it. So now they had to go to the back of the house with a garden between them.

It might have only been a garden between them but there was a big difference between the two gardens. The Mouhumes who had gone to the higher garden had to fathom out how to get around the back of the house to meet the others.

The house had been empty. Most of the contents such as the old carpets and broken cupboards were blocking the walkway at the side of the house. The rubbish was attracting vermin: rats and mice. This was not something two Mouhumes wanted to come across by themselves. The smell coming from the carpet was terrible.

They had to decide and decide quickly if they wanted to go that way. It would be the quickest but not the healthiest for more than one reason. Whatever they were going to do would have to be quick as more and more lights were being turned on in the houses. From previous experience this could only mean one thing, animals: dogs and cats would be coming out of the houses. No doubt some of that smell belonging to dogs.

Created and written by I C Henderson

Adventure of the Mouhumes
Jack and Annie's new
Visitors

They looked at each other with disappointment on their faces. They knew that Rug would be at the back end of the house now and waiting for them. They would just have to go over it. It was almost as high as the door. It had just been thrown out of the house in a heap.

Rug was at the back of the other house in the garden looking for the two Mouhumes. He knew they should have been there by now, so he decided to go and look for them as he went into the next door's garden he was still expecting them to appear at anytime. As Rug walked around the corner his eyes could not believe what he was looking at. It was a mountain of rubbish and even from where he was standing the stench was overbearing. He had to grin; the two who had gone that way were now falling from the heap then running as fast as they could from it, stopping just in front of Rug.

The rotten carpets together with the smell of old food, cigarette smoke and also dog and cat scent, was more than they could put up with. They had never come across anything like this before.

Rug tried to keep his distance from the two Mouhumes but they kept getting near him as they tried to tell him what it was like. It got to the stage where Rug had to tell them to go back to camp and get cleaned up which they agreed without question. The smell was turning their stomachs. As quick as they arrived they returned to camp only this time they left the way Rug had arrived they were not going over that heap again.

The only thing was, this left Rug with only one Mouhume for help. Still he was not going back. What danger could there be? He thought all the gardens are similar, a dog here, a cat there and humans coming into the gardens putting food out. It was nothing he had not seen before; it was just like that on the other side of the street.

Created and written by I C Henderson

Adventure of the Mouhumes
Jack and Annie's new
Visitors

He would just have to be careful and as there were only two of them there would be less possibility of them being seen. So eventually they went down to the hedge weaving in and out until they reached the bottom of the hedge.

At the end of the garden there was a large grassed area open to any amount of danger. It was no good for a Mouhume to attempt venturing across it so there was only one thing to do and that was to go as he had intended out of sight.

As they travelled down another four gardens they could hear water running. It was not that far away, maybe two or so gardens away. The noise of humans going out to work made them find cover for a while. They might have lived in the woods but they had come across the same thing at certain times of the day. All they could do was hide and hope that nothing would come along to hurt them. All they could do was to rest, have a snack and a drink from their pouch. Time went by slowly. Humans were going to work and young humans were going to school then finally things went quiet.

At least on the other side of the road this did not last as long. The humans seemed to be heading towards this side of the road for some reason.

Now Rug could now move on. Rug and his companion decided to head towards the water to fill up their water pouches and collect any food they might find. They were only two gardens away from the sound of water when they came across a garden with a gate. The gate was leading on to the big lawn area. This was not strange in itself but what was happening was!

Rug and the Mouhume with him stood back in astonishment. They had never seen anything like it. The Mouhume with Rug rubbed his eyes not once but twice. He also pinched Rug's arm to see if he was awake. Rug turned and slapped him over the head. Yes he was awake and yes what he was seeing right in front of his eyes was happening.

Adventure of the Mouhumes
Jack and Annie's new
Visitors

Rug was, in a way, pleased the young Mouhume nipped his arm because he was also wondering if he was dreaming. Now he had to make a decision, what could he do?   Was he to go and show himself or was he to stand back to see what was going to happen next. His thoughts were all over the place. He was just about to step out when his arm was pulled back.

The young Mouhume pulled him back and whispered they should stay and observe for a while. Rug knew this was right but did not like hearing it from a younger Mouhume. Still he nodded.

As they watched it became even more astonishing. Things they had never seen or heard of were happening right in front of them. They stayed hidden in the bushes and long grass that was growing at the base of the prickly bush. Rug wanted to know more about what they were watching but they would stay hidden, just for now.

As they watched, a Mouhume called Woozy was pulling the gate open he was also getting help from a creature Rug had never seen before. They seemed to be working hand in hand. The Mouhume was on the ground pulling the rope and the other creature was pulling the catch open.

It was an old gate that was held on to a brick wall, one of the rusted hinges just holding on. It looked like it was ready to be pulled off once and for all. Rug wondered if that was what they were trying to do, pull the rotten gate away from the post. But why would they do that?

Created and written by I C Henderson

Adventure of the Mouhumes
Jack and Annie's new
Visitors

He could see no reason. If the gate was open, the garden would be open to any predator. Then before his eyes a dog came running straight towards Woozy. Rug pulled his sharp thorn out, ready to go and attack the dog.

He jumped out from the hedge and headed towards the dog. Then he stopped. The dog with slaver drooling and dribbling from its mouth licked Woozy from toe to head. Not once, but twice covering him with its dribble. Woozy just rubbed its muzzle as if he was its friend.

Rug stood watching then, it was even more remarkable than he imagined. He could see a young Mouhume sitting just behind the dog's ear; he stood there almost frozen to the spot when the dog charged towards him, lifting her front paw up and knocking Rug backwards onto the ground.

Woozy, still wiping the slaver from his face and body, saw what happened. He called for the dog to stop. The fairy nearby was translating so that the dog could understand. By this time she was standing over Rug, her hot breath upon him. Rug, at this time, closed his eyes thinking that he was going to be killed.

Created and written by I C Henderson

Adventure of the Mouhumes
Jack and Annie's new
Visitors

The young Mouhume who was on the back of the dog looked down, Woozy ran over and helped Rug to his feet. Without thinking he started to tell Rug the fairy had called the dog off. Then he told Rug the dog was called Tilly and the young Mouhume was Dash, the son of Ruddy.

It was a lot to take in but Rug listened. The other Mouhume came out from hiding. This made Woozy feel a little insecure. Woozy was still wet from Tilly. His rabbit fur jacket looked as if it had been in a pool of water and it weighed him down slightly. A fur jacket wet was not the best for fast movements but he knew that Tilly and Starlight were nearby, if needed.

Starlight landed beside Woozy. She was almost twice the size of any Mouhume and her strength more than ten Mouhumes together. She liked Woozy and he liked her. They often spent days together with Dash and Tilly. The four, over the last week or two, had become almost inseparable. First thing in the morning and last thing at night, only parting when Tilly had to be in and when Starlight needed to re-energize. That would be at least twice a day, depending on what they had been doing.

Making herself invisible took a lot out of her. It took a lot of energy and could drain a fairy a lot. That was something they would only do in extreme circumstances.

Woozy started to tell Rug that they had missed him but also said they did not know that if they went back to the park whether they would end up fighting or killing each other so they thought it best to stay away.

Woozy knew that Rug was stronger and more than capable to beat him so he just had to play it down as he did not know what Rug was after. More importantly, was he here to hurt Dash. After all, it was Ruddy he had not wanted in the commune.

Created and written by I C Henderson

Adventure of the Mouhumes
Jack and Annie's new
Visitors

He had to think quickly. If he headed two more gardens down he would be in the fairies community then the next garden down it would be his. What could he do?

He walked away from Rug and Rug's friend towards Tilly. Tilly bent her head down. He asked Dash if he could get off Tilly and run home with Starlight following him but also asked Starlight to make sure that no one was following them.

Starlight agreed she knew what she had to do. Dash just thought that he had to go home but Starlight knew that she would have to get Ruddy and the others. She had not known all that had happened but she knew enough to get Ruddy and anyone else that was willing.

Dash ran home as quick as he could. Starlight went back and forth, keeping an eye on him but also back tracking, making sure they had not been followed. When Dash got to the big shed he ran straight down into the basement.

Starlight had an idea where Ruddy might be at this time. Two of her other friends followed her; they knew by her expression that something was not right. Starlight went straight to the garden where Buster lived. Tilly lived there as well but Starlight often opened the gate for her so her and Dash could go for a run. Buster was happy enough spending his time in the garden with Ruddy and the other Mouhumes who came in the garden.

Ruddy and her friends were trying to find out how the hedgehog got into the garden. It was every Tuesday without fail, Buster would then roll it around the garden getting his face and paws covered in quills.

Ruddy had tried to tell Buster, with the help of Glow, to leave it alone but the temptation was too strong. He had to roll it around then the hedgehog would walk away amused with itself.

Created and written by I C Henderson

Adventure of the Mouhumes
Jack and Annie's new
Visitors

Starlight landed on top of Buster's head. She knew that Ruddy would not be that far away. Buster froze to the spot with surprise. This had been the first time a fairy had ever landed on him.

Starlight started to call for Ruddy and Glow. Glow came out from part of the hedging with Ruddy right beside her. Starlight told them what was wrong and also told Ruddy that she had sent Dash home to safety.

Before Ruddy could do or say anything Starlight and Glow had picked her up and were taking her to where Woozy was. This would be the quickest way. The other fairies followed and some got there just before Ruddy. They kept themselves out of sight.

Glow and Starlight made themselves transparent. All Rug could see was Ruddy flying just before she landed. The surprise, in the way she came, was something words could not explain.

He had never seen a Mouhume come from out of the sky before. Rug and his follower looked at each other and went onto their knees bowing their heads. This would be a tale that no other could live up to.

Ruddy had her hand on the handle of her sharp thorn, ready to strike if needed but to her surprise Rug was full of apologies. He told her that he had acted wrong, made so many mistakes and needed guidance. He wanted Tube and Ratty and any other leaders to help him.

She knew by his stance and how he asked for help that he was telling the truth. If he had been there for any other reason he would have more than one Mouhume with him. In fact, he should have had more with him on an ordinary outing. She found that, in itself, strange.

Created and written by I C Henderson

Adventure of the Mouhumes
Jack and Annie's new
Visitors

Time was getting on and they weren't under any covering. This is not something that you would say out in the open but ideally they needed to be somewhere that would hide them from view.

The fairies that had hidden themselves flew off after having a quick look around. They could see no danger so reported back to Ruddy but they were still out of sight. Not even Ruddy could see them but she had started to learn their ways: a little tap on her shoulder or a whisper in her ear. She would take Rug and his companion to a garden not that far away from her home but far enough away that the fairies would know if they had visitors.

Tube and Ratty came Rug was clearly happy to see them. He started to tell them about his new home whilst the Mouhume he was with went to fill their water pouches up. He told them all how he had made a big mistake.

He also told them how he had gone back to the park and those who had been too weak were now in good health. They had more than enough food and they understood that it had to be stored away in case of poor weather.

It was Ratty who explained to Rug about the strain of what had happened and the lack of food. That had been the main reason why tension had made everyone act out of character at that time.

They showed Rug their new home. Tilly went back home with the help of Glow and Starlight to open the gate. Tube kept quiet about the dogs and the fairies. At this time it was not essential to say anything so none of the Mouhumes from the shed camp said a word unless they were asked.

His head had enough to take in, what with finding them and telling them about his own adventures. So asking about things like the dogs and the fairies with Woozy at this time was not top of his

Created and written by I C Henderson

Adventure of the Mouhumes
Jack and Annie's new
Visitors

agenda. Some things he even doubted. Had he seen them really or was it some sort of hallucination?

Rug stayed the rest of the day with Tube and Ratty exchanging accounts of what they had seen and difficulties they had to overcome. What had once been one big community was now split into three. Other Mouhumes who had been made to go in another direction might have made another home, unaware that Tube had escaped from danger and now they were all in different locations.

Tube and Rug had both thought of this. They also talked about one day they would like to send out a search party to locate any Mouhumes that might have been split up. They sat for a long time talking about that more than anything else. How long would it take? How many would have to go from each camp and their food supplies?

It was time to go. Rug gave Tube and Ratty a big hug. He was so happy. In the next few days they come back and forth, to each other's camp and even to the park. All of them were now happy about where they were living.

Created and written by I C Henderson

Adventure of the Mouhumes
Jack and Annie's new
Visitors

Chapter 24
The attack

IT WAS NOT long before they were disturbed by the telephone, just like the day before.

Jack was the one to answer, but this time he was not as considerate as last time. As he got up he was in a foul mood. And not frightened to let Annie know.

"This damn phone I was having a good sleep and…! It should be in the bedroom not the landing!"

That would save him getting out of bed.

Then he answered the phone, not in the best of ways.

At this time Annie was waking up. Rubbing her eyes and stretching. With a big yawn, she asked, who was on the phone, as she could hear Jack talking.

Just then he looked in the bedroom with the telephone still in his hand. He pointed to it and beckoned her to come to the phone.

As she got up she whispered "who is it?" Jack shrugged his shoulders.

Annie looking slightly nervous took the phone off Jack, and spoke into the receiver. "Hello who is it?" Annie asked in a nervous way her voice shaky.

"Hello, it's me Sharon I'm just ringing to see if you're feeling any better? And if you will be back at work soon?"

"When do you want me back Sharon? Can I have a late start; I'm shattered and in desperate need of some sleep. We had a late night again and just woken up"

Adventure of the Mouhumes
Jack and Annie's new
Visitors

"I hope that you are not drinking too much. And have a hang over do you?" Sharon laughed in the squeakiest way.

Then Sharon went on to tell Annie what shifts she would be on, but she could still have some time off. Then they discussed what day and time Annie would be starting back,

Annie agreed when she would start back. They said their goodbyes and hung up.

In the meantime Jack was back in bed, as he was ever so tired. Annie not having any of this went over to his side of the bed and pulled the blanket back. She rubbed Jack's head with the knuckle part of her hand. This didn't go down well; Jack jumped to his feet and in right stomp went to get his dressing gown, which was over the chair near the dressing table. Annie smiled to herself and got her own dressing gown. She then followed Jack down the stairs.

As they went into the living room Jack looked at the clock. With a sigh he told Annie to look at the time. They both were getting run down with the lack of sleep.

The time was six pm they had gone to bed around ten am.

Annie asked Jack "If it's all right could we have our tea and then go back to bed. And not watch the Mouhumes, if the telephone rings don't answer it. I'm fed up with not having a good night sleep"

Jack agreed and they start making the tea (Annie) while Jack sneaked into the conservatory. Jack was obsessed with the Mouhume's; he wanted to know as much about them as he could. If he could he would not leave the conservatory.

Created and written by I C Henderson

Adventure of the Mouhumes
Jack and Annie's new
Visitors

Just as well he has Annie to keep him right. Annie had an inkling that Jack might be in the conservatory, so she crept around the side of the door. Sure enough there he was. So Annie in the loudest way she could possible screamed at him.

"Right you get yourself into the dinning room, get the table ready right now!"

Jack must have jumped nearly three meters into the air.

Annie could hardly keep her laugh in. Jack, like a young schoolboy, caught with his hand in the sweet jar, scurried into the dinning room as quickly as he could. Still shaken, the colour ran out of his face. Like water coming out from a watering can.

Jack then started to put tablemats on the table and the salt and pepper cellars. Just as he was doing that Annie ran to the conservatory window and banged on it hard. Jack was still not right from the first fright Annie gave him. Now his stomach was doing summersaults.

In a shaky voice he asked Annie "what's going on? What's happening? Why are you knocking on the window? Are you trying to frighten the Mouhumes?"

Annie replied. "There's a cat and it's after the Mouhumes. I think that it might have caught one."

Annie with a towel in her hands went out into the garden, to chase the animal away.

At this time Jack was at the conservatory window looking as sad as Annie was cross. Annie was having a bit of a job trying to chase the cat away. She beckoned to Jack to come and help her. Jack was in a right state.

Created and written by I C Henderson

Adventure of the Mouhumes
Jack and Annie's new
Visitors

What with Annie, and now this, his nerves were shot. He thought that he was going to have a heart attack. He was now feeling as weak as a kitten. He needed to sit down. This left Annie alone to sort the cat or kitten out herself. She finally got the cat to leave but she had her work cut out. When she got back into the house she was cross with Jack for not helping.

"Jack where are you? Why did you not come to help me?" Annie full of temper stormed into the conservatory.

She got a bit of a fright, as she saw poor Jack. It was clear to see he was in a lot of pain. She went to see if see could help him in anyway. But he was looking unwell and painful; Annie went for the painkillers from the kitchen, hoping these would help him.

The thing was they would take some time to work. And to see Jack hurting so much was upsetting for Annie, She found the painkillers in the cupboard above the fridge, which was where they kept all the medical stuff.

Jack was aching, but it was not all from his back. He was having a lot of pain from his chest. The fright that Annie gave him earlier set the pain away in his chest. He was unable to talk; the chest pain was too much. He could not tell Annie what was wrong. Annie sat down with him, until she thought he looked better; there was nothing that Annie could do. After a short time, she just got on and did the tidying up in the kitchen.

She was still able to see Jack, she had the doors open. And one of the kitchen windows looked straight into the conservatory.

After some time, Jack was able to get up out of the chair, and move about. He was still in a lot of pain, but he felt if he moved it would ease, this sometimes helped but not always, as always Annie would tell him to sit down and take it easy. And as always Jack would tell her, that he would feel better if he moved about. The

153

Adventure of the Mouhumes
Jack and Annie's new
Visitors

more Annie went on telling him to take it easy, the more Jack would get cross.

But this was Annie's way as she new that Jack would go the opposite way, his determination would beat the pain.

They are always like that; they would not let the other one pamper them too much, as they had friends who would just love to be pampered? And that would just put more pressure on the other partner, in no time at all Jack was back in his fighting sprit, he had plenty to say to Annie, about giving him a fright.

"Annie you're to blame for me being in pain, when you frightened me earlier, you sent shock waves all over my body, I tell you what, I thought I was going to have a heart attack"

Annie just laughed at him and told him that he was a softie.

"You're a right softie aren't you; I think you were just trying to get out of setting the table for tea."

"Never mind that how's the little Mouhume? You said that the cat had one. And killed it but if that happened… the cat would not have stopped so long"

"I think the cat must have dropped it, I could not see anything in its mouth, it seemed to want to have a good look around the pond. It was definitely looking for something, I thought the cat had one; yes I'm pretty sure that it had one in its mouth. That's when I ran out; it might have dropped it by the time I got there"

Jack was concerned that if the cat had seen the Mouhumes, it would be back and they might leave.

The telephone started to ring; Annie looked at Jack as if to say are you going to answer it. But as usual Jack just sat there. Annie went to answer it. Annie, shaking her head as she went.

154

Adventure of the Mouhumes
Jack and Annie's new
Visitors

"Hello! Its Brian" she told Jack, She stood and listened to Brian. She did not do much talking herself. She then hung up.

"That was Brian; he wanted to come around tonight. He rang his dad up and his Father thinks his Grandfather left his studies. Paper work and that, it might be in an old box or something at his father's home.

Jack was nodding his head as he was making his way to the back door; he wanted to go to see if the cat had hurt any of the little Mouhumes.

In the drawer next to the back door, there was a torch he got it out and tried it, it worked. Not that he needed it as it was still light enough.

"I'm just going to see if there is any sign of the Mouhume. That the cat had." Then out he went.

Annie was not long following him, as she knew he was still not right from earlier.

When they got into the garden, they looked near the pond. Jack had his torch pointing towards the area near the waterfall. Then suddenly a head poked through the hedge. Jack with fright dropped his torch; it was their next door neighbour.

Old Ted he was hard of hearing, so straight away, Annie and Jack, knew that they would be spending their time repeating themselves.

Jack was not having a good time, there seemed to be fright after fright; it was not having a good affect on him.

In his old squeaky voice, Ted asked if they had seen his kitten, as it was the first time he had let it out and it was a bit of a

Created and written by I C Henderson

Adventure of the Mouhumes
Jack and Annie's new
Visitors

livewire, he told Jack and Annie it was climbing the curtains in the house, so he had let it out to burn some energy off. Jack nodded to Annie as if to say she should go and talk to Ted. Ted must have been in his kitchen looking out, but with the kitchen light on he would not have seen what was happening.

"You go and talk to Ted; I will look and see if I can find this poor little thing" Jack went around the pond. He started to move the flowers and plants with his walking stick.

Annie was talking to Ted, or more like shouting as Ted was as deaf as a door post,

Jack could not make out what was being said as Annie was shouting and Ted was talking at the same time as Annie, Ted was never one for talking quietly. So the racket they were making was somewhat distracting. Ted would get on about the garden he had when he was younger. (Just three years ago) at his old house he would just go in the garden at night leave a picture of what he wanted, and say out loud "please can I have this done for me" and it would be done. He said it was the fairies; he even brought some little garden ornaments from where he lived.

This was the first time, Jack and Annie really took any notice, and listened to what Ted was saying.

At the same time they looked over the hedge. It was true the ornaments were as life like as anything they had seen before.

Just then Ted's wife Linda came out, she looked as mad as a ships cat.

Her long grey hair looked like it had never been brushed. If you spoke to her all you might get in was a "hello" you could not get a word in. She would have you there for the best part of the day or night, you would never get away. She would keep you talking all

Created and written by I C Henderson

Adventure of the Mouhumes
Jack and Annie's new
Visitors

day if you were unlucky, and did not have an escape plan. That would be you stuck.

Annie did not feel comfortable where she was, and always tried to get out of the way as soon as she saw her.

Jack thought she was good to talk to, as he would get out of doing any jobs. As always her hair was grey, wild and bushy as if she had been pulled through a hedge backwards.

"Hello dear Linda how are you doing on this fine evening?" Jack said in a happy way.

In the meantime Annie looked around the pond to look for the Mouhume. She was bending and looking in the flowerbed moving the plants ever so careful. Then all of a sudden there was a loud scream.

Annie jumped up to see what was wrong; she could not do anything for laughing. Jack had found the kitten or the kitten had found him and had run up the outside of his pyjama trousers leg. Its claws must have been as sharp as anything.

"Don't you hurt my kitten" shouted Linda in her witchlike voice.

This was all too much for Jack. Things just weren't getting any better for him.

The cat at this time was sitting on his shoulder purring, and rubbing its head on Jack's chin. Jack would never hurt the kitten, but Linda was not to know. Jack pulled the kitten off his shoulder and passed it over the hedge. Linda got hold of it put it down on the grass.

157

Adventure of the Mouhumes
Jack and Annie's new
Visitors

"You poor little thing what has the nasty man done to you? You will be all right come in the house, and we will tell dad off for letting you out of the house" And off Linda went kitten in tow.

Ted was looking as worried, as a man waiting for the gallows.

"I better get myself back in, and not get her any angrier; she is not one for having a bit of fun." Then Ted went in to face the music.

Not a happy man he had only let the kitten out as it was climbing the curtains. In the similar way it had climbed Jack's leg.

Annie was still laughing at the same time looking amongst the plants.

"Annie can you come in the house, I want to talk to you?"

Annie looked at Jack, what could he want now? She thought to herself. Anyway she went into the kitchen and taking her shoes off, she asked what he wanted.

"Jack what on earth do you want? Are you all right? You have had some bad frights tonight" Then she started to laugh again.

"Be still woman I want to try something tonight, I need you to help as I have an idea where the Mouhumes might have come from"

Annie looked a bit confused and wondered what Jack might be thinking. Or what he might have her doing. With a big sigh she asked.

"Come on then, tell me what you're going to have me doing tonight…"

Created and written by I C Henderson

Adventure of the Mouhumes
Jack and Annie's new
Visitors

Then Jack reminded Annie, what old Ted was saying in the garden about the fairies. The way he would leave a picture of a thing he wanted, like that one in his garden. It s so like that castle from Alice in wonderland.

"Palace not castle" Annie interrupted Jack and corrected him and put him right.

"Well never mind the small details in a name, the fact of the matter is, it was built for him the next day and in every small detail"

Jack determined to have his say; then carried on trying to finish what he was wanting from Annie.

"I'll try again will you just let me say what I would like you to do… right then, as I was saying, could you find a picture or a photo of something. That you might like in our garden. And I'll dig up some clay from the bottom of the garden"

"Look Jack I do not think you are up to digging, do you? I will dig the clay up, off you go. In the cupboard at the bottom of the stairs you will find a small box of photos. There are also some magazines, which might have something in we might like."

Then off Annie went, into the old washhouse at the top of the garden near the back door, they now called it a shed, that had some garden tools in, Annie went to get the spade to dig up the clay.

It did not take Annie long to get a good bit of clay. She ended up having to use the wheelbarrow.

Annie was not one to make the job last any longer than she had to. She pushed it up the garden and left it near the pond, then went into the house to see if Jack had found any good photos, and to see if the pictures in the magazines would be any good to use. And get an idea what they might be able to use for their garden.

159

Adventure of the Mouhumes
Jack and Annie's new
Visitors

"Have you found anything Jack? Do you really think this might be the work of the Mouhumes?"

Annie was getting really excited. She thought their garden could do with some lifelike ornaments. Annie was in the kitchen washing her hands at the sink.

Jack was sitting at the table looking through the photos and the magazines. Jack started to put the photos that they had collected, over the years to one side. Then putting them in different piles. They had photos from all around the world.

He was making a pile of the ones that he would like in his garden, cutting some out of magazines, by the time Annie had washed herself and dried her hands, Jack had a large amount, which they could look through.

"Annie look at the ones I have picked, out of the magazines, see if there are any you might like to have. I'll look through the photos that we have.

"We can put them in two piles, the ones we want and the ones we don't"

"Jack do you think that Ted might be wrong? I know that the Mouhumes are supposed to be clever, but are they that clever?"

Then Annie shrugged her shoulders as if she was not certain. But she would go along with it as Ted did have some wonderful ornaments in his garden.

By the time they had picked the pictures, the ones they wanted, and the ones they did not, time was getting on.

"Right let's have a good look at the ones we have picked" Said Jack all excited.

Created and written by I C Henderson

Adventure of the Mouhumes
Jack and Annie's new
Visitors

This must have taken another twenty minutes. They looked at each picture and photo, making another pile, narrowing that pile down until finally, both Jack and Annie agreed which one they wanted.

"That's wonderful it's fantastic, I would be happy with that in my garden. Jack this is wonderful" Then Annie gave Jack a small kiss on the side of his cheek. Jack in his boyish way went all shy, and put his cheek on his shoulder.

"So we agree this is the one we want, you would not mind if this one goes in the garden?" Jack knowing fine well that Annie liked the photo they had picked.

"Jack I would love it, I do hope they build it for us"

"Right then lets go out and put the clay and the photo near the place we want it to go, and hope that Ted is right and we have not wasted our time. Annie do you know where you would like this wonderful ornament to be put"

Annie looked out of the kitchen window, towards the bottom of the garden, studying the garden and muttering quietly to herself.

She was not going to just pick any old place just for the sake of it. It would have to be in a good spot. In an area where you would see it from all angles, then her face changed to a smile. She knew the spot, where the ornament would go.

"Right Jack I do believe I know where we can put it. I think you would like the spot as well."

Jack knew that it would not matter if he liked it or not, he would not have much say in the matter anyway. "Yes Annie lets see and I am sure wherever you have picked. It will be all right. And it will be just right"

Created and written by I C Henderson

Adventure of the Mouhumes
Jack and Annie's new
Visitors

Then they went out, and went to the spot Annie had picked. They (Annie tipped the wheelbarrow and the clay poured out) then Jack put the picture out on the top of the clay.

"Let's go in Annie and sit and watch to see what happens"

Then Jack held Annie's hand with a big smile on his face. Annie was excited too, but at the same time she was getting tired, she had to go to work the next morning.

Annie had some ironing to do, as well as other jobs around the house.

When they went into the house Jack went straight into the conservatory. Annie went upstairs and into the bathroom to get washed.

Jack not knowing, that Annie was getting washed. (And as always, he wanted something). Asked Annie to put the kettle on, and if she would make a cup of tea.

Not getting an answer he got up and went into the kitchen, he looked around then looked out of the window.

Concentrating, looking towards the wooden shed, at the bottom of the garden, looking at something moving around.

"What are you up to now?" Annie asked as sharp as anything. That made Jack jump, the colour from his face disappeared again. His legs started to wobble. Annie got a fright herself and grabbing hold of Jacks arm helped him to the chair in the dinning room.

"I've had it! .Are you trying to kill me or what? I do not know what you think you are trying to do but I tell you what… I've had more frights today that would last anyone a lifetime"

Created and written by I C Henderson

Adventure of the Mouhumes
Jack and Annie's new
Visitors

"I think its time we both have a little supper, and after that go to bed as the last few days have been long. It has taken it out of us, time we had some rest, what do you think Jack?"

Jack was looking as if he had not had any sleep for weeks. So he nodded his head and went to the dinning table and sat down.

"Ok let's have an early night; I think you might need it as much as me Annie"

Annie got the teapot, and a plate of sandwiches, then got the cups, which she put on the table. It did not take long for them to eat the plate of sandwiches; Then Annie got the plates and put them into the sink, ready to clean.

They finished their cups of tea Annie started to wash the empty cups and plates. She wasted no time in getting cleaned up. Then they went up the stairs to bed.

As Jack was going up the stairs he knew if Annie had a chance she would want to be in the bathroom first. He himself wanted to use it; he had to put his thinking cap on. Annie was in front of him, as he got near the top of the stairs Annie was turning into the bathroom, the telephone was on top of the landing on the little table, which was always being knocked over.

This was his chance. So with one almighty stumble he knocked the table over.

"Annie! I have fallen and knocked the telephone over, can you help me?"

Annie quick as a flash came with her reply.

"If you think I'm going to fall for that one, you can think again. I have another thing on my mind and that's not picking the phone up"

Adventure of the Mouhumes
Jack and Annie's new
Visitors

Then Jack with a little soft voice told her that he had knocked the table over. Also the vase was knocked over.

Then all you could hear was a loud scream from the bathroom. The door swung open and a look of thunder on Annie's face. Jack looked as if he was going to be beaten, the fear on his face, words could not describe.

"Right what have you done to my vase? My great aunt left me that if it's broken I'll give you…"

Jack pulled it around from his back, with a nervous look on his face, his chin on his chest. Annie was ready to jump on him; Jack started to laugh then showed Annie, that it was alright. Then he put it in her hands, then hurried into the bathroom.

As he shut the door he told her, he had to get her out of the bathroom somehow.

"You know you would be in here for the best part of the night, I don't have time to hang around the bathroom… like some sort of…"

"Don't be silly I never take long in the bathroom and…"

Just then Jack interrupted her. "You never take long? All women take a long time getting ready, doing their hair and things; you're not like us men, straight to the point"

"I'll give you straight to the point when you come out of there…"

She started to tidy up the table. She asked Jack if he had heard anything from Brian, as he seemed interested in the Mouhumes and was supposed to be coming that night.

Created and written by I C Henderson

Adventure of the Mouhumes
Jack and Annie's new
Visitors

Jack through the bathroom door, told her he had not heard anything. "Maybe he's been grounded" Jack said laughing.

Annie not amused by Jacks remark told him that she did not find that funny.

Jack came out the bathroom and straight into the bedroom
"I am ready for bed, a good nights sleep is what's needed, what time do you start tomorrow? Annie"

"One o'clock tomorrow afternoon till ten. I do not like that shift but it will give me a chance to have a good sleep. What will you be up to? Have you any plans to do anything?"

"No I have no plans I might go round to see Ted, he might be able to help us with the Mouhumes"

"Ted does not know about the Mouhumes does he, come on Jack lets settle down and go to sleep, you do not look well and I need my sleep, good night Jack"

They settled down and in no time at all they were both asleep.

Adventure of the Mouhumes
Jack and Annie's new
Visitors

Chapter 25
Disappointment

THE NEXT TIME they awoke it was ten o'clock the next morning, as always Jack was the first one up, his back was giving him a bit of trouble, as it all ways did after laying down for a long time. He struggled to his feet and stretched out, that sometimes helped him. But this morning it did not. He looked at the clock and saw the time; he rubbed his eyes and gave Annie a little knock on the side of her shoulder to waken her.

"Come on Annie its time you were up so howay and get the kettle on please"

Annie poked her head out from the covers, one eye open she looked terrible.

Jack shuddered, Annie put one of her feet out of the blankets to see how warm the room was. That morning was not the warmest of mornings. So her feet went straight back under the blankets. Jack started to put his dressing gown on; he was struggling as his back was stiff.

"Come on Annie lets see if the Mouhumes have made your ornament, how way hurry up!"

Jack wanted to go down the stairs the same time as Annie to see the expression on her face. Annie was up like a shot, once she was reminded about the ornament. She took no time getting ready her clothes were on in a manner that Jack had never seen. They went down the stairs together. Annie told Jack the best place to see the ornament would be from the conservatory. So that was the first place they went to.

With being cool that morning the windows had condensation on, so they could not see properly through the windows.

Created and written by I C Henderson

Adventure of the Mouhumes
Jack and Annie's new
Visitors

"Go and get a cloth Annie so we can see what we are looking for"

Annie took no time at all; straight into the kitchen and under the sink, she got a cloth.

"This will do the job Jack, I'll bring the dish in for the condensation, I get from the windows"

Jack not one for waiting, had already used his sleeve from his dressing gown. But the window was still not clear. It had a smudge. Jack had made the glass worse. When Annie came back from the kitchen and saw the state of the window, she was not at all happy.

"What do you think you are doing? Can you not wait? Get out of my way and sit down, I'll turn the heater on, that'll help keep the windows clear"

Annie not wasting any time had the windows as clear as fresh air. You could not see one smudge.

She stood back "There you are as clear as anything; now then let's see this wonderful ornament"

As they looked they moved around the conservatory then looked at each other, with confused expressions on both their faces. What could have happened there was just a pile of clay that Annie had poured from the wheelbarrow. There was no ornament.

"Well that's good just a heap of clay, what do you think might be wrong?"

Annie was unable to answer; Jack was really upset and disappointed. What was wrong why did the Mouhumes not make the ornament? She just could not understand.

167

Adventure of the Mouhumes
Jack and Annie's new
Visitors

"Why have they not made it for us Jack? What could we have done that have upset them?"

"Do you not think the kitten might have frightened them? They might have left for good. I bet that's the last we see of them! Annie I feel really sick and disappointed"

The telephone started to ring Annie went and answered it, she shouted through to Jack, and told him that Brian was on the phone, and he was coming over to see them. Jack asked Annie if she had told Brian what had happened the night before. Annie nodded and said her goodbyes to Brian.

"He was disappointed to hear what had happened, but he still needed to come over to show you some of his granddads work.

Look I must get ready for work myself; maybe it's a good thing that they have disappeared! We were running our self's down with the lack of sleep"

Jack not at all happy that the Mouhumes, might have had disappeared; he knew that Annie was not happy, and she was just putting a brave face on. Annie was getting herself ready for work and tidying up, the way she was tidying, told Jack, that she was upset. When she was upset or angry, she kept herself busy.

"Annie what time did Brian say he was coming? And if you could can you bring some of that Ham from your store. Give yourself a rest and Ill make you a cup of tea"

Annie stopped and looked at the clock, and told Jack she has not got much time before she would have to leave for work.

Jack was in the kitchen and making the cups of tea, putting the biscuits on the tea plate Annie at this time was sitting at the table. Not looking at all happy.

Created and written by I C Henderson

Adventure of the Mouhumes
Jack and Annie's new
Visitors

"Come on lass put a smile on your face you will turn the milk sour. You'll be back before you know it"

Annie smiled and shook her head, if it was just work that was on her mind... The poor Mouhumes what had happened to them? It must have been terrible for them. Was it just the cat or was it something else?

Jack and Annie had their tea and biscuits.

"Look at the time I must go Jack. Will you be all right? If you need me just ring up at work and I will be back in no time at all"

"Annie I will be all right, don't worry Brian is coming, he will make us a sandwich won't he?"

"You have the cheek to ask as well"

Annie got her things ready for work, took something out the freezer for teatime

"That's for tea so leave it alone" she then put it into the oven, because she new Jack would not cook anything, and it was out of harms way, she got her bag and keys

Then Annie went to give Jack a kiss on the cheek, Jack smiled as Annie went out the door.

Created and written by I C Henderson

Adventure of the Mouhumes
Jack and Annie's new
Visitors

Chapter 26
Lights

IT HAD NOT been that long ago when Jack had put traps around the garden near the pond and in the greenhouse. He had placed most of them around the pond, some down the garden path and some around the hedging leading up the garden. In fact, any place that a small animal might use as cover.

The one in the greenhouse had killed one of the Mouhumes. They had tried to get his body out but the trap was too strong for them. Jack had found it, but just picked it up looked strangely at it, then buried it around the back of the greenhouse.

The Mouhumes, knowing how dangerous these traps were, set each trap off with sticks then took the food that had been placed in them

They now had garden lights that turned on as soon as it went dark. This made it more difficult for those who went out on a night time hunting spree. After a few days had passed, they got used to the lights and just went about their jobs as normal.

As they carried on doing what they needed to they took no notice of Jack in his chair looking out. He sat there most times throughout the night and day, hardly ever coming into the garden, so they saw him as no danger.

The grass was starting to get long. Ted, next door, kept his grass short. Most gardens had short grass, just one or two let nature take its course.

In a way the long grass gave them some cover. Some of the Mouhumes from the park group were coming. They were going to show them how to fish. The Mouhumes had already tried fishing in their garden but it was more luck than skill if and when they got anything.

Adventure of the Mouhumes
Jack and Annie's new
Visitors

It was a full moon and the lights around the pond gave them plenty of light. The park Mouhumes had watched the humans' fish and tried to copy them. They might not have had fishing rods but they made do with what they could find and became quite good at fishing.

In the garden the Mouhumes would turn the mice and rat traps over and go onto the water using them as rafts. This was a good way to go onto the water. The park Mouhumes had never used a raft before so this was new to them but their fishing skills were outstanding. They no sooner got out on to the water and started fishing when they pulled a fish out of the water.

Some of the Mouhumes had flowers on top of their head. This helped with camouflaging. They mostly had dandelion flowers on their heads but almost anything would do, depending on what area they were in.

At this time Jack was looking out the window. The Mouhumes took no notice. They knew he was there and that he was not to be feared. He was harmless, apart from setting the traps.

It was good that the lights attracted insects such as moths and other flying bugs. The Mouhumes could, if not for themselves, use them as bait to catch other food stuff like fish and mice. Birds would often fall prey to the traps when the Mouhumes used insects as bait.

The lights had been there for only two nights but the Mouhumes took advantage of this. Even the hedgehog came in after the insects the Mouhumes had put out for him. Glow asked the hedgehog if he would stop going to Buster's garden as he was getting hurt by the thorns coming out of him.

The hedgehog explained why he went to see Buster. The reason was that Buster did not hurt him but helped to get any loose

Adventure of the Mouhumes
Jack and Annie's new
Visitors

quills out. It was hard to find a way to get them out. Buster rolled him by shoving his face onto him and patting him using his paw which helped to pull the quills out. They needed to be removed so that new ones could grow.

The Mouhumes said that they would be more than happy to take them out for the hedgehogs, because they could be used to help protect them. The quills were long and strong and if they needed to be shorter they could be cut easily.

Once again it had been Ruddy who had made the connection between the two creatures. Something else the community would talk about. It was amazing how she could bring two different worlds together. They worked hard so they could all benefit.

She had made friends with the fairies, Buster, Tilly and now with the hedgehog. Her personality just shone. That was why all the Mouhumes loved her. She would fight without fear to help another Mouhume and even her new friends.

It was Starlight who noticed that Jack was looking a bit flustered. Jack's wife was standing next to him. She looked as if she was laughing. What could have made Jack so restless? He was pacing the floor and going in and out of one room to the next.

Starlight pointed this out to Glow. The two of them went to the window to see if they could hear anything. It became clear that Jack was not happy that a fish had been pulled out from the pond.

They flew back to the pond to tell those that were there to go, to leave quickly as Jack was not happy. The lights had been put there to watch them. Their faces were that of disappointment. They had just thought of Jack as there, nothing more. Just there doing no harm but he was watching them.

In a split second nothing was to be seen. They had all gone back to the shed. Some were in the shed, in a doorway they had

Adventure of the Mouhumes
Jack and Annie's new
Visitors

made with the help of the fairies. That was something else the fairies were good at, making things.

Some of the Mouhumes went under the shed into the hideaway in the burrow. The shed was a perfect place to hold a meeting. It was all but empty. Some drawers were near the main doorway and there were bits of tools lying around but the floor space was almost clear.

In here it could hold a large number of Mouhumes. It was dry so they would use that for any meetings, if and when it was needed. A large space and the drawers were a good place to stand on. They were above everyone else and he or she could be seen and heard.

The safety of the community was now in question. Why had Jack put lights up? If it had not been for Starlight and Glow they would have never known that Jack was upset about the fish.

The traps also came up in the debate. Why had he put them out with food? When the food was taken it killed the taker!

These were all reasonable questions. Nobody could answer in a positive way. Starlight did not want any harm to come to any of the Mouhumes. She came up with an idea. The fairies would, in turn, watch Jack and his wife, Annie, listening to what was being said. Each day they would report back to Tube for him so he could decide what might be best.

Starlight did not like the idea of Woozy and her being parted. She was willing to do anything to keep them together. She also knew that Glow had a good friendship with Ruddy; she also would not want that to be ended.

Glow, at that time, went back to her community. There were more fairies than Mouhumes so there was more than enough to help spy on Jack to see what he was preparing. Was he out to hurt

Created and written by I C Henderson

Adventure of the Mouhumes
Jack and Annie's new
Visitors

the Mouhumes or not? The Mouhumes agreed with Starlight they would give it another day or so to see Jack's intentions.

Two fairies, at a time, went to the conservatory where Jack spent most of his time. They would listen to what was being said. When they were relieved from their positions they reported back to Tube and two other senior fairies.

This went on all night, as long as Jack was sitting there with Annie talking. The fairies moved around the roof of the conservatory taking in everything that was talked about, some of the things they had no idea about.

The next day they would have to try to explain to Ted their concerns. For long enough they had tried to communicate with Ted but he could just not understand. This time he was needed, to see what and if he could stop Jack's bad intentions with the Mouhumes.

They had to observe tonight. This was new to them. They had nothing to do with humans apart from Ted. Not even Ted's wife had seen them. They were reluctant to let anyone or anything see them. They had too many bad experiences so they found it was best just to hide away until now. Since the Mouhumes came they had let Buster and Tilly see them, even the hedgehog was now in the group.

This got the fairies colony worried where it might be leading. They had never been seen by humans or any other creatures and all of a sudden they were socializing with allsorts.

Some had made it clear in meetings they started to doubt things, things that where now putting them in danger. They would still help for now, just in case they were wrong. A big if! Looking at all that had gone on. They would look as if they were doing all they could to help the Mouhumes.

Created and written by I C Henderson

Adventure of the Mouhumes
Jack and Annie's new
Visitors

Some were ready to go to their own world but even that had been compromised due to the fact that Ruddy had been shown it just before she had her baby. So all they could do was gather evidence all night and see what the next day would bring before they would decide what to do.

Two of the fairies crept in one of the bedroom windows that were open ever so slightly. It was just enough room for them to squeeze in. They heard Jack and Annie coming up the stairs, Annie laughing as she came up.

The fairies hid on the curtain, blending in with the patterns. Jack and Annie got themselves into bed. Annie, now and again, burst into laughter about the look on Jack's face when the Mouhume pulled the fish out of the water.

Just as things went quiet Annie would start laughing. Jack telling her to stop, this went on almost all night: in a way that was a good thing, as the fairies could get a better understanding of Jack and Annie.

This would be something they would report back: Annie found it amusing whilst Jack was upset that one of his fish had been taken. In their opinion, Jack and Annie were not at all bad humans. They cared for the creatures in their garden but would they care for the Mouhumes the same way?

The streetlight was glowing through the curtains. The two fairies were still hidden in the design. They took it in turns to fly around the room looking around to see what they could see trying to find out what sort of people Jack and Annie were.

After nearly being seen a number of times each, they decided to go but not the way they had came in. They decided to go downstairs and look around the rooms.

Created and written by I C Henderson

Adventure of the Mouhumes
Jack and Annie's new
Visitors

They had a good look around. There was nothing they could see nothing out of the ordinary but now they would have to find a way out. They checked the windows in the living room but they were all locked.

Even the window at the bottom of the staircase was locked. They started to get worried as they could hear movement from upstairs. They flew into the kitchen area but the windows in there were also locked.

They were now in need of energy. One of the windows in the kitchen area looked into the conservatory. As they looked through the glass they could see that one of the windows was slightly open, the catch had not been put down properly. Maybe due to Jack and Annie going to bed laughing and otherwise distracted they had forgotten to close it.

The door that led into the conservatory was slightly open. Though not big enough for them to squeeze through but maybe they could pull it open? These two fairies were smaller than most, they were not as strong as the others and now they did not have sufficient amount of energy to blend into the background.

As they tried to pull the door open they could hear footsteps upstairs and the creaking of the floorboards. They were starting to get worried that they might be seen.

Some Mouhumes had seen them trying to pull the door open but how could they help? It would be almost impossible to help! They stood watching thinking about what they could do. After what had happened to Jumper, Ruddy and the others it had been forbidden for any Mouhume to enter into a human's house.

It was early morning so finding a fairy would be hard to do. Even in the daylight, if they did not want to be seen, they would have no chance. One of the Mouhumes had some twine but could

Adventure of the Mouhumes
Jack and Annie's new
Visitors

he throw it high enough so they could scale the height they would need?

No matter what they did they could not get the twine anywhere high enough. A number of Mouhumes were looking to see if they could find a fairy. As it was still early they would not even be at the bush were they recharged in daylight?

The fairies in the house had been resting all day. That was why they had been chosen to watch Jack and Annie that night but they had misjudged how much energy they had used.

One of the Mouhumes had an idea. In Jack's garden was a cherry tree. One of the branches had been sawn off by Jack the year before and it was trickling out sap, sticky sap. The Mouhume got some flower heads and filled them with sap. It had to work he passed them onto other Mouhumes who carried the flower heads up towards the conservatory.

Time was against them. Even outside they could hear movement upstairs. What they did next was nothing they had seen done before, but they had to do something. Some of the Mouhumes climbed onto the outside window ledge. The flower heads were passed up; the Mouhumes on the window ledge then got handfuls and threw it on to both the window and onto the white plastic frame. Then, in turns, with hands full of sap they attempted to scale up the window but they just slid back down again.

The plastic frame seemed to have had a better hold. They took it in turns as soon as they got so far up they slid back down. But each time they were getting a little higher until finally they reached the window that was slightly open.

The twine was passed up and attached to a screw holding the guttering. Four Mouhumes with clean hands ascended up the side of the conservatory. It took two of them to pull the window open.

Created and written by I C Henderson

Adventure of the Mouhumes
Jack and Annie's new
Visitors

Once it was open they attached some more string and climbed down. There were four of them in the human's house with panic in their hearts. It was not just for the fact that if they were found by the humans but the fact was what would happen when Tube found out.

They rushed to the door. Now the two fairies where lying on the floor, plain to be seen by all. They had used all their energy. By luck and luck alone they were smaller than most fairies.

Two of the Mouhumes picked up one each and put them over their shoulder and with a Mouhume behind taking some weight they climbed the twine passing the fairies down to the other Mouhumes who were waiting.

The Mouhumes had to scale down the outside with their feet that were now covered with a little fur from their clothing, wiping away the sap. The last one undoing the string and making the final descent using all his body hoping to clean away any last marks, hoping he was not going to fall to a certain death. Luckily as he fell, the fur from his clothes clung to the sticky sap. Not all the evidence was wiped away but they had no more time, a dark streak was now left on the white plastic.

As the Mouhumes ran to hide they heard Jack in the conservatory. They were still in sight but hoped they had not been seen. Some went next door to put the fairies near the energizing bush, before they eventually all returned to the shed.

Created and written by I C Henderson

Adventure of the Mouhumes
Jack and Annie's new
Visitors

Chapter 27
The Gathering

THE NEXT DAY was the strangest yet! Some Mouhumes stayed near the pond. Hiding in the shrubbery watching the room where Jack sat looking out. That morning he had only stayed in the room a short time.

The fairies that had been in the house were still weak so not much was asked of them. The Mouhumes who had gone in the house and those who helped them were now being questioned. They knew they would be in trouble and there was one punishment that they dreaded and that was to be expelled from the Mouhume communities.

It had only happened once to their knowledge, back in the old home. Five Mouhumes had gone into a house and had been seen. That, in turn, put the whole community in danger so they were banished never to return.

The five had been going into a house where an elderly human lived. They thought they were helping, by doing little jobs such as helping to stitch anything that needed stitching and cleaning up around the rooms.

One day, however, the human set a trap and tried to follow them back home. They had discovered that by stopping for a rest, as the day had been hot, they had left footprints: on the bottom of their feet was white dust.

The human had kept his distance but they had seen the human hiding behind a bush so they had to change direction. For days after the human kept going there, looking around and hoping to find them.

What had been a good deed had confined them to camp for days. Only Mouhumes keeping watch were out, the rest hidden

Created and written by I C Henderson

Adventure of the Mouhumes
Jack and Annie's new
Visitors

away in camp until the human stopped looking for them. The stress they had been under was something they never wanted again.

The odd Mouhume still went into houses but never took anything or helped in any way so that humans wouldn't know they had visitors. This was different, Jack had seen them and they had seen Jack. Right up until he saw them fishing, the two worlds just got on doing their own thing.

It was later that day the fairies held the gathering in the big shed. They reported what they had seen and what they had heard. They also thanked the Mouhumes for helping them get out of the house.

Tube sat with a stern look but never said anything. He knew what they had done was brave. He had been up the garden and he had seen there was a number of tell tale signs.

The only thing was, had Jack seen the tell tale signs? It had been reported back to Tube that Jack and Annie had left in the car some time ago. Tube had asked Glow and Starlight if they could help clean the mess on the side of the white wall.

They agreed but it took some time. The Mouhumes could not do a lot as the window was now closed. They could not even fasten the cord. They had not seen the screw the Mouhumes had tied onto the night before.

So the fairies cleaned up for them and now it was the fairies who had called the meeting. They were unhappy about everything that had been happening: dogs, hedgehogs and the coming and goings of Mouhumes from different camps.

The fairies were concerned about their own well-being. They felt the Mouhumes had not done anything but bring potential danger to their door.

Created and written by I C Henderson

Adventure of the Mouhumes
Jack and Annie's new
Visitors

They were open about each concern and explaining why: the hedgehogs eat insects, worms, and any other meat they can get a hold of including dragonflies. Which were part of the fairy family but not yet evolved.

Not even the best Mouhume could defend themselves against a hedgehog. If the hedgehog wanted to harm them they easily could. At this time they did not need to harm the Mouhumes as the Mouhumes were feeding them but if food was to run short they would, without hesitation, feed themselves on whatever was around at that time.

Tube looked worried about what was being said. He had the same thoughts himself when they discovered that fairies were close to them. He could understand the concern the fairies had. The last few days had been nothing but discovery. They were opening worlds that would normally avoid each other.

Every concern was opened and each one was put to discussion. In each case it was the fairies that had the worry and it was the fairies that had lived in harmony with humans.

Although the fairies did say in their defence, it was only Ted that they had made contact with, not even Ted's wife had ever seen them and they had lived alongside them for a number of years.

The only contact they made with other creatures was only when needed. If it had not been for Ruddy and Capheus, contact between the Mouhumes and the fairies would not have happened and if not for the Mouhumes, the two dogs Buster and Tilly, would not be aware of the fairy world.

It all came back to Ruddy: her inquisitive ways, wanting to explore all aspects of the surrounding areas and her fearless and reckless ways were, once again, being questioned. All Glow wanted to know was whether the Mouhumes would stop letting

Created and written by I C Henderson

Adventure of the Mouhumes
Jack and Annie's new
Visitors

other creatures into their world, and stop letting others know they even existed?

Tube nodded. He knew they were right again. Then came another truth. It had been all one-sided. The fairy community had been helping the Mouhumes with anything they could not do themselves and at the same time putting their own health at risk. They had asked for nothing in return but now it had to stop.

The shed was almost full of the Mouhumes. Glow was putting up a good argument just her and four other fairies. Glow was around the same size as a Mouhume in height, two others were half the size but the one standing out of sight was bigger than Starlight. What ever war wounds Glow had, this fairy had more. With just one look at her you could tell that she was fearless and stronger than any other fairy.

They said what they would like from the Mouhumes and that was for the Mouhumes to stop letting anything and everything know about the fairies, it was not a lot to ask!

Tube had not let the woodland Mouhumes know about the fairies and he had not let the parkland Mouhumes know. As far as he was aware they still did not know but they were right the dogs now knew and the hedgehog knew.

He agreed without putting up any debate. He then told the Mouhumes the two fairies had reported back and that as far as they knew the humans, Jack and Annie, seemed to care about some of the creatures in the garden, more than others.

At this time they would have to try to hide away and keep out of sight until they knew what would happen next. He reminded them the last few times Jack had not been sitting in the window. He had come back with things that could be, in all probability, a danger to the Mouhumes. Things like the rat trap and the lights.

Created and written by I C Henderson

Adventure of the Mouhumes
Jack and Annie's new
Visitors

Just as Tube was about to say something else a Mouhume came running in and reported that there were now three humans sitting looking out of the window. When asked what they were doing he was told just sitting looking out.

Tube looked at Glow but did not say a word. This was something he needed to know but he also knew that Glow was right. The Mouhumes had done nothing for them except bring them nothing but danger.

Glow had not seen Tube look at her with want in his eyes. She had her back to him. She was talking to her friends and then they were off.

It was now evening the light was dull. It had been a long discussion and now it was time to get food, after all they were now under the cover of darkness. The fairy community would now be out of sight. Darkness was not a friend of theirs. It wore them out, as those two fairies the night before had found out.

Tube wanted to go up the garden and see what was happening. He wanted to know who was sitting looking out of the window. There were around six Mouhumes there already. They could not understand what was being said but they might have some idea just watching.

The Mouhumes went about their business, collecting food and other stuff. One or two of them were watching Jack and Annie and this new human. The humans were watching them. Now and again the humans were getting up and going into another room adjoining the conservatory.

It was clear to see they were talking and sometimes pointing towards where the Mouhumes were. As daylight came the Mouhumes finally went back under the shed to rest. Only a small number of Mouhumes stayed out in daylight.

Created and written by I C Henderson

Adventure of the Mouhumes
Jack and Annie's new
Visitors

Those in the conservatory went so the area was now clear. That day they did not see Jack or Annie. The car that had brought the other human had also gone. The Mouhumes now knew how dependent they had been on the fairies and how much they needed their help to understand what was being said.

The rest of the day was as normal as it could be. The fairies kept themselves to themselves, as did the Mouhumes.

Created and written by I C Henderson

Adventure of the Mouhumes
Jack and Annie's new
Visitors

Chapter 28
The autopsy

THE LAST FEW days had been somewhat strange to say the least. And all of a sudden it came to an end, nearly as quick as it had started; this would leave a hole in their lives.

No way could they tell anyone, as no one would ever believe them.

Jack started to wash the cups and plates that they had used for breakfast. Then the front door bell rang, Jack started to dry his hands with the towel as he was going to answer the door.

He opened the front door, to his surprise it was Brian.

"Come on in Brian I thought you would be coming later, I did not expect you this early, you have your hands full do you need a hand?"

"No I will be all right Jack. But I have found something interesting in my grandfather's papers. I'll just get them in order for you to look at and see what you think"

Jack told Brian what had happened the night before, about the cat and what old Ted had been telling him and Annie. And how now they think the Mouhumes had disappeared.

Brian started to sort his papers out, which would take some time, as there were a lot of them. Brian's Grandfather must have studied the Mouhumes for a long time. After some time Brian was ready, he was not the most organised man, but he did like things in order which when doing it himself, he seemed to mess things up.

"Right then Jack, I think I have it in the order, which you will need to look at"

Created and written by I C Henderson

Adventure of the Mouhumes
Jack and Annie's new
Visitors

As they started to look through the document, Jack's face brightened up.

"Your grandfather was some man; he had the Mouhumes a right kingdom. Look at this"

There was an old photo and it showed the things which could only be described as wonderful. To be a part of this would have brought happiness to anyone's heart.

Brian and Jack looked through the documents for the best part of the day. Talking and discussing the Mouhumes and bouncing ideas off each other. Then all of a sudden Jack jumped up.

"I tell you what! … I might have one down the garden; I think I might have killed one in a rat trap"

The look on Brian's face must have been one of shock. Jack started to explain how he thought that he had mice and rats running around the garden, so he placed the traps to try and catch them.

Brian was shaking his head in disgust, what on earth must he be thinking about Jack?

"Right then, I think we need to go and dig this corpse up, to see what we have. Can you show me where you buried it; how long ago did you find it in your …trap?"

"It would be some time ago, I cannot remember. It was when we started to see the things running around"

"Mouhumes…!" Brian interrupted sharply.

Jack did not say anything, he was aware that Brian was not happy, that one of the Mouhumes might have been killed accidentally by Jacks traps. Jack was putting his boots on in the kitchen, when he looked over to the professor who was sitting in

Created and written by I C Henderson

Adventure of the Mouhumes
Jack and Annie's new
Visitors

the dinning room; he was looking at Jack, shaking his head in disgust.

"Right then come on I'll show you, but it has been some time I don't know how well it will be…"

Brian interrupted sharply; his tone would frighten the life out of anyone. "It's not going to be well its dead!" he said.

They went down to the bottom of the garden, towards the greenhouse.

"It's around the back of the greenhouse; there is a spade just as you open the greenhouse door, if you would be so kind" Jack said with a smile on his face. Brian opened the greenhouse door, and went in, it's quite big and everything was in its place. Quite tidy, he had a look around then he saw the spade in the corner, along with other garden tools.

"Come on are you going to stay there all day?"

Jack thought he would try to make Brian get a move on; the professor looked through the glass at Jack, in the most shocked way, then picked the spade up and came around the greenhouse to the side where Jack was standing.

"Right it's around the back, I will show you, but you will have to dig it up as my back is playing up today"

The look on Brian's face was a picture, not at all happy with the thought of getting dirty. But he would have to go along with it, as Jack looked to be in pain. Jack pointed to a spot and told Brian that's where he thought he had buried it. Brian looked at the spot where Jack had pointed, then he give a sigh and put his spade on the spot, with his foot he pushed the spade into the soil, he then pulled back the soil from the ground, the two of them (Jack and

Created and written by I C Henderson

Adventure of the Mouhumes
Jack and Annie's new
Visitors

Brian) looked as if something might jump out, and grab hold of them.

"Get hold of that stick, and poke it in to the soil and break it up, you will see if that's the spot" Jack told Brian, as if he would not know what to do.

Brian picked up the stick Jack was pointing at, started to move the soil on the spade.

"Nothing on that one, if you put the soil over there, out of the way and you will have to do that each time" Jack all of a sudden the expert, telling Brian as if he was the beginner.

Brian not wanting to get into an argument, just carried on and each time Jack telling him what to do, after sometime and a large pile of soil, and a large hole Jack put his hand on his head.

"I remember its not there, it's over there silly me, that's where I buried the wife's woolly hat"

Brian looked a bit concerned, wondering why on earth anyone would want to bury a hat; anyway he had more interesting things to dig for, and took no time in starting to dig where Jack had pointed to. This time it had to be the right place. As he had dug just about the entire garden behind the greenhouse, Brian had no sooner stuck the spade in the ground when he saw what they were looking for.

The two of their faces lit up, this was the first time either of them had come in contact with a Mouhume, Jack had already been in contact, but not knowing what he was looking at was not concerned. This time he wanted to know as much about the Mouhumes as much as the Professor. Brian cleaned the soil from the little body as gently as he could so not to disturb its little delicate body.

Created and written by I C Henderson

Adventure of the Mouhumes
Jack and Annie's new
Visitors

"I think we had better get this in the house, and have a good look at it, will that be all right with you Jack? The cold weather has helped to preserve the little body"

Jack agreed and the two of them went into the house, Brian carrying the Mouhumes body, when they got into the kitchen Jack got some kitchen roll, and placed it on the worktop to help to keep it clean. Brian put the body on the paper roll,

"I'm going to have to go to the car, to get my bag as I have some tools in it, which will make this easier to do. Jack will you not touch or move it please? As I will have to do some tests on it"

Jack nodded and went to the door with Brian, so that he would not get tempted to touch the little thing.

Jack could see Brian's car from the back door. Brian pulled this large black bag out of the back of his car.

"Jack can you clear the table as I will need some space to do what I need"

In no time Jack moved Brian's grandfather's papers and had the table clear. The professor wasted no time and got on with his work.

Some of the things he pulled out from his bag you would expect a doctor or surgeon to have. In no time at all, the entire table looked like an operating theatre, a large white cloth had covered the table and all the tools placed out. Brian was putting some white gloves on and wearing strange looking glasses.

"Right Jack if you could bring in the specimen after you put on the gloves, then we will get started and find out more about this wonderful…"

Created and written by I C Henderson

Adventure of the Mouhumes
Jack and Annie's new
Visitors

Just then he stopped as he did not know what to call it, was it an animal are what? No doubt they were about to find out what it might be.

Brian got his sharp scalpel and a small pointed pair of pliers and just about to start to make his mark.

He gave a large gasp just as he was about to make his first cut in the fur, It seemed to slip away, with fright he jumped back, this also give Jack a fright. They looked at each other, in what can only be described, as shock. Jack had not seen what Brian had seen, but the way Brian had jumped back had given Jack a fright.

"What's the matter Brian what's wrong has it moved? Is it still alive?"

"Not likely it's been in the ground for a long time, the fur it's not attached to the rest of the body… its"

Brian could hardly tell Jack what he thought or what seemed to be the answer, so he tried to explain what made him jump.

"I think the best thing is to do this step by step as I will need you to be my assistant. I will tape record everything I do as I am doing it, so will you be all right to help?"

Jack not sure what he might be letting himself in for, but still wanting to know more about the Mouhume's, agreed.

"I don't know what to do, so don't get impatient with me ok Brian?"

Brian reassured Jack and told him that all he has to do is pass, and move things as he asks him. Brian got a tape recorder from his bag, then turned the tape recorder on and spoke as he started to do the autopsy on the small body.

Created and written by I C Henderson

Adventure of the Mouhumes
Jack and Annie's new
Visitors

"Right Jack if you could pass the magnifying glass, and position it just here and press that. That should hold it just right, and then we will get started."

As he started to pull the fur off the Mouhume with his fine pliers, he started to talk step by step saying what he was doing.

"I am starting to hold the fur apart as it would seem, that it is not connected to the skin, there seems to be a stitch near the seam, Jack if you would be so kind to hold the magnifying glass a little closer" Jack moved the magnifying glass closer.

"Yes there is a stitch and it would look like a knot holding the middle of the two ends together. At first it would seem this is part of the animal but at a closer look it is clear to see that it is from another animal"

Brian then took a small sample and put it in a test tube, marked a label then stuck that on the test tube. Brian then explained to Jack, when working with wild animals in the countryside his work needs to know what they have been eating. And the only way they can do that, unless they have been watching them for some time…is to open them up.

"The only way is an autopsy, that's when we come across animal's that have been found. Sometimes I take samples, and as I have done here put them in a test tube and then take them to my lab. Looking at the fur on this little one, I am sure it is fur from a rat. But I will know for sure after I have run some tests on it, the DNA will tell me a lot"

Jack asked if he would be able to still keep it quiet. And how long will it take for the results.

Brian explained that he had a lab at home; and often did any tests he had to do there; he was more than welcome to come along and watch.

Created and written by I C Henderson

Adventure of the Mouhumes
Jack and Annie's new
Visitors

"Right then back to the autopsy I will pull the fur coat back and see what is under. This is strange! Look there! Yes, like there is a fine fur growing under what can only be described as a fur overcoat. Can you see Jack? This has a rat's coat to help keep warm"

Jack looked and nodded, as there was nothing that he could say that would make any sense. He was amazed that a little thing would be able to kill another animal then skin it and make a fur coat, what would Annie say? She was not one for cruel and unnecessary killing of animals.

In the meantime Brian was carrying on doing what he had to do.

"I believe the cold weather has helped to prevent the decay. This small body is still in good condition; I believe the Mouhume found the cold weather too much and needed a fur coat or other clothing to keep warm"

At this stage Jack moved closer to have a better look, his head only a short distance from the poor thing.

"! Jack would you be so kind to move out of the way, as there is still a lot of work to be done"

Brian was not too happy that Jack nearly knocked him out of the way; he wanted to get on, to find out as much as he could about this wonderful creature. Jack gave an apology then moved back to where he was standing. Brian then started again, and as before started to talk and say everything that he was doing, and what he could see, no matter how strange it might be.

"Right we have discovered that it has what would seem to be a fur coat on. Which at this stage might be from a rat? I am about to

Adventure of the Mouhumes
Jack and Annie's new
Visitors

undo the bow and slip this coat off to see what is underneath" Brian with his fine pliers undid the bows, three in total.

"It would seem the bows are only over the waist and chest area I'm going to pull one of the arms out of the sleeve"

Brian as gently as he could, so that he would not break the arm, using his fingers so he could feel and know how much pressure he could use, gently pulled one sleeve over the arm. He then gave a big sigh, as when he was pulling the sleeve over the arm he had been holding his breath. The arm was in good condition to Brian's surprise. This would be the first time anyone would have seen the real appearance of a Mouhume. It had small hands no bigger than that of a mouse, but similar to that of a human's hand.

"Jack can you put the magnifying glass just over the hands please. As I think if we have a closer look we can see what sort of life it might have had. Have you seen this it has what would appear as if the little fellow might have what looks like clay on his hand?"

Then Brian looked at Jack in an uncertain way, with a nervous voce asked if he would not mind, if he could take this body to his laboratory.

Jack still not wanting the thing to be public knowledge, told Brian that would be all right but he would have to keep it quiet. Brian agreed, as he wanted to learn as much as he could about this creature.

The back door then opened, the two of them looked as if they had been caught with their hands in the sweet jar. The look of horror on their face's when they saw who it was coming in, not even a knock on the backdoor and not a word even as he came through the kitchen.

Adventure of the Mouhumes
Jack and Annie's new
Visitors

Jack in a stuttering and nervous voice asked what was going on. "What do you think you are doing? Just walking in like that? Not even knocking, what's going on?"

A little old voice spoke in a discontented and disapproving way.

"What have you here? You think that you have found a missing link do you?"

Brian not knowing what to say are do looked at Jack, with a lost look on his face.

Jack not showing any kind of emotion and himself, not knowing what to do or say did nothing and said nothing.

The little old man from next door, old Ted was seen in a different light. Ted walked into the room, looked at the table, and asked why they had killed this little creature.

Jack not wanting Ted to know what was on the table tried to stand in the way. Ted asked again, what were they doing with that creature on the table?

They had no idea what to say, as they did not expect anyone just walking in, catching them doing an autopsy on the dining room table.

"Www what are you doing?" Jack stuttered, not a lot of sense coming out of his mouth.

"What is this then, what do you call this?" Ted asked again, his face looked angry his tone when speaking was forceful.

Brian jumped in to the rescue, or so he thought. "This creature is called a Mouhume, what concern is it of yours?" Brian

Created and written by I C Henderson

Adventure of the Mouhumes
Jack and Annie's new
Visitors

stood tall, blowing his chest out as if he was in one of his classrooms.

"Don't stand there as if you have found the missing link, who do you think you are? And how do you know its name" Ted asked in the most disapproving way.

"Well my Grandfather told me their name, as he discovered them when I was a child, this might not be the missing link? But who knows what it might lead to" Brian answered proudly.

"Suppose that's as good as any name as any" Ted replied in a content way.

This took Jack and Brian aback, it was as if Ted had came across them before, by this time Ted was at the table, looking at the thing, he even looked upset as if he had lost a pet.

Jack just put it down that he must be an animal lover. He must be emotional; he had a soft spot for animals.

Ted said something to the little Mouhume, but Jack and Brian could not make it out what he had said, so they just ignored him.

"Would you like a drink of anything? Tea, coffee…anything" Jack asked not sure what was happening with Ted.

Ted looked up towards Jack, Ted nodded than he sat down on the chair at the table, Brian sat near Ted at the table.

Jack still not knowing what Ted wanted to drink, turned the kettle on, he knew if Ted did not want a hot drink he would have one himself, no doubt Brian might want one. Just in case he thought, he'd get him a glass of water as he was waiting for the kettle to boil; Jack placed the glass of water near Ted on the table, and sat down, as the kettle was not ready.

Created and written by I C Henderson

Adventure of the Mouhumes
Jack and Annie's new
Visitors

"Well Ted you looked a bit upset there for a minute, how are you? Do you think that you have seen one of these things before?" Jack asked with doubt in his voice.

Ted looked at Jack but before he could answer the kitchen door opened, in came Annie hands full of shopping. She looked into the dining room and saw Ted sitting there at the table.

"Hello Ted, how are you? Jack can you come and give me a hand?" Then she saw that Brian was also there.

"Sorry Brian I did not see you, how are you?" then Annie saw what was on the table, her heart sank her legs felt wobbly. Jack saw this and he jumped up and helped her to sit down at the table.

"What's wrong? Annie are you ok, can I get you anything? You're tired; I bet you've worked yourself sick today" Jack asked, not seeing the obvious, that maybe Annie was surprised to see Ted, also the table was like an operating theatre,

"Never mind me what's going on here, sorry Ted, but how are you involved in this? Where did you get this? This thing on the table what is it?"

Annie had just walked into the middle of an autopsy and had no idea what was going on in her house, what on earth was going on when she was at work? She wondered. Jack tried to explain in his own way but no doubt he would get Annie's back up.

"Annie can you remember when I first thought that we had mice? And I got something, in the rat trap in the greenhouse, you never saw it, I buried it round the back of the greenhouse. Anyway I remembered and Brian and me retrieved it,"

"Brian and I" Annie corrected his English. Then she realised what as on the table! She felt sick, the thought of the poor thing being killed in a rat trap, by Jacks traps, the colour drained from

196

Adventure of the Mouhumes
Jack and Annie's new
Visitors

her face! She looked at Ted. He looked no better than she did; she wondered what he must been thinking.

"Annie look at it! Its wonderful, its not what you would think, go on then look" Jack was keen on the fact, that it was nothing Annie and himself had thought. It was completely different in every way.

"So you are doing a post-mortem on my Dining room table? Are you, I shudder to think what goes on when I'm not home" Annie was angry with the thought of some dead creature lying on the table, she started to feel sick then she jumped up and ran upstairs, went straight to the toilet.

Downstairs they could hear her vomiting; Jack in his daft way shouted from the bottom of the stairs and asked what was the matter? Brian still in the dining room looked at Ted, then turned his eyes towards the door leading to the hall, as if to say that it was obvious what the matter was.

Annie could not stomach the fact of what was going on in her house, and the problem was lying on the table.

Brian asked Ted how he was feeling. Ted told Brian that he was ok, that he would be going home shortly. Jack came back into the room, and having no expression on his face, asked what they thought was wrong with Annie.

"It might be the fact you have a half done post-mortem on the table" Ted snapped.

"Not at all Annie has a cast-iron stomach, it will be something she has eaten at work, not a silly little thing on the table would make her poorly" Jack was convinced that it had something to do with what she had eaten at work.

Created and written by I C Henderson

Adventure of the Mouhumes
Jack and Annie's new
Visitors

"I don't know Jack, I have seen the hardest characters, be sick at a post-mortem, will we go? I'm sure she might have something to say about all of this" Brian was not wanting to stay, as he was convinced Annie would be upset, at what they had been doing in her absence, so he started to tidy up hoping to be away before Annie came down stairs.

No luck, the passage door opened Annie walked in, she glared at the three of them; they all looked away, so as not to make contact with her eyes.

Bang! Her hand slapped the table; the three of them jumped so high they nearly went through the ceiling. Annie smiled as the shock on their faces was a picture.

"Aaa Annie don't do that, I nearly had a heart attack, are you ok now? This must have upset you; I know this kind of thing is upsetting to most people" Brian said, trying to avoid a telling off. But had he? He would soon find out, Ted still looked as if he was ill, was this was due to the fright or the creature on the table?

Annie looked at all of them, her eyes saddened, the whole idea was a lot to take in, where was it going to stop? One day they had discovered a small creature, the next thing two other people were involved. How could they now keep it quiet?

Ted could see what Annie was thinking, so he spoke up, and told her that he could not and would not say anything, at his age people would think that he was going senile, or was… senile.

That made them all laugh, at the look of Ted, you would all ready think that he had gone in the head. He then told them that he would go and he would see them the next day as this was something that he needed to talk to them about.

When Ted had gone, Annie asked why they had to do this on her dining room table, could Brian not have done it anywhere else,

Adventure of the Mouhumes
Jack and Annie's new
Visitors

all she got was blank looks from the two culprits, she told Brian to get cleaned up, which he did, not needing telling twice, Jack was disappointed at the way Annie was acting, but did not say anything.

Annie laughed to herself; she thought Brian must be feeling like one of his students, as he was always telling someone off.

"Bet you haven't been told off in years, now you know how I felt when Jack and I came to your classroom at the museum, what will you do with the body?"

They could not decide who should have the body, as Jack was not happy, if Brian took it someone might see it, after a long and hard talk they decided to put it in an air tight jar, left it under the staircase, A cool dark place to help keep it as near perfect as possible.

Brian got all of his equipment; they then arranged to see each other in a day or two.

Brian had left his Grandfathers papers, on the sofa in the living room, this did not go down well with Annie as she did not like things left lying around, she picked up the papers with a struggle, there was a large pile, then put them in the cupboard at the bottom of the stairs, along with the Mouhume. Annie then told Jack to tell Brian to come and get them as soon as possible.

Jack rang Brian straight away as he could tell Annie was upset, he spoke to Brian they made arrangements for the next day.

Time was getting on, Annie had to be up early the next morning, so the pair of them decided to go to bed, as both of them had been busy that day, it did not take them long to fall asleep as the two of them were worn out, with all the going's on over the last few weeks.

Created and written by I C Henderson

Adventure of the Mouhumes
Jack and Annie's new
Visitors

Chapter 29

THE NEXT DAY Jack waited for Brian, but he never came, so Jack just pottered around the garden picking up bits of rubbish, and leaves, from the tree at the bottom of the garden, the tree was in the garden that joined his, but the leaves always came into Jacks garden. They never seemed to land in his neighbours' garden, this annoyed Jack, because his neighbour never had to tidy them up, they had laid there all winter, Jack would have normally picked them up but due to his injures he had not been able to.

Jack looked at his watch, he knew that Annie was due in from work, so he put the rake away in the greenhouse, then made his way up the garden, so that he could get cleaned up before Annie came, he knew that she would moan at him, for not taking it easy.

He heard a car pull onto the drive; he popped his head out the door to see if it was Annie, yes it was, on time as always, he quickly dried his hands then hung the towel on the hook near the back door, just before Annie came in, as always her hands full of shopping.

"Are you all right Jack? How has your day been have you had much company?" Annie not giving Jack much time to answer the first question rolled on asking the next.

Jack told her that he had not had any company that day, Brian had not came, nor had Ted been around, so he had been bored all day, Annie sighed for him.

"You poor thing, have you been bored?" Annie asked nipping his cheek, then rubbing his ear.

"Here I have had a long day, you have no idea, what its like sitting around not doing much, its not that I do not want to, but I cannot" Jack was starting to feel sorry for himself, so Annie told

Created and written by I C Henderson

Adventure of the Mouhumes
Jack and Annie's new
Visitors

him to get up stairs and bring some washing from out of the bathroom, so that she could turn the washing machine on.

When Jack was up stairs, Annie started to put the shopping away; she found it easier to do when Jack was out of the way,

Annie got on making the tea, as she knew that Jack would be ready, and probably not had anything, as he would be too busy with the Mouhumes.

Jack brought the dirty washing down, he give it to Annie, and told her that when she was busy that he would have a look down the garden, Annie put the washing in the washing machine, in the mean time Jack went down the garden.

Annie could see him from the kitchen window; she was wondering what on earth he could be up to now? He was looking around the greenhouse then he went into the greenhouse, she could see that he was concentrating hard on something, what was he doing? What was that? She would have to go down and see for herself, she put her old shoes on (her garden shoes) and down the garden she went.

"What are you up to now? I hope we are not going to let these things control our lives and time" Annie was not happy as the Mouhumes had taken over their lives, Jack had spent too much time on these, she thought it was time to get on with their own lives.

So she was going to give Jack no peace, until he got them out of his head, and they got back on with their own lives.

Annie was hoping that Jack had not found any more Mouhumes; she knew that it would take all of their time up, which she did not have the time or patience for.

Created and written by I C Henderson

Adventure of the Mouhumes
Jack and Annie's new
Visitors

As she drew nearer to the greenhouse her heart went faster, butterflies jumped in her stomach, she could see what Jack was looking at.

"Oh no Jack what's happened!? No please not that" Annie said this as she stopped in her tracks, right outside the greenhouse door.

Jack looked up at her, from inside the greenhouse, with a look of surprise, and the same time horror.

Annie had an old glass vase, which had belonged to her Grandmother; Jack had put it into the greenhouse before his accident, when the conservatory was being built, along with some other things in a cardboard box.

"Look Annie I can explain, I had put them down here when we were getting the conservatory built, there was nowhere else I could put them for safe keeping"

Annie was in a right old temper now, seeing that her vase was left in an old box, in the greenhouse over the winter, she was too frightened to look to see if it was damaged, she asked Jack to take it out of the box, as it was laying on top of the other things in the box. Jack lifted it out, then he unwrapped it from the newspaper, which he had not over done. Annie watched hoping that it had not been broken, as Jack unwrapped the newspapers from the vase; he looked up towards Annie then smiled.

"Its ok Annie, look its ok, I knew that it would be safe down here"

Annie sighed with relief. "Thank God I love that vase, give it to me, do not bring anything out of the house unless you ask me first ok … Jack ok?"

Created and written by I C Henderson

Adventure of the Mouhumes
Jack and Annie's new
Visitors

Jack was looking in the box, to see what other things he had put in, so he was not listening to Annie.

Annie went back into the house with her vase; she began to wash the vase in the kitchen sink. Once it was cleaned and dried she placed it in the conservatory, on the coffee table in the centre of the room.

Jack still in the greenhouse, was going through the box and had not noticed that Annie had gone, and probably had not heard what she had said, he just carried on looking in the box, and there were all sorts of things, so that kept him occupied for some time.

The next thing Jack knew was that Annie was calling him, for his Dinner. After they had Dinner, they got cleaned up (Annie as usual).

That night not much was said, they had both had too many late nights and it was catching up on them, they were sitting in the conservatory, Jack was glancing out of the window from time to time,

"Annie where did you put that vase?" Jack tried to start a conversation.

"Do you not take any notice of anything!?" Annie snapped. "It's right in front of you on the coffee table. I'm going to bed I have an early start again tomorrow" Annie said as she started to get up.

"You have so many vases from different relatives; I cannot keep up, which one is from which, Aunty or Grandparents"

Annie had no reply, then told Jack that she was off to bed, and told Jack that he had better not be too long. Jack sat there for a little longer hoping that the Mouhumes would come, but deep

Adventure of the Mouhumes
Jack and Annie's new
Visitors

down he knew they would not, so it was not long before he himself went to bed.

Before he went to bed he made himself and Annie a cup of Horlicks, so that they could relax and maybe have a good night's sleep, the last few nights that they had gone to bed early, they had not slept properly. As he went up stairs to bed, he started to whistle so that Annie would not fall asleep, before they had their drinks.

"Annie look at what I have for you" Jack said as he walked through the bedroom door, the bed was behind the door so he could not see if Annie was asleep. As he came around he put the cups on Annie's drawers next to the clock, he give her a little poke, Annie turned around to see what was wrong.

"Jack what have you there?" Annie asked as she rubbed her eyes, she had fallen asleep, and Jack had just woken her up.

"I've made a drink for you this will help you sleep" Jack said with a smile on his face, thinking that he had done a good thing.

"Jack I had fallen asleep, thanks anyway"

Jack could tell that Annie was upset, so he asked her if he should take it back downstairs.

"No Jack I will drink it, you have gone to the trouble to make it" Annie said as she reached and held Jacks hand, she gave him a smile, just so he knew that she was not angry with being woken up. They drank their drinks, in no time at all they both settled down and were asleep,

Created and written by I C Henderson

Adventure of the Mouhumes
Jack and Annie's new
Visitors

Chapter 30
Quiet Days

THE NEXT TWO days the Mouhumes and fairies did not see one another. The fairy world could keep out of sight but still watch the Mouhumes. They watched the Mouhumes trying to communicate with other creatures they could not understand.

The fairies wanted the Mouhumes to see how much they needed them. Buster and Tilly, as friendly as they were with the Mouhumes, lost that connection due to not understanding what the other wanted.

The fairies would normally translate for them, but now they had lost that and had to find another way to understand each other. That was not a bad thing as they were starting to depend on the fairies more and more. Now they had to do what they had always done and that was to learn fast. About the world they had not just discovered but made for themselves.

Ruddy was trying to make friends with the kitten that belonged to Ted. She knew that if she could not make friends with it, as it got bigger it would be a deadly enemy. She gave herself a week to have it as a friend or she would have to try and kill it.

The kitten grew bigger each day; it was exploring the area with more and more interest. It was looking into every corner whilst on the prowl. At this time it was still playful but Ruddy knew it would only be a matter of time before instinct would kick in and it would be killing. She had a son to take care of, so she wanted to keep her distance from any danger that might come near. So making friends with it was one way.

Glow and other fairies stayed out of sight, watching all the time to see the true Mouhume and to see if they had any other ideas. They watched Ruddy the most, as she was the fearless one. They wanted to know if it was right what some Mouhumes had

Adventure of the Mouhumes
Jack and Annie's new
Visitors

said, unaware they were being listened to. She was a killing phenomenon they would say. She killed anything in her way without hesitation no matter what.

There were parts Glow had seen: her reaction, her speed and her strength. But that was not all of Ruddy. She had something else. Something she had not seen in her own kind. She had a want to get along with others, but some did not see this. They had put her upon a high platform, so no matter what she did she would be liked or disliked.

.

Glow could not believe herself. She had almost blamed Ruddy for the mishaps. Ruddy was the only common denominator in all those so called friendships, or those who had been enemies, such as Rug

Ruddy was teaching her son Dash how to catch a bird, what size it should be and so on. It was the same with fishing: it was no good trying to catch a fish that was as big as them, because it would pull them into the water. That was something a Mouhume would never survive as a Mouhume could not swim. They had no ponds or lakes where they had lived.

The fairies had little time for birds, birds often went after fairies to kill and eat them. The fairies had little hope against a bird on ground or in the air, no matter what size the bird was.

Whilst the Mouhumes were being watched, the fairies had seen that a small number from this community were going to the woodlands community and also to the parklands. They had all started to keep in contact with each other on a daily basis. This was good to know. It gave the Mouhumes strength in numbers if needed. The Mouhumes had no idea how many fairy communities there were. This was something fairies did not want to share.

Dash was distracted. His mother was crouching down behind a flowering shrub ready to attack a bird when he went to look in the

Created and written by I C Henderson

Adventure of the Mouhumes
Jack and Annie's new
Visitors

pond, something had caught his eye. He was standing on the edge of the paving stones that went around the pond, surrounded by a border with flowers and plants. Dash was bending over the edge looking into the water when something knocked him in. A toad, it had been startled and jumped out from behind the plants around the pond.

Dash yelled for help, but Ruddy was now in a conflict with a bird. She would be the only Mouhume close enough that would put her life at risk for another.

Starlight heard. And without hesitation she was at the pond trying to pull out Dash. At this time Ruddy had seen what was happening and quickly was on her way. Starlight's wings got soaked as she tried to pull Dash out from the water. Now she was in need of help, she could not open her wings as wide as she would have liked, and was struggling to get on the path around the pond. She got as near to the edge as she could, but her wings were now weighing her down and the clothing Dash had on was pulling the two of them down.

Then a hand grabbed hold of the two of them trying desperately to pull them out. It was Mousey holding onto them at the same time. His body was leaning backwards holding on to the two of them. Their heads were now just above the water.

The fish swimming below were taking a nibble at their feet but not getting a hold properly. Each time the fish was pulling them back under the water, each time almost pulling Mousey in too.

Glow arrived and could see this, quickly she pulled out Starlight. She dropped her onto the dry path. Then back to pull out Dash at which time Ruddy had landed too.

It had all happened in a moment. Starlight was like a wet rag, as was Dash. The two of them were on the dry path lying in a pool of water. Ruddy seeing to her son whilst Mousey and Glow saw to

Adventure of the Mouhumes
Jack and Annie's new
Visitors

Starlight. What a day it had been, once again, the fairies put their own well-being at risk to save a Mouhume.

Mousey was a hero that day, not just in the eyes of the Mouhumes but the fairies also thought of him as a friend. He could have let go anytime as he too was in danger, danger of also being pulled in, but he had held on to the two of them, not favouring one more than the other.

Celebrations were cut short when the man who had been there the other day talking to Jack and Annie came back. That had been when the dead Mouhume was dug up from the back of the shed. This was alarming for the Mouhumes and they needed to know why? So what they did was to get Ted to go and see. But as none of them could speak to Ted, not even the fairies, how could they get him to go around to Jack's house?

Ted had some plant pots with soil in them but nothing planted in them. It was just dry soil. So the Mouhumes wanted a sign for Ted to see. They started to empty the soil from the pots just by picking it out by hand, or anything that could scoop it out, then they threw it onto the patio. When there was enough they spread it like a fine dust, then they used their feet to make an arrow-like mark pointing to Jack's house.

The fairies would have to get Ted's attention. There was only one way they could do that. Ted had a bell on the outside wall; this was for the fairies when they needed Ted. They would swing on the string until it rang. Ted being a little hard of hearing, sometimes it would take longer than other times.

They rang it hard and fast until Ted came out. They waved at him to follow them around the back garden then they pointed to the ground with the arrow. Flying over the hedge they waved for him to follow. Ted went as quickly as his old legs could carry him around the front then straight into Jack's kitchen. There were voices louder than normal coming from Jack's house.

208

Adventure of the Mouhumes
Jack and Annie's new
Visitors

Ted came out. He was only in Jack's house for a short time. The fairies could not hear what had been said so could not tell the Mouhumes anything. The plan was for one fairy to follow Ted into Jack's house but Ted shut the door behind him as he went in.

They would have to wait and hope that Ted would tell them but Ted sometimes just thought they would know about things so he would not say anything. Not just that but anyone watching or listening might think that he was talking to himself. He was always conscious of that. His wife Linda had often found him talking to himself and would give a comment about him talking to himself but in reality he was talking to the fairies.

There was no news so they would just have to wait to see what the outcome might be. There was one thing that was learnt that day: both sides helped one another without thinking.

It was near the end of the day and the darkness was cutting in. They parted as normal. The Mouhumes knew that most of the fairies needed to settle down at night, although some still had enough energy until early morning. Tube understood this and knew that this would be something he would have done if he was the leader of the fairy colony.

The Mouhumes returned to the sheds they held discussions about what had gone on with the fairies and the human called Ted, Tube listened but one thing kept making him laugh was Mousey's story about being thrown away. When, in fact, he had been pulled out of harm's way and had passed out in shock.

Mousey's explanation was, that his mind was going that fast he could foresee it and only days earlier Ruddy had been dropped from a great height so it was not far from being the truth. It could have happened!

Created and written by I C Henderson

Adventure of the Mouhumes
Jack and Annie's new
Visitors

It was only later, after he passed out, he found himself in the outhouse. He woke up to find Ruddy standing over him but she was looking poorly.

Then a fairy came to in to see if we were better. Then I was told about what I had done: I had unknowingly walked into the resting area of the fairies that needed re-energizing from the sunrays. That's what they do, they re-energize from the sun, two or three times a day.

That's also how they can hide. They imitate what they are near, making it almost impossible to see them.

Mousey went on with many more interesting accounts of what he now knew. Even telling Scallop what he had learned in the short time he was with the fairy called Glow.

It was a lot to take in for Tube and Ratty and some of the other leaders. Why would they tell others of their weakness? What would they benefit from it? They had no idea who the Mouhumes were, so why tell them?

Ruddy was next telling them of her account. How she sensed something behind her, how she was taken into the air with a vice-like grip. No matter how hard she tried to break loose she could not. Then she was dropped but it was no ordinary drop, she was spun so that she could not do anything to help herself.

Then the next thing she was saved by Capheus. "He was injured by helping me. I felt under the weather after that and that was why I went out of the way from everyone anyway. The next day I went to see what these creatures were."

"It took time but then they showed themselves and took me somewhere. All I remember was that I was shown some place that I could not describe and colours that I have never seen before and could not even explain what they might look like. Things were

Created and written by I C Henderson

Adventure of the Mouhumes
Jack and Annie's new
Visitors

there but not really there. It was all too much then I passed out. The next thing I knew I was with baby and they took care of me until you came for me."

Tube and Ratty were astonished. Mixing with other creatures and getting help from outside was not the Mouhume way. Though, if they wanted to stay there they would have to try and work together and the way forward was with Ruddy, Mousey and Scallop. As it was now these three who had the most contact with the fairy world.

Created and written by I C Henderson

Adventure of the Mouhumes
Jack and Annie's new
Visitors
Chapter 31
Jacks new discovery

ANNIE HAD TO start early that morning, it was probably the first time she was awake before Jack, she knew that the last few days would have taken it out of him, so she let him have a lie in.

Annie was in the kitchen making her breakfast, when she heard Jack upstairs moving around, she knew that it would not be long before he was down, so she made him a cup of tea.

Jack was upstairs, looking for his slipper, he had kicked it off the night before and had no idea where it had gone, he was always doing that, and every morning was the same, Annie knew that in a moment he would be calling for her to help him find it.

Sure enough he was at the top of the stairs, calling for her, Annie smiled, but she would still tell him off, for not putting his slippers together.

After some time looking for Jacks slipper, they came down the stairs, Annie true enough told Jack off, and Jack apologised, Annie knew that night would be the same, Jack would take his clothes off, and they would just be dropped anywhere.

It was time for Annie to go to work, she said goodbye to Jack and asked if he would be alright, Jack told her that he would be alright and not to worry, Annie could not help but worry as just a few days before she left him alone, when she came back he was helping to do a post- mortem, when she came back from work, she wondered what she would come back to that night.

Jack feeling a bit stiff, as he always did in the mornings, was stretching all of his body, arms, back, legs. The morning was bright and the sky was clear, it looked as if it was going to be a warm day, it was still early so he sat in the conservatory, with his cup of tea, wondering what he would do that day?

Created and written by I C Henderson

Adventure of the Mouhumes
Jack and Annie's new
Visitors

He was sure that no matter what he would do that day, it would be boring compared to the last few weeks, so he sat trying to decide how he would fill his day.

He just happened to turn his head towards the garden when he noticed Ted, over the hedge, Jack stood up to have a better look, he was wondering what could Ted be doing in the garden this early in the morning?

Jack watched for a short time, then decided to go and ask, there was a bit of dew on the grass, so he looked for his shoes like his slippers he had taken them off and they were scattered, somewhere in the kitchen, he had no routine, so by the time he found his shoes, Ted had gone back into the house, Jack still looked over the hedge, to see if he could make out anything.

"Can I help you?" came a voice from up the garden, which startled Jack, Jack looked up towards the voice, it was Ted.

"I was just looking for you, I was wondering what you were doing? If you might" Jack stuttered, "Today you might have time for a cup of tea or something?"

"No I have nothing to do today, yes you could come around if you like, later Linda is going out, and so I would be left alone and probably bored" Ted was never bored, Jack would soon discover. They stood talking for a little longer, Jack then took his empty cup back into the house, as he approached the back door, he could hear the telephone ringing, he kicked his shoes off in a fashion, then ran into the living room. He answered the phone, and to his surprise, it was Brian. "Hello stranger! I thought you had abandoned us, what happened yesterday then?" Jack thought he would poke some fun at Brian, for not turning up the day before.

Brian then explained that he had forgotten that he and his wife were having guests around for dinner. He had forgotten to ring and let him and Annie know.

Created and written by I C Henderson

Adventure of the Mouhumes
Jack and Annie's new
Visitors

So he asked if it would be alright to come around and pick up some of his Grandfathers papers, Jack agreed, then he remembered that he was going next door to Ted's, so he told Brian if he got no answer, just to come around to the back and he would see him and Ted in the back garden, Brian agreed and that was that.

It was getting really warm and sunny outside, so Jack put on a tee shirt, and even some shorts, the only problem he had was finding his flip flops, no doubt he would have taken them off, the same way he took everything off, he remembered that Ted a few night's earlier was telling him and Annie about fairies, so he thought he would take some of Brian's Grandfathers papers around for Ted to look at, Jack was sure Brian would not mind Ted having a look at them, after all Ted was now involved as he had walked in on them two days ago.

Jack went to the back of his house, to see if Ted was in his garden, Ted was sitting on his patio chair, Ted told Jack to come around, and he would get some cold drinks from the fridge for him.

Jack asked if it would be alright if Brian came later, Ted told him that would be fine, Jack told Ted about Brian's Grandfather's paper's, and asked if he would like to have a look at them.

Ted said that he would love to have a look at them, Jack told Ted that he would be straight around, sure enough he was around like a shot, Jack only took a hand full as there were too many for him to carry, and he knew that it would take more than a short time sitting outside to read them and take it all in.

When Jack went around the back of Ted's garden, Ted was waiting and there was a cold drink on the patio table. "There's a drink for you, do you need a hand with all that paper?" Ted asked as he was making room on the table.

Created and written by I C Henderson

Adventure of the Mouhumes
Jack and Annie's new
Visitors

Jack told Ted that he was ok, then he put the few papers that he had, on the table, he explained that there were more around home, but he thought that he had brought enough for now.

As Jack sat down, he looked around Ted's garden, it was beautiful, the plants were starting to bloom, it was a picture.

Ted took no time in starting to read Brian's Grandfather's documents, they dated back to the early thirties, it would seem that Brian's Granddad, went into documenting every thing that he had done with the Mouhume's, Ted seemed interested his head was in the book, some of the documents were in books, some were written on bits of loose papers but they were all in order.

Jack got up and was looking around the garden he could not get over how good it looked, it had to be the best garden Jack had ever seen, everything was positioned just right, Jack came back to the patio table, and picked up his drink, Ted was still reading, he had got through best part of the pile, that Jack had brought round.

As Jack was sitting looking around, he suddenly noticed something was on one of the plants, it was or, looked as if it was flapping in the soft breeze, Jack looked at the other plants but none of them were moving, this had Jack puzzled, he sat for some time, his eyes fixed on this plant, it stood about one meter high, it looked similar to that of a foxglove, but Jack new that it was not one of them, Ted's head poked above the book he was reading, he looked at Jack then he looked at where Jack was looking, then he knew what Jack had seen, Ted still did not say anything, he watched Jack watching the plant, Ted was waiting till he knew Jack had worked it out.

Then all of a sudden it was obvious Jack had worked it out, Jacks face was all excited he was like a small child, wanting a present but having to wait, his body was shaking with excitement as it did most times, but he knew he could not jump up and frighten it away, Jacks shaky hand touched Ted so that he could get Ted's

215

Adventure of the Mouhumes
Jack and Annie's new
Visitors

attention, Ted looked over the book knowing fine well what Jack was going to tell him, but he played daft.

"What's wrong Jack? Are you all right Jack? Is there something stuck in your throat? Can I help you?" Ted wanted Jack to tell him what he had seen, Ted knew that he could not tell Jack, Jack had to tell him.

Jack did not know how to put it into words so he pointed, to where he was looking, Ted turned his head and looked, just a quick glance, as he knew what it was, he had seen it so many times before, Ted nodded then put his head back into his book, hiding so that Jack could not see him laughing.

Jack was beside himself wondering if Ted had seen what he had pointed too, so he nudged Ted again, then pointed again, this time Ted answered.

"Yes I know they are beautiful aren't they" then Ted went back into his reading.

Jack not sure that Ted was aware of what he had meant, asked Ted if he knew what he had meant. Ted looked up and asked Jack to explain in his own words what he had seen, if he could tell him from the start.

"Well Ted I was having a look around your garden, at your plants, than I sat down just drinking my drink that you'd made for me, I just happened to look up then I saw it" Ted interrupted, and asked what had he seen, Jack started again.

"I will describe it as I saw it, it looked like a leaf was fluttering in the wind, but when looking at the other plants, their leaves were not moving, I must admit I could not feel any breeze on my arms, so I knew something was not right" Jack stopped; Ted could see that he was getting uneasy, so Ted asked Jack just to carry on.

216

Adventure of the Mouhumes
Jack and Annie's new
Visitors

"Jack you look restless, I'm sure whatever it was can be no more strange than that of the Mouhume's"

Jack started again, this time he was determined to tell Ted what he thought he had seen, and nothing was going to stop him this time.

"Right then something was waving it looked as if it was some leaves, but no other leaves were moving, so I was trying to see why it might be moving, at first I wondered if there was anything blowing on that plant, like a clothes drier." Ted looked at Jack confused, Jack knew even saying that, sounded silly, so he was not surprised at the look Ted gave him, so he thought that he had better carry on.

"Well there was nothing that I could see, so it had my attention, the more I watched the more I could make out, then it moved around, then I could see what it was, or what it looked like" just then a voice from over the hedge from Jack's garden interrupted Jack from carrying on.

Brian had come and he was looking for Jack, he had remembered that Jack had said that if he was not in the house, that he would be in Ted's garden, Brian had not wanted just to walk into someone's garden without being asked, so he thought it would be better poking his head over the hedge so that Ted could invite him around, which Ted did.

"Hello Brian are you coming around?" Ted asked.

"Yes how will I get around? Will I come around the front then around the back" Brian asked unsure, probably wondering if there was a gate in the back garden to save him walking around the front, but he was not that lucky, he would have to go back out the way he came and then around the front of Ted's than around the back to where Ted and Jack were.

217

Adventure of the Mouhumes
Jack and Annie's new
Visitors

Jack at this time was getting really brassed off at being interrupted. Ted could see that Jack wanted to tell him, but he asked if he would not say anything just for now and he would explain later, Jack unwilling agreed, he was bursting to tell someone, but he would have to wait.

When Brian came to where they were, he noticed straight away that Ted was reading his Grandfather's documents, Ted noticed the look on Brian's face so he asked and hoped that he did not mind him reading them, Brian not too happy but unwilling to spoil the mood, nodded and told Ted that it was ok, in the mean time Jack had taken his eye off the thing he had been looking at and it had disappeared.

Brian sat down near Ted, then asked what he thought about the documents? Ted told Brian that his Grandfather had gone to a lot of trouble, learning about the Mouhume's, Brian noticed that Jack was not saying a lot, so he asked him if he was all right, Ted looked at Jack as Brian asked and shook his head, as if not to say anything about what he had just seen, Jack understood so he did not say anything, but told Brian that he was feeling a little bit under the weather.

Time was getting on, it was near dinner time Jack was getting a little hungry, so he stood up and told Ted that he was popping back around home for a bite to eat; Brian had an attempt to drop a hint that he too was feeling a little hungry.

"Jack would you be alright on your own? As I can see that you are moving with difficulty, I know what I could do, I could come around and make us both a bite to eat, yes I'll do that for you" Brian thought that he had put it across good, and that it would be a done deal, so he was getting up thinking that he would go around to Jacks for a bite to eat, Jack not wanting to put anyone to any trouble said that he would be ok and told Brian to stay and talk to Ted.

Created and written by I C Henderson

Adventure of the Mouhumes
Jack and Annie's new
Visitors

"No Brian you stay here I'll be ok, Ted and you can sit and talk about the Mouhume's and decide where they might have gone"

The look on Brian's face was obviously that of disappointment, Jack stood up looked at Brian, Jack give no sign that he had noticed the expression on his face, Jack turned to Ted and smiled, Ted then knew that Jack had heard Brian and understood that Brian was hinting to go with Jack for a bite to eat , and that he was just having a bit of fun with Brian, by acting as if he had not heard what he had said, Ted was still unsure that Jack would not say anything about what he had just seen so he also asked Jack if it was ok for himself to go with him, Jack even put Brian out of misery and asked if he would like to go with them.

Jack told them that would be all right, but he was not sure if he would be able to feed them all, as he was feeling unwell. Brian then interrupted again seeing a chance that he still might get fed, and told them that he would be glad to cook for them or make a sandwich, Jack nodded he saw that would be a good idea as he and Ted could talk about what they had seen in Ted's garden.

Jack told Brian, where everything was what he needed, for their lunch, Jack and Ted went into the conservatory, Brian could not hear them talking, as he was busy, and they were talking quietly, Jack asked Ted if he could tell Annie what he had seen, Ted told him that only people who see them need know, they only let you see them if they think you are good and will not hurt them, Jack then asked why not tell Brian as he is a Professor? Ted then explained, that they are a shy creature and only a few people have ever seen them, once they have shown themselves you will see them a lot more, you could be standing looking at them with someone at the same spot and only you might see them, they can hide on any plant.

Brian came in the room then sat down near Ted; he then asked what he thought about the papers? Ted told Brian that his Grandfather had gone to a lot of trouble, it looked as if he might

Created and written by I C Henderson

Adventure of the Mouhumes
Jack and Annie's new
Visitors

have helped them to evolve, Brian when told this was a little confused, he was under the impression that he and Jack were the only ones apart from his Granddad to know anything about the Mouhumes, So how would Ted think that his Granddad had helped them to evolve.

Brian then got up and went back into the kitchen, to finish the lunch, but all the time he wondered what Ted had said, he could not understand? How would he know, did his Grandfather help them to evolution, his documents gave no indication of this, so how would Ted come to this judgment or even think this? After sometime Brian just dismissed this and came to the conclusion that Brian must have read it wrong or misunderstood it.

Brian put the food on the table, then called for Jack and Ted, to come from out of the conservatory, the two of them came into the dinning room, the table was set, it looked good, Brian was a dab hand, he had done a lovely lunch, it took no time for the three of them to clear the lot, neither Ted nor Jack volunteered to do the washing-up, so the dishes where left in the sink.

They all went back next door to Ted's, Brian had left his Granddad's paperwork on the patio table, after all that was the main reason why he had came, when they got around to Ted's, Ted asked if they wanted a drink, Brian and Jack both agreed, that they would have one, Jack sat on the same chair as before, hoping that he would see what he had seen earlier, Ted did not take long as he did not want Jack to be tempted to say anything to Brian, Ted brought a tray with the drinks on, a nice cool glass of lemonade each.

The three of them sat for sometime talking, about all sorts, not just the Mouhumes, they talked about, all the things that had ever been written, which might have been mistaken for a Mouhume, Ted came up with something which surprised Jack and Brian, he said what if everything that had been written, might be

Created and written by I C Henderson

Adventure of the Mouhumes
Jack and Annie's new
Visitors

true, but in some cases they might have added or missed out something.

This got Jack thinking, could Ted be right, had all the nursery rhymes, fairytales be true, Peter Pan, Thumbelina, Cinderella, Sleeping beauty, Elves and the shoe maker. Were all of these stories based on real things?

Jack was beginning to think, after seeing what he had in the last few weeks, thinking about these stories they all had a lot in common, had they told what they had seen in a story? After all it could be true, because Jack could see some of the characters, out of some of the stories, yes he thought to himself, theses stories must be true, Jack then looked at Ted and nodded, Ted's eyes gave the response that he knew, that Jack understood.

Jack needed to talk to Ted without Brian being there, there was a lot he needed to know and ask, Jack was bursting, he needed to ask but he had to wait, until Brian decided to go.

How long would he be what was keeping him, he had his Granddads documents, why was he not going now, he was a Professor, he was a busy man how way go, Jack thought to himself his impatience starting to show.

"Are you going?" Jack asked looking at Brian.

"No I have the day off, I thought I would stay a little longer as there is so much to talk about" Brian answered, not the response Jack wanted, but he would have to but up with it.

Jack did not want to go into the conversation too much so when Brian asked anything he would give only one word answers, or even say that he could not remember, even when he wanted to tell him more , but he had other thing's more impotent to ask Ted.

Adventure of the Mouhumes
Jack and Annie's new
Visitors

Ted at this time, was smiling to himself as he could tell that Jack was getting frustrated, it was obvious that he did not want to get into a long debate, about the Mouhume's. Brian was the only one not to have realized, so he carried on asking questions, he must have thought that Jack had amnesia, or bad eye sight, on some of the things he should have seen.

Time went on, Brian's mobile phone started to ring, Brian stood up then walked down the garden to answer it, Jacks face was stressed, Ted laughed at Jack, Jack whispered to Ted. "How long to do you think he will be?" Ted laughed even more, as he could see Jack getting more and more frustrated.

Brian came back up the garden and told them that he was called away, his wife wanted the car. Jack sighed with relief, his moment had arrived not before time, Brian asked if it would be all right if he came back the next day after work as he had some ideas he wanted to put forward to Ted, Ted agreed he told Brian that he found some of his Grandfathers documents interesting, Jack in a hurry nearly pushed Brian to his car, telling him that he should not keep his wife waiting, he grabbed hold of his arm and walked him to the car, Brian not knowing what to make of it, just put it down to that Jack was looking out for him, so that he would not get told off from his wife.

Jack came back to Ted's garden, after seeing Brian off, Ted was sitting in his chair, waiting for Jack.

"Right Jack if you could tell me what you thought you might have seen earlier, in your own words" Ted asked Jack in a way, that he was, or might be unsure.

"I've been dying to tell you, hold on Ted you know what I saw don't you" Jack stopped was Ted not sure or was he playing games? Jack's head was confused. Brian sat for what seemed like a life time, no Jack was sure that Ted knew what he was going to tell

222

Adventure of the Mouhumes
Jack and Annie's new
Visitors

him so Jack started to tell him exactly what he had seen and he was not bothered if it sounded silly.

"Right as I was saying before, I was sitting looking around your garden at your plants and ornaments, thinking how nice they looked and nothing out of place, then suddenly something took my eye"

"Something took your eye? What do you mean" Ted interrupted knowing fine well what Jack had meant.

Jack was not put off by Ted's interruption, so he carried on, as he had to say what had happened and seen.

"Something caught my eye, it was fluttering only in one spot, nothing else was moving , I know this because I looked around the rest of the garden, the harder I looked the clearer it became, the more confident it seemed to become, I'm sure it even smiled at me,"

Ted stopped Jack again asking what smiled at him, Jack knew that Ted knew what he was talking about, or he thought he did, no he was sure so he carried on with his tale, not answering any of Ted's questions.

"It was hiding around the back of the plant that one there" Jack pointed to a plant which looked a little like a foxglove.

"Then it slowly came around the front, half its body still behind the stem of the plant, but it was clear to see what it was, man it was beautiful, better than anything I have seen before in books or any ornament" Jack was stopped again.

"In your own words Jack, describe it as you saw it" Ted asked again.

Created and written by I C Henderson

Adventure of the Mouhumes
Jack and Annie's new
Visitors

"At first it looked like a giant…" Jack stopped again he did not want to get the description wrong or make it sound like any other thing.

"Well I suppose if you had to compare it with something it would be a dragonfly, the same but different, do you know what I mean?" Jack stopped; Ted nodded for him to carry on.

"It had big green wings, clear but still you could see the colour, two larger at the top two smaller under the larger ones, you would not believe how lovely it was to see, I can not believe how fantastic it was" Jack looked at the spot where he had seen the creature, it had gone, but then it dawned on him that Ted had probably all ready seen them himself, as he was always on about how that the fairies helped him in the garden.

Ted stood up and nodded to Jack for him to follow him, they went down the garden path just a short way, then Ted stopped he stuck out his hand flicked his fingers, then six fairies, came and landed on his shoulders and arms, Jacks eyes lit up, Jacks world had changed the things he thought were stories, fairytales, where now real, he thought how, why had he not seen all of these things before.

Why was Ted so involved with the fairies? How did the Mouhume's live along side the fairies, what was the connection? Jack had so much to ask, he had no idea were to start, just as well, because Ted was going to tell him.

Created and written by I C Henderson

Adventure of the Mouhumes
Jack and Annie's new
Visitors
Chapter 32
Fairy tale

"JACK I SEE that you have a lot to ask, you must have so many questions to ask, I will save you the time, lets go and sit" The two of them went back up the garden to the patio, they sat down, Ted began to tell Jack how he got involved with the fairies, and how the Mouhume's came to be part of his world.

"Jack it all happened thirty-years ago, I had been paid off from work, the factory I worked in was closing down, I had a lot of time on my hands so I would go for walks, do the gardening, jobs in the house, just to keep busy. Anyway one day when out for a walk, the strangest thing happened I heard what sounded like a bird squeal, like a hawk or something you know what I mean" Jack nodded so Ted carried on; Jack did not want to speak as he wanted Ted to tell the story.

"Well, I looked over what was an old bridge, it was a place where I would walk, and it took me over a railway bridge, I looked down into the gorge, yes it was a hawk, or some kind of hunting bird, I'm not too good on the types of birds, anyway it was after some thing, hot on its heels, at that time I had no idea what it was, but I was soon to find out, the thing came straight for me, you had to see it to believe it, the two of them coming at me, well I froze, I was unable to move, nothing like this had ever happened to me" Ted stopped and rubbed one of the fairies which was under its chin, then he carried on.

"Coming at me like two bullets, one went to my left the other to my right, the bird hitting my shoulder, with its wing, which knocked it off course, anyway I turned around to see where they had gone, the bird flew away, but I could not see the thing it was chasing, I lost sight of it, so I just carried on and went on my way, I had a jacket on it had been a little chilly when I went out that day, but after what had happened with the bird, the sun started to come out, I was starting to feel warm so I took my jacket off, gave it a

Adventure of the Mouhumes
Jack and Annie's new
Visitors

shake, well the surprise I got when…" Ted stopped his face was glowing, his eyes were bright sparkling, as he looked at Jack and his little friends, he started again, he could see that Jack was keen on learning what happened next.

"to my surprise it was or had been on the back of my jacket, it fell off when I shook my jacket, it had been hurt and was clinging on my back, probably to get its strength back, as it was puffing and panting, it was clear to see that it was tired, I picked it up ever so gentle, placed it on my jacket, it lay there like on a king size bed, the poor thing was too tired to attempted to fly off, Linda my wife, at that time was a veterinary nurse, so I rushed home, carrying the delicate little thing, when I got home, Linda had already left for work, there were no phones at that time, well not that may, not many homes had one, anyway so I left the tiny thing on the sideboard, then ran after Linda lucky for me she had not gone far, she had been waiting for me getting back, but could not wait any longer and left" Ted stopped for a drink, then he carried on.

"You have no idea how hard it was to get her back home, can you imagine how hard it was to get her back home, your standing on a street asking for her to come home to have a look at a creature which no one had ever seen, then it was that all that about the fairies at the bottom of a garden, from the two girls who had taken a photo, well Linda thought that I must have bumped my head, I nearly had to carry her back home, anyway she finally came back with me, when we got back home well…" Ted stopped again; Jack could tell that it was a bit emotional for Ted, so he asked if they should stop, Ted refused, he told Jack that he would be all right. So he carried on.

"My heart sank when we walked into the room where I left the fairy, it had gone! my jacket was still there, the look on Linda's face, would frighten anyone, she thought that I had got her home on a false pretence, I tried to explain , she would have none of it, anyway I picked my coat up, and went to hang it up on the back door, there it was hiding in the fold of my sleeve, it poked its head

Adventure of the Mouhumes
Jack and Annie's new
Visitors

out ever so shy, I turned around to Linda look there it is look, Linda came and looked, she could not see anything, she gave me a right telling off, then she went to work, was I seeing things was my mind playing tricks on me, all of these thing ran through my mind, no of coarse not, I could see it but for some reason it would not show itself to Linda, she has never seen any of them even to this day, but since that day they have lived with me, they come and go, but this one and that one have never left me" Ted pointed to one which was on the table, there was one on his arm, eating some sort of berry.

"I must be like a hotel for the fairy world" Ted said laughing, Jack could see that the fairies for some reason looked at him with passion, loyalty, why had they taken up with Ted, why were they now showing them selves to Jack? Jack wondered, why they had never shown themselves to Linda why only him? Why just Ted?

Time was getting on Annie was due back from work, but Jack was too interested in talking to Ted, Jack was wondering how the Mouhume's were involved with the fairy's and Ted, were they friends or what? Jack new that all creatures, had enemies, the fairy's had birds chasing them, that's how Ted found his first one, so were the Mouhumes friends or what, he was not sure if he should ask or not, so he thought that he would leave things as they were, so that he would not upset Ted, after all Ted knew about the Mouhume that he had on the table, maybe Ted would bring it up as he was talking.

Jack could hear someone in his back garden; he jumped up looking over the hedge, half expecting to see Annie, to his surprise and horror, he got a big fright, it was a dog, it lived a few doors down the road, it was always getting out lately, it was a bad dog everyone said, Jack tried to tell it to go away but it paid him no attention, it was sniffing around the garden, Jack was worried that it might have the scent off the injured Mouhume, so he hurried back around to his house, the dog was a white English bull terrier, it even had a black eye like that one out of the film Oliver, but on the other side of its face, he was a big brute, every one around that

Adventure of the Mouhumes
Jack and Annie's new
Visitors

area was frightened, not that he had ever bitten anyone, but he would bark and that was enough, to stop you in your tracks.

Jack came around from the front way, he picked a brush up which he used to brush the yard, to try and get the dog out the garden, soon as the dog saw Jack and brush it came running at him and started to bark, then Jack shoved the brush straight at the dog.

The dog grabbed hold of the brush and shank his teeth into it and snapped it like a twig, in his big powerful jaws, Jacks legs went like jelly, he was unable to move, his legs would not let him move, the dog leaped up on him, the wall behind Jack was helping to keep him on his feet, the dog rubbed his head under Jacks hand as if to say that he wanted a stroke, Jack at this time was unable to look down, he was unable to bring himself to look, Jack felt the dogs heavy breath on his hand. The dog then sat down its tail wagging than he started to bark, Jack slowly looked down, the dog was looking up at him, Jack slowly put his hand down to stroke it, the dog again leaped up towards Jack, both Jacks hands grabbed the dogs head, the dog started to lick Jacks belt, that was when Jack realized that the dog was not going to hurt him, Jack began to stroke the dog, then he heard someone behind him.

"There you are, what are you doing" it was the lady from down the road, the dog's owner, she had left him out in her back garden but someone had left the side gate unlocked, the dog had pulled it open, and took himself for a walk, "he's let himself out again its his way letting me know that he wants to be out"

Jack at this time was bending down stroking the dog, the dog loved it.

"He's not as bad as he looks is he? He's friendly what a lovely dog" Jack could not get over how nice the dog was, by this time the dog was lying down getting his belly rubbed.

Created and written by I C Henderson

Adventure of the Mouhumes
Jack and Annie's new
Visitors

"He is like that dog out of that film, you know the one" Jack could not remember the film, he had taken to the dog and was not concentrating, he knew the film and the book but the dog had taken his attention.

"Oliver" the dogs' owner spoke up.

"Yes that is it Oliver, what is the dogs' name?" Jack asked still making a lot of the dog.

"Bulls eye" the lady said.

"What a good boy bull's eye" Jack started to talk to the dog.

"No he is called Buster, I thought you wanted to know the dogs name from the film" the lady put him right.

The dog Buster loved the attention he was getting from Jack, Jack also was enjoying the dogs company, Buster was muscular, he had shoulders on him that would make any body builder proud, but at the same time he was as gentle as a baby, except when he jumped up at you, his weight knocked you back no mater how strong you might be.

"I have another one at home a bitch, she would have been with Buster, but the door had blown shut, she would have frightened you, when they are both together they fun fight all the time with each other" Jack was not paying much attention but out of politeness, he would say something.

A car was pulling up on the driveway, Jack still playing with the dog paid it no attention, the dogs' owner told Jack, but he was too involved with Buster, it was Annie she had finished work, she was a little confused to what was going on, the dogs owner introduced herself.

Created and written by I C Henderson

Adventure of the Mouhumes
Jack and Annie's new
Visitors

"Hello I am Kez I live down the road, my dog got out and paid your garden a visit" Kez stuck her hand out to shake Annie's hand, Annie still unsure stuck her hand out, and introduced herself, Annie asked what was going on, Kez told her that her husband was nervous when he had first seen her dog, Buster in the garden he tried to chase him with a brush, but Buster thought that he was playing with him and broke the brush, Kez flicked her fingers and Buster came directly to her side, Jack was amazed that a dog as powerful was as gentle, the power he must have in that body, Jack thought to himself, Kez apologised and told them that she must go, she nodded to Buster, and he followed by her side.

Annie asked Jack what had been happening. Jack had a day that was nearly as strange as when they first saw the Mouhumes, but he had promised Ted that he would not say a word, so he told Annie that he had seen the dog in the garden and tried to get him out.

"With a brush" Annie interrupted.

Jacks reply was with excitement, he told Annie that the dog grabbed the shank of the brush and it snapped, in his jaws, like a twig, Annie asked why was the dog in the garden, Jack then realised that the dog had been sniffing around the pond, that had been why he had came and tried to chase the dog, Jack asked Annie if she would come to see what he was sniffing.

Annie not wanting to, made an excuse to go in the house to get changed, Jack nodded and went to have a look himself, Ted popped his head over the hedge he did not say anything, he put his finger to his nose and touched it twice, as if to say, say nothing, Jack shook his head in away that Ted knew he would not say anything to Annie.

Jack started to look where the dog had been sniffing, there was nothing out of the ordinary so he looked over the hedge to see if Ted was still there, Ted had gone in the house, Jack looked

Created and written by I C Henderson

Adventure of the Mouhumes
Jack and Annie's new
Visitors

towards the plant where he had seen the fairy, then suddenly he jumped, Annie had grabbed his leg as if a dog would have, Annie had to sit down she laughed so much her sides were hurting, Jack was not at all amused, he asked Annie to stop frightening him, and get on looking for the Mouhume, Annie asked what he was looking at in Ted's garden?

"I was just looking to see if Ted or Linda was there" Jack answered nervously.

Annie went over to the hedge to see for herself, but she could not see Ted or Linda, so she had a look around the garden from over the hedge, Jack at this time was around the back of the greenhouse, which also went around the back of the shed, Annie turned around expecting to see Jack but he was not there, Annie shouted for Jack asking where was he, Jack could not hear, or he was not paying attention, as he was looking for signs of the Mouhumes.

Annie decided to go into the house to see if Jack had gone in, after all he often would start a job then disappear when Annie came, so this was nothing new for Annie.

When Annie went into the house she was expecting to see Jack sitting in the dinning room, but he was not so she went to the bottom of the stairs and shouted up to see if he was there, but she did not get a reply, this was worrying for Annie, Jack had disappeared, he was there one moment, then he wasn't.

You could understand Annie, getting worried after what had been happing the last few weeks, all sorts of thoughts was running through her head, she had to sit down what could she do? She thought of phoning the police, but how would she sound? She could not tell anyone about the Mouhume's, they would think that she was cracking up, as she had no proof, what was she to do, the moment she had turned her head Jack had disappeared, Annie wondered what was going on in her garden.

231

Adventure of the Mouhumes
Jack and Annie's new
Visitors

"Right" she said to herself, I will ring the police, just as she got up to go to the telephone, she heard the back door open, she ran into the kitchen, to her surprise and relief, Jack was standing, his hands covered in mud.

"What have you been doing Jack?" Annie snapped.

"Never mind me where were you? You said you were going to help me look around the garden" Annie not wanting to tell Jack that she thought that he had disappeared into thin air, went to the back door had a look out, the path was covered in mud.

"I hope that you are going to clean that mess up! I do not know how you are going to, seeing that you broke the brush playing with that lady's dog" Annie not giving Jack time to answer, went on giving Jack a right hard time. "I bet you where chatting her up, funny how I go out and a woman is here when I get back"

Jack at this time was confused, so he didn't give her any reply, he just asked her to go down the garden with him, he knew it would be pointless to answer her when she was in this mood, he did wonder what had happened to get her in this temper, but he left it alone and did not ask.

Annie followed Jack down the garden around the back of the greenhouse, Jack pointed to the side of the shed, Annie at this time had calmed down, if anything she look unsure, maybe a little worried.

"Go on woman, have a look" snapped Jack.

"You have gone quiet now what's the matter?" Jack was getting his own back at Annie after she gave him a telling off for no reason.

Created and written by I C Henderson

Adventure of the Mouhumes
Jack and Annie's new
Visitors

Annie, not sure what she was meant to be looking at, turned back to Jack, the expression on her face was obvious that she had no idea what she was supposed to be looking at.

"What" Annie asked, shrugging her shoulders?

Jack pointed to a small hole in the side of the shed, Annie could see now what Jack was pointing at, it was a small hole but not just any type of hole, that you might expected, from an old shed or the wood that had not been treated properly, this hole was perfect this hole had not occurred accidentally, it was a half circle, with a door, it looked as if it was four inches tall by three inches wide.

Big enough for a Mouhume to enter, was this where they had come from or was this where they had moved to?

Jack had not been in the shed since his accident, which was now coming up to a year, so he would not know what was in there, Jack asked Annie to go and get the key for the shed from the kitchen, they had a hook with all the keys on in the kitchen, Annie not too keen on finding out what was in the shed, asked Jack if they would not be better off leaving it alone.

Jack shook his head, then beckoned Annie to hurry up, his hand pointed to the house, Annie knew that he would not be put off, so she reluctantly went on her way, but not as quick as Jack would like.

Annie knew if the Mouhume's were in the shed Jack would spend all day and night watching them, she hoped that if they had been in there they might have gone, Annie went towards the key hook near the doorway going into the dinning room, there were six sets of keys on it, the hook held eight, so there were two missing Annie checked her pocket, she still had hers she had not put hers away so she hung her keys up straight away, so she would not forget.

Created and written by I C Henderson

Adventure of the Mouhumes
Jack and Annie's new
Visitors

Annie looked along the keys to see if she could find the keys for the shed, there were three keys on the key ring, one for the door the other two for things in the shed, Jack still down the garden was getting impatient, he did not want to shout just in case he frightened whatever was in the shed, so he hurried up the garden the best he could, as his back was hurting, what a sight, he was wobbling as he went up the garden path, then he stumbled on the lawn, as he was doing that Annie just happened to look out the window, Annie stood laughing, she was still chuckling when Jack finally came in. Jack not at all happy, that Annie was standing in a fit of laughter at his misfortune.

"Annie have you stood there all this time? Having a giggle when you know that I was waiting for you" Jack asked not in a bad way but not at all in a cheerful way. After Annie stopped laughing, she passed the keys to Jack, Jack looked at the keys; Annie asked him what was the matter? Jack told her that he was just checking that it was the right set of keys; Annie would often give the wrong keys to Jack,

"This would save time" he told her.

"if I had gone down the garden to the shed and had the wrong keys I would have to come all the way back up wouldn't I, the way my back is just now, I don't need to be running up and down the garden" Jack started to get a little cross, Annie knew that his back must be giving him some trouble, as he always got angry when he was in a lot of pain, Annie knew it would be no point in telling him to sit down. She would have to have a reason which had nothing to do with his back; otherwise he got even worse tempered when being pampered, so she left him to get on with it.

Annie thinking that she should maybe do something asked if he would like a cup of tea, Annie knew that he would never say no to a cuppa.

Created and written by I C Henderson

Adventure of the Mouhumes
Jack and Annie's new
Visitors

Jack was just about to go out the door when Annie ask him, Jack stopped in his tracks, the way he pulled his face, he stood for a moment half in the doorway half out, his body not knowing which way to go.

As he was deciding Annie poured the drinks out, that did the trick Jack was at the table before Annie had time to get the biscuits out of the cupboard, Annie placed the biscuits on the table then went back to the kitchen for the drinks, she took her time so that Jack would have a longer rest, she new that soon as Jack was finished he would be down the garden and into the shed, Jack did not take long to finish his drink and biscuits, he stood up picked his cup up and took it into the kitchen, Annie knew that he had not rested as long as he should, and that once he was in the shed he'd be there all night, what could she do to stop him?

"Jack have you not done too much today? Come in you can look tomorrow, its not as if they are going to run away, if they are living in there, they're not likely to move tonight for no reason" Annie tried to talk some sense to Jack, but she knew that when he was like this he would take some convincing.

Jack looked at Annie, she could tell that he was thinking it over, so she thought that she should give it another go.

"Jack come in how way you look as if you are in pain" Annie thought she must have done enough, just as she turned away to go back into the kitchen, Jack was on his way down the garden, keys in his hand, he had to find out if they had moved into his garden shed.

Annie turned around expecting to see Jack behind her, so Annie looked out of the window to see Jack on his way down the path heading towards the shed, luckily she still had her shoes on, she hurried out to catch him up, Annie hurried down the path , not wanting to shout out, she thought if there was anything in the shed, she did not want to be the one that frighten them away, so as she

Created and written by I C Henderson

Adventure of the Mouhumes
Jack and Annie's new
Visitors

got closer to Jack she slowed down, Jack must of heard her he turned his head he put his finger to his lips as if to imply that he wanted her not to speak, as he approached the door, Annie was not faraway from Jack. Jack looked at the keys, he stopped for a moment, he hesitated then he turned towards Annie, Annie was surprised that Jack stopped, she did not know if she should stop Jack, or tell him to open the door.

Jack after some time wondering if he should or shouldn't go into the shed, finally decided that he would, he whispered to Annie to come to his side, Annie was apprehensive, Jack could tell from her face, so he did not say anything, as he did not want to get into a discussion.

Time was getting on and it was getting darker, not that it was late at night but it was getting cloudy and the light was dull.

Adventure of the Mouhumes
Jack and Annie's new
Visitors
Chapter 33
Buster

IT WAS RUDDY who seemed to be the bond between the two different worlds. It took no time for her to be back on her feet. Her baby was now walking. She had plenty to show him. Dash she called him and he was just like his father, Jumper, in so many ways. She had seen no reason to live after he was killed, that was why she had attacked everything in her way but it was different now. She had a son who depended on her.

A few days earlier she had even taken him to see Buster and Tilly. They loved him. Tilly let him sit on her back and hold onto the fur around her neck, not that she had much loose fur, so sometimes he would hold onto her ears.

Buster was Ruddy's friend. Sometimes Glow would come and spend time with them. She could talk to both of them and she would be the intermediate between the two. This helped the two dogs get to know them. Ruddy tried to go to see Buster and Tilly every day but sometimes their human would be there so she would have to stay hidden in the shrubbery.

Back in their Garden, Jack would often come into the garden putting out new or setting the traps, in different areas of the garden. The Mouhumes were not sure if the traps were set there to hurt them or to prevent other animals from getting the food. After all, the Mouhumes now knew how to set them off without being hurt and then to take the food. They thought that Jack must be like Ted. Ted looked out for the fairies.

Some of the Mouhumes were around the pond. They could hear talking from next door, so they popped their heads through or around the hedge to see who it was. Ted and Jack were sitting there talking. The Mouhumes could not understand what was being said, they looked around the garden to see if any of the fairies were there but they could not see any so they went back to the pond.

Adventure of the Mouhumes
Jack and Annie's new
Visitors

The pond had lots of different plants growing in and around it. There was a good covering to hide amongst and a waterfall which came out of a castle. It attracted all sorts of creatures: toads, frogs, newts, dragonflies and even a grass snake. The birds would swoop down for a drink. The pond itself was a haven for most wildlife or so it would seem.

Ruddy was showing Dash around the pond. She needed to show him all the different creatures that lived around the pond. She did not want what had happened days earlier to happen again some of the other Mouhumes were also there collecting insects, another good source of food for them. It gave them protein and that, along with other foods they were now having, it helped them survive that much better.

Ruddy was going in and out around the plants showing Dash the way up to the waterfall. It had rocks and plants growing all the way up, almost hiding the castle walls. It was a wonderful sight for man or creature.

Next door Ted was with Jack having drinks and chatting about all sorts of things. The fairies were hiding out of sight. One or two were now near Ruddy, showing themselves now and again, as if they were playing hide and seek.

Everything was peaceful. There was nothing to fear or to be concerned about. There was only the slightest breeze that was barely moving the leaves on the plants. You could hear the sound of the waterfall and the birds and chatting that came from next door.

So this would be a good time to show Dash around the pond. She showed him the little hiding holes, the top of the castle where the water came down from and the collection of water at the top that housed frogs and toads and newts. It formed a pool then it overflowed down into the big pond where the fish lived and the dragonflies would swoop down for a drink or insects.

Created and written by I C Henderson

Adventure of the Mouhumes
Jack and Annie's new
Visitors

Glow came and tapped Ruddy on the shoulder. This gave her a fright but she was still getting used to her new friends and their ways. Glow started to tell Ruddy that one or two fairies were showing themselves to Jack. Ted had asked them if they would so that he might understand our ways.

Ruddy looked puzzled. Glow was just starting to explain when a slight sound came from the hedge separating the two gardens. It was Ted's kitten, a black cat and it had mischief in mind. The cat with its sleekness went through the hedge, scarcely making a sound, slowly creeping towards the pond.

Another fairy had seen what was going to happen so came to inform Glow. Glow told Ruddy to hide as soon as possible which she did. Ruddy placed her body in front of Dash, protecting her son holding her thorn in her hand ready to strike. Glow and the other fairy flew off, informing the rest of the Mouhumes who were at the pond. They were off leaving Ruddy and Dash. There was nothing they could do with this young cat.

The Mouhumes ran through the top of the gardens heading to the only safe place that Glow told them about. The other fairy, just above them, told them what she needed them to do. She was bigger than Glow and full of colours, you could easy mistake her for a flower. She was called Bouquet. She could blend in with most flowers, making her almost invisible and that was without using her ability of disappearing.

Glow flew down to where Buster lived. He was, as normal, sniffing in the flower area looking for what ever he could find. Tilly was pulling at a rope hanging from a tree, this was how she played, pulling and tugging at the rope. Glow went straight over to Buster and told him that Ruddy and Dash were in need of his help straight away. Then Glow flew over to the gate. It had some heavy rope over the top of the gate which also looped over the fence post.

Created and written by I C Henderson

Adventure of the Mouhumes
Jack and Annie's new
Visitors

Glow pulled hard at the rope trying to loosen it but it was harder than she thought. Buster also used his muzzle under the rope at the post end along with Glow. Eventually they got it off. Then Glow pulled the gate open, just enough for Buster to put his nose in between the gate and the fence post, pushing it open.

Buster ran up the street towards Jack's house. When he got there, the gate to Jacks garden was almost open. Bouquet and one of the other Mouhumes were trying hard to get it open for Buster.

Created and written by I C Henderson

Adventure of the Mouhumes
Jack and Annie's new
Visitors

Bouquet had opened the catch on the gate, the Mouhume holding the string that Bouquet had tied on the gate and was pulling it open with all his might. Buster, the same as before, opened it with his head and followed the fairy to where Ruddy was.

Glow returned to where Ruddy was. The kitten had not found her yet but had found a toad that had just jumped onto a Lilly pad with a beautiful yellow flower. The toad sat very still, watching as if it knew the kitten could not reach it.

Buster came around the pond like a bull in a china shop putting his head into the plants even though he was not really sure what he was looking for. The kitten, as quietly as it came, turned around and quickly went the same way back home.

Buster was still poking his head into the plants and rustling through them. Suddenly he found what he was looking for. Ruddy came out of her hiding hole with Dash. Ruddy rubbed Buster's nose and thanked him. Then suddenly they heard shouting. Jack came around to the pond with a brush that had been at the side of

241

Adventure of the Mouhumes
Jack and Annie's new
Visitors

the house. He poked Buster with the brush end, almost knocking him into the pond. Buster put his head down, and his tail high up in the air, wagging it. He started to bark at Jack. Jack again pushed the brush into Buster. Buster grabbed hold of the brush shank. Then with his strong jaws he snapped it. Jack fell backwards on to the fence. Lucky for him the fence kept him up. Buster jumped up at him putting Jack's hand into his mouth. Jack almost passed out. Buster then put his front paws back onto the ground letting go of Jack's hand he then licked it, to Jack's surprise.

Jack started to stroke Buster. Buster loved getting all this attention. Then he heard his mistress calling for him. Kez his owner had heard Buster bark so came looking for him to see what he was up to. She explained to Jack that he was a friendly dog. As they stood talking, Annie arrived home. Buster got even more attention. Kez then said that she would have to go back home as Tilly had got out as well. So she called for Buster who followed her back home.

Created and written by I C Henderson

Adventure of the Mouhumes
Jack and Annie's new
Visitors

Chapter 34
The shed

THERE WERE TWO locks on the shed door, one of them was a padlock, Jack unlocked the door lock first, then just before he put the key into the padlock, he gave Annie a smile, as quietly as he could he unlocked the padlock.

The excitement Jack had built up… he was ready to burst. As he pulled the door open ever so slowly so that it did not squeak, he knew that it was always rusting up and he had not been in there for some time, so he knew that it was a possibility that it would have stiffened up due to the bad weather they had over the winter.

He would have oiled the hinges before the bad weather but his accident stopped him doing most things that he would have done before winter.

Jack was right the door had stiffened up and he was right to pull it slowly, he was having a bit trouble opening the door, the door got so far then it stopped it would not move any more.

Jack could not open it, he did not have the strength, not that the door was too stiff, but he was still weak he had not recovered as well as he had thought. Ever so quietly he asked Annie to have a go to open the door.

Annie reluctantly went to the door she pulled the door, it was even stiff for her, with one almighty pull she released the door. The door hinge made a loud cracking sound, louder than they probably would have wanted.

Jack and Annie stood at the door both looking into the shed, nether one saying a word. It was getting darker; it was clouding over and it was starting to rain, not heavy rain, but big drops it was obvious that it was going to get harder.

Adventure of the Mouhumes
Jack and Annie's new
Visitors

The two of them went into the shed for shelter from the rain. This was the first time Jack had been in the shed for a long time, as he looked around things seemed to be still in place, as far as he could see, as it was getting dark ever so quickly, due to the time of day and the rain, Jack remembered that he had a torch in one of the drawers, next to where he was standing at the entrance, as he looked in the drawers for his torch, Annie looked around the shed unsure what she was looking for as she never went into the shed, she could not tell if anything was out of place, so she looked to see if there was any tell tale signs, of anything living there, Jack was still looking for his torch.

"Jack I think that we should leave it for now it's too dark, let's go and come back tomorrow morning" Annie knew that they were wasting their time looking when it was this dark.

Jack pulled something out from the drawer, it was his torch if it would work or not was another thing, it had been in there in the damp and cold for a long time.

He turned it on nothing not even a small dot of life in the bulb; Jack was disappointed all his hopes seemed to have disappeared. The clouds cleared a little, the moonlight gave them some light, not much, just enough so they could see each other. Annie could tell from the look on Jacks face that he was devastated, time was ticking Annie knew that if they left it till the next day they would never find out if the Mouhumes had been or were still in the shed.

"Just a minute I'll go and get the extension cable from the house, Jack are you listening stay here I'll not be long" Jack stayed in the shed Annie was all but running up to the house, she did not even take her shoes off as she went straight through the dinning room, then in the living room to get to the hallway, to get to the cupboard at the bottom at of the stairs, not taking anytime she pulled anything and everything out of the way, until she found the extension lead.

Created and written by I C Henderson

Adventure of the Mouhumes
Jack and Annie's new
Visitors

They had a table lamp in the living room, she picked it up ran into the kitchen plugged in the cable ran all the way down to the shed, unrolling the cable as she went, the table light in one hand, the way she did this was unbelievable. Jack still in the shed trying to see with the little light he was getting from the moon. Annie put the light plug into the extension lead.

"Are you ready Jack?" Jack nodded; Annie took a deep breath, she was slightly out of breath not with running but more with the excitement, Annie then turned the light on, the shed lit up as did Jacks and Annie's faces.

As they stood looking from the doorway into the shed, it had been clear to see that something had lived in there. Jack was the first to go inside, Annie still was at the doorway holding the lamp high so the light shone down.

It was a good light coming from the lamp, Jack frantic to see what had been living in his shed, looking all over to see what signs were left, as he was looking at a pile of leaves, and wondering what they were doing there, something caught his eye at the side of him to his left, he did not want to turn around too fast as to frighten it away, so he slowly turned his head around, on the floor next to where the wheelbarrow would stand, but was not as it had been left out around the back of the shed, after Jacks accident, then Annie had used it for the mud when they thought that they would have an ornament made (but never did) there on the floor was a hideous mischievous looking thing, not at all bothered about Jack standing only a few feet away.

Jack pointed to Annie to have a look, as she did her face all of a sudden had a nervous look on it, the thing on the floor looked up at the two of them and just carried on eating, what looked like a large cake that someone must have put out for the birds.

Created and written by I C Henderson

Adventure of the Mouhumes
Jack and Annie's new
Visitors

Annie was a little squeamish she put the light on the drawers inside the shed, then she stood back out of the doorway back outside in the rain.

Jack not too sure if he should hit the thing or watch it to see what it would do. It never moved from the spot, not because it was frightened but because it was still eating not at all distracted by Jack standing near it.

Jack edged his way towards the door, and then went out to where Annie was standing.

"Annie what do you think it is?"

"I don't know Jack, is it not one of them Mouhume's?" Annie did not look at it long enough, to tell what it was, or what it was not.

"Will I hit it?" Jack asked

"No! You will not… get back in there and see what it is" Annie snapped at Jack.

Jack slowly walked in, he picked up a trowel off the wall hook, he went near the thing, as he stood over it his hand tightened around the trowel, it then turned its head looking up towards Jack. With an expression on its face what looked like a smile, Jack's hand moved back with the trowel. Annie had seen this then she stepped back into the shed.

"Jack don't… don't hurt it!" Annie thought that Jack was going to hit it with the trowel, so she came in to stop him.

Jacks hand went near the thing (the one with the trowel in it) it was not to hit it, but to use it to pick it up, as the trowel got near to the creature he half expected it to run away, but it just stayed there, this surprised Jack. Why had it not run off? It did not look

Adventure of the Mouhumes
Jack and Annie's new
Visitors

hurt or even frightened; its face looked somewhat contented. Jack felt a little uneasy that it looked unmoved; most creatures would have hidden away as soon as the shed door opened.

But…this had not moved it had just carried on eating, why had it not run away?

It looked harmless, even cute, Jack moved the trowel towards him, he nudged the trowel under this creature , so that he could have a closer look at this little mischievous creature, it still did not make any attempt to try to run off. Jack picked it up and moved the trowel near to his face, so that he could have a good look at it, hoping that it would not run away. Not that it could as it would have fallen onto the floor.

As Jack's head got nearer to the trowel, he could look at it better; it was doing the same to him. It was if it was examining him, as much as Jack was looking into the nature or condition, of this extra ordinary thing.

He could not make out if it was a Mouhume or not, it did have some similar things about it, but was a lot fatter obviously a good eater as it held onto its food still.

"Jack what's wrong?" Annie asked as she came back into the shed closer to Jack, she could see that Jack was looking at it intensively. Annie did not know why.

Jack did not say a word, he put his spare hand up to stop Annie getting any closer to him and this thing that might be a Mouhume, it started to carry on eating not at all concerned by Jack or Annie, being there.

The rain had started to come down harder then ever, the light that they had in the shed had just been a bedside light and not that bright.

Created and written by I C Henderson

Adventure of the Mouhumes
Jack and Annie's new
Visitors

It was really dark outside now, Annie looked up the garden the kitchen light was on but it looked dull, as the rain was coming down so hard.

"Jack… how much longer are we going to be down here?" Annie wanted to go back into the house but did not want to go by herself.

"Can I bring this up to the house?" Jack pointed to the thing on the trowel.

Annie looked at it, she was not sure if she wanted in the house. She nodded reluctantly. Jack went to the shed door, looked out saw that the rain was lashing down.

"We will give it a minute to die down" Jack not wanting to get wet, told Annie. Annie agreed.

Then Annie spoke up, she told Jack that she did not think that it was a good idea to take it into the house. Jack thought it pointless to have come down to the shed in the bad weather. Just to leave it there.

"Annie what have we come down here for? If not to see what was in here, do you think that I am going to stand in here frozen… in the damp just too…" Jack stopped he was lost for words.

He knew that Annie was right, but the thought of losing or not seeing these little creatures. Did not fill him full of hope, what was he to do? He knew he needed, wanted to know more about these things.

If he took it into the house he would get wrong, Annie was giving him a nasty look. So he did not want to give her any reason for her to get annoyed with him. Annie could see him hesitate.

Created and written by I C Henderson

Adventure of the Mouhumes
Jack and Annie's new
Visitors

"Come on I want to go in the house, so hurry up you no what you have to do for the best" then Annie went on her way, towards the house. She stopped again then with one almighty sigh. That was that Jack knew he would not be able to reason with her. He looked up to her. Almost tears in his eyes, he was torn what was he to do? This little thing in his hand looking quite happy and not at all afraid, He turned back looking towards the shed.

With one big groan he walked back into the shed and put it back from where he had picked it up. It looked up at him then carried on eating the last of the cake. Jack knew that there were others in the shed but he did not want to frighten them.

Annie was in the kitchen looking down the garden from the window, the rain had not stopped in fact it started to come down even harder than before. Jack came up the garden path stiff from the cold and damp, his body looked as if he had been beaten up. Annie turned the hot water heater on so that he could have a bath. This sometimes gave his body a little heat and would ease him up.

Jack came into the kitchen dripping wet, he was soaked to the skin, all of his cloths were sticking to him.

"Annie come and give me a hand" Jack asked as he tried to pull his wet jacked off.

"My hands are cold I can hardly move them" Jack said in a pitiful way.

Annie came straight to him and shut the door behind him, she helped him to get undressed in the kitchen, then she covered him with a large towel. And helped him up the staircase by now he was in a lot of pain his joints had become rigid and it was clear to see that he was in a lot of pain.

Annie sat him on the edge of the bed, and ran the bath for him, the water was warm it took no time at all to heat up, it was not

Adventure of the Mouhumes
Jack and Annie's new
Visitors

too hot as where you would have to put cold water in to cool it down, but it was warm and that would help Jack to warm his bones and joints, she helped Jack into the bathroom he was moaning and groaning.

"You're like an old man not a forty year old" Annie knew this would give him a bit of fight and he would help himself a little.

Jack straightened himself up and pulled himself up onto the stool near the bath, he sat there for a little, then he got up and got himself into the bath.

The moans he gave would have the neighbours thinking that he was getting murdered,

Annie was soon to tell him to stop moaning and shut up.

She was concerned as she could see that Jack was in more pain than normal, she rubbed his back for him. To help put some heat in his body, but it would seem that it was not working. And she even tried to take his mind of things by telling him what she had done at work that day. But nothing was working he was in too much in pain.

Annie was getting worried the painful look on Jacks face was nothing she had ever seen before; she asked if he would be all right for a moment. He snapped out and told her that he would.

Annie went down stairs and into the living room and rang for an ambulance; she needed to get him to Hospital as soon as possible, he looked so poorly she knew that he needed help.

Suddenly there was a bang upstairs, and a loud and terrifying scream from the bathroom. Annie ran up the stairs two at a time. She got into the bathroom to see Jack lying on the floor moaning and groaning. She tried to help him up the best she could but he was not helping himself, no matter which way she moved him he

Created and written by I C Henderson

Adventure of the Mouhumes
Jack and Annie's new
Visitors

shouted out in pain, she went and got more towels and his dressing gown to help keep him warm, she tried all ways to help him, but nothing was helping

There was a knocking at the front door; Annie left Jack as comfortable as she could under the circumstance. She knew that would be the ambulance, she hurried down the staircase and answered the front door. She was right it was the ambulance men. She told them that Jack was in the bathroom and pointed up to the staircase.

"First room on your left" Annie told the men as she stayed at the bottom of the stairs.

She could hear Jack complaining and asking them what they were doing. She could not hear what they were saying but she knew that Jack would be telling them that he was all right. So she shouted up the stairs.

"Don't listen to him, I have never seen him so poorly" As she said that her head sank into her arms, it was if she had just realized how ill he was. The ambulance men came down the stairs with Jack on the stretcher. He looked worse than he was just moments before, his face colourless and the look of pain. They asked Annie if she was going to the hospital with them. She asked which hospital they were going to take him.

"The General is that ok?" One of the ambulance men asked Annie.

Annie nodded as she put her shoes on. Then she put her jacket on, Jack's health was getting worse by the minute.

They hurried out the door and took no time in getting Jack to the hospital. The siren screaming as soon as they had Jack in the back of the ambulance, Annie was sitting holding Jacks hand, holding back her tears. His hand went limp it was ice cold. Annie

Created and written by I C Henderson

Adventure of the Mouhumes
Jack and Annie's new
Visitors

began to sob, the Ambulance man jumped to Jack's aid. Annie could not control herself any longer she cried hysterically. They soon arrived at the hospital the medical staff waiting to take Jack into the accident and emergency department.

Annie was taken into a room at the side of a corridor; a nurse stayed with her and made her a drink from the kettle in the room.

Created and written by I C Henderson

Adventure of the Mouhumes
Jack and Annie's new
Visitors

Chapter 35
The First Meeting

THE MOUHUMES HAD all gone back to under the shed. A lot
had happened. Tube was now wondering if staying there was a
good idea. Yes they might have good allies in the fairies but they
seemed to be finding trouble every day.

Ratty came to see Tube: he could see that he was troubled. He
also had an idea what it would be about. All this new stuff was a lot
to take in. Ratty had also thought was it worth while?

All they had to put up with in their last home was second
nature. Yes it would have to be a gathering but Ratty had made his
mind up he was going to leave. Some others had also made their
minds up. Not just from this camp but from the woodland and the
parkland camps too. Some from those two camps wanted to move
on and getaway from the humans.

So before Tube could say anything Ratty told him that he was
going to leave. He had no idea where he was going but in a weeks'
time he and some others were going to go to find, a place away
from humans.

Tube was disappointed Ratty had already arranged to go
without telling him. They had been friends from a young age. They
had helped each other countless times and now Ratty wanted to go
by himself.

Tube nodded as if to say he understood but the look on his
face was that of sadness and disappointment. Ratty saw this and
was quick to tell him that he wanted the both of them to leave and
set up elsewhere. Tube could not hide his delight, he smiled from
ear to ear and gave Ratty a "never before" big hug.

Tube hardly ever, if not never, showed his emotion to another
but this was a big thing. Another adventure with new, exciting

Created and written by I C Henderson

Adventure of the Mouhumes
Jack and Annie's new
Visitors

discoveries and what could be better than doing it with a companion that you had shared all your experiences with.

They sat talking in the chamber under the shed trying to work out how and when they would inform the others to see who wanted to come with them and who wanted to stay. Then they had to discuss the food supplies: what they could take and what they would leave.

Ratty told Tube that most of the food was already worked out, depending on how many were staying and leaving. It had been a week or two ago that Ratty had decided to go: he had been gathering and collecting food and hunting equipment.

Tube was taken aback with all this, how had he not noticed? All this was happening with his best friend and he had not seen any signs. Ratty started to tell him there had been a lot going on and with Tube being the leader he had not wanted to burden him with anything else so he had corresponded with the other two camps.
It was not going to be something that was … he stopped he could not explain what he meant. It was not going to be something like sneaking out of camp with food provisions and the rest waking up to half the camp gone.

As they were talking a young Mouhume came to inform them that Jack was looking round the back of the sheds. He was in the greenhouse then at the back of the sheds then back in the greenhouse and then back around the sheds.

What could he be looking for? The Mouhume then told Tube that Jack had just gone back towards the house. What could they do? What should they do? Tube told all the Mouhumes to stay under the shed and to be ready at the escape exits.

They asked if they had to escape where should they go? What direction they should take? How many should there be in each group? They could not all run in the same direction as it would be

Adventure of the Mouhumes
Jack and Annie's new
Visitors

easy for any enemy to see them. That was why they needed different escape routes so they could travel in different directions. It might take longer than other routes but it would be safer for all to do it that way.

Ratty and Tube hid under the shed listening for any sound that might be a human. The sky had gone dark: big black clouds had filled the sky. It was going to rain and rain hard. Tube could tell from the smell in the air. It was going to be a night that no Mouhume could travel.

Then he heard Jack and Annie coming down the path talking quietly. The shed door was being forced opened. There was a loud cracking sound as if something had been broken. It was the door, it had not been opened for a long time and the hinge had rusted. Then the sound of drawers being opened and shut was heard, what could he be doing? Then they heard footsteps going back up the garden.

They must have given up, Tube thought. So Tube went into the shed from the side where they had made a doorway of their own. As he crept in he could see a silhouette at the doorway. He could tell that it was Jack from the outline. He was not moving just standing in one place as still as a statue. What could he be doing Tube thought? Ratty was just about to come into the shed the same way as Tube did but Tube stopped him.

More footsteps were hurrying down the garden. Tube was now getting worried. He had no idea what was going to happen. They then turned a bright light on. Tube had never been this close to a bright light being shined into his eyes before. He could not adjust to the bright light; he just flopped to the floor rubbing his eyes. The light was being moved around the shed to lighten up different areas. Ratty could see a light was being shone inside the shed from the breaks in the floor.

Ratty was worried for his friend Tube, what was happening? Dare he open the door to see what was happening? He stood listening. He could hear Jack talk to Annie but he could not

Created and written by I C Henderson

Adventure of the Mouhumes
Jack and Annie's new
Visitors

understand what was being said. He heard something being moved; maybe it was being picked up? It sounded like a metal object, the sound of scraping slightly on the floor.

Tube sat there holding onto some food that he had. He was too frightened to drop it but still looked at Jack not knowing if he should run or stay. He looked around the door that he came in, it was now shut. He had told Ratty to shut it. He looked at the main doorway where Annie and Jack were standing; if he ran he would have to run between their feet. He decided to stay. They had seen him anyway, he was feeling tired and what would be would be!

Jack looked at Annie. He asked her if he should hit it with the trowel. She told him not to. He bent down, Tube closed his eyes; fear was running through his body because he did not know what Jack would do. Jack put the garden trowel near Tube. Tube, at one stage, thought that Jack was going to hit him. Jack gently moved the Trowel under Tube. Tube adjusted himself but was still sitting and still holding onto the food. Jack was now holding Tube up in the air looking at him. So Tube looked back at him. He could see every detail of Jack's face as could Jack see every detail of Tube.

Annie and Jack started to talk to each other. Tube had no idea what they were saying so he had a bite of the food he had, it was no good sitting hungry. Tube had put a lot of weight on lately. He had not needed to hunt like the other Mouhumes. Food at this time was plentiful. It had got darker now and the rain was coming down harder than ever. Jack was turning one way then the other way as if he was going to take Tube out in the rain, then he turned back into the shed. The rain was coming in the doorway wetting Annie and Jack. Rain was hitting the trowel and wetting Tube too. At this point Tube was looking for a way to get off the trowel. If only Jack would keep still but he was turning too fast for Tube to jump.

Tube knew that Jack had seen the fairies at Ted's house. That was one of the reasons why he had not run away when Jack came into the shed but he had still taken a risk. After all, Jack had put out

Adventure of the Mouhumes
Jack and Annie's new
Visitors

traps that had killed one of the Mouhumes. Jack started to bend down placing the trowel on the floor. Tube stayed there for a little while, not knowing if he should get off or not.

Annie had already gone up the garden and Jack started to follow. He shut the door on his way out. He was not as quick as Annie as he walked up the garden. He got soaked. The Mouhumes under the shed could see this but they did not know Jack was in poor health and was going to get worse with every step. The cold rain was affecting all his joints and bringing with it more pain. By the time Jack got to the top of the garden he had slowed down, his body was now finding it very hard to move.

The Mouhumes under the shed could not see what happened next to Jack and they were not really concerned either. They all came together to talk about what had just happened and that was the only concern they had at this time.

Created and written by I C Henderson

Adventure of the Mouhumes
Jack and Annie's new
Visitors
Chapter 36

THE NEXT DAY the rain had stopped. The ground was wet and in some areas soaked with pools of water all over the place. At the back of the shed there was a deep hole that Jack and Annie had dug days earlier now it was full of water. The Mouhumes had no idea why the humans had dug a hole that deep, had it been to try and catch a Mouhume? If a Mouhume had fallen into the hole it would have been hard but not impossible to get out. They had no idea why they would do such a thing, now the clay on the lawn was a right mess! Jack and Annie had dug the hole; they had pulled out some clay and put it on the lawn hoping that what Ted had told them may come true, that they would wake up to an amazing ornament but so far this had not happened. The only thing there was a big mound of mud.

Ratty was told while the talks were taking place in the shed that Jack and Annie's house had blue flashing lights outside. Two Humans had gone into the house and someone had been carried out. They did not know who it was that had been carried out. They were expecting to see Jack or Annie that morning but there was no sign of them, not even in the conservatory.

Ratty was not too worried about this news. He and Tube had other things to attend to and the weather was not something they wanted to be out in. Most of them would be stopping under the shed or in the little shed for cover. The fairies would not be out in this either as their wings would get wet and they would not be able to fly. So Ratty and Tube knew they could not ask them what had happened in the house.

It would be too risky for a Mouhume to go and inspect the house or would it? Ratty had an idea. Would it be a risk as Jack and Annie had seen Tube and not hurt him? It would be an idea to put to Tube. Tube was now back in the shed alone, waiting for Ratty to arrive. They had a lot to talk about this had been something that had kept Tube awake all the night. He wondered if it was the right

Adventure of the Mouhumes
Jack and Annie's new
Visitors

idea. In a way he had hoped that Jack would hurt him then the decision would have been made for them, from that action alone.

But Jack had not hurt him and this had troubled Tube. If they moved away and came in contact with other humans, would they be the same as Ted, Jack and Annie? The human over the road killed the birds and rabbits by using poison which would then kill any other animal that ate them. That was not a human they would want to come into contacted with.

Tube wondered if there was a place that had no humans or was it just a hope of something better than what they had? He had all these thoughts going through his mind. He knew that Ratty was determined to go away and start again but was there such a place? Tube knew that food here was plentiful. Yes it had risks but so did everywhere. Here they had allies with the fairies, Buster and Tilly. Jack had not hurt him so … Ratty arrived then so he no longer had time to think of the question what if?

Ratty was full of enthusiasm. The weather outside might have been wet but this had not dampened Ratty's mood. He had a lot to talk about and things to sort out with Tube. Although as he approached Tube he could tell that Tube must have had second thoughts. Tube's face could not hide how he was feeling.

Tube told Ratty what he had been thinking. He told him all the good points and the bad points. He trusted Ratty and his opinion, but this time Ratty was not thinking as he would have normally. This time he was not looking at it as he would have most things that might have a serious outcome for the Mouhumes colony.

Ratty told Tube his thoughts and pointed out the danger if they stayed. If the fairy clan decided to turn on them what could they do? They had no idea how many fairies there were and they could attack without being seen. Ratty had a good point. Tube had talked this over with Ratty many times. They had no idea what or

Adventure of the Mouhumes
Jack and Annie's new
Visitors

where the fairies went on a night time or when the weather was bad. Yet the fairies knew where the Mouhumes would be almost all of the time.

Tube reminded Ratty the fairies had openly told them almost everything right from the beginning: how they got their energy and strength, how they could do some things but not others and they told them of the weakness that they had. Ratty listened and agreed with most things but then put doubt in when there could be something that might have been misleading:

"Why would another creature tell you all their weaknesses when you have just met them?" Ratty asked "if not only to mislead you or maybe for us to tell them about our weakness"

Tube had talked many a time about this not just with Ratty but other Mouhumes. Each and everyone had always thought the same, that it might be a trap. Then the truth came out. Ratty thought that if he and others from the park and the woodland left to find a new home and those who had stayed here got attacked by the fairies because the numbers were small then word would get back. They would then know nothing could be trusted again.

Tube's head fell into his chest: his thoughts, his wants, it no longer mattered. He would stay with who wanted to stay. Ratty could not go anywhere yet, the weather was not good enough to travel in. It would be the next day he would be more likely to go, if not, the day after that. Tube would help Ratty get everything he needed for the journey. This would be a sad day for the two of them. They had always been near each other side by side in all sorts of adventures.

Ratty had always known that Tube would not go. Tube was looking his age now. Ratty was a little younger but Tube, with all the battles his body had been through, was now showing tell tale signs.

Created and written by I C Henderson

Adventure of the Mouhumes
Jack and Annie's new
Visitors
Chapter 37
Jacks wellbeing

JACK COULD SEE a bright light, it was not getting bigger or brighter but seemed to be getting smaller, his mind was doing overtime, if he was dead should the light not be getting bigger? Then suddenly it was as if he new if the light went out that would be it. He give one almighty scream. Then everything went blank.

It seemed a long time had passed when he finally opened his eyes, the bright light dazzled his eyes, his eyes could not adjust to the light, he had to close them, then as before it all went blank.

Annie was still in the small room at the end of the passageway, the nurse trying desperately to console her, but having no luck.

"Is there anyone that I can call for you Annie?" the nurse asked in a soft caring voice. Annie shook her head; the nurse got her some more tissues to wipe her tears.

"Will it be alright if I… go home?" Annie just got the words out then started to cry again. The nurse put her arm around Annie and held her to try and comfort her.

"Just wait for a little longer" said the nurse as she did not think that Annie should leave, in the condition she was in.

Jack opened his eyes again; the room was glowing white, his eyes still finding it hard to adjust to the brightness of the room. He thought to himself this must be heaven everything is bright white.

"I've gone to heaven I wonder when I am going to see anyone, a distant relative, or maybe the boss himself, no he will be too busy for the likes of me" Just then he was interrupted.

Created and written by I C Henderson

Adventure of the Mouhumes
Jack and Annie's new
Visitors

"HELLO Jack…it is Jack? How are you?" A man who was standing in a white coat asked.

Jack could still not focus too well, but seeing this man in a glow made him jump a little, "Where am I?" Jack asked with a weak and panicky voice.

"Your in hospital, you must have been over doing things, you had us worried for a time, but we've got you under control now" the Dr told Jack in a strong and confident voice.

Jack felt silly as he had thought that he had died, and had gone to heaven, so he did not say anything to the Dr as he did not want to appear to be daft.

Annie still in the small room, not knowing that Jack had come around, and was recovering not too far away from her, was still under the impression that he had died on the way to hospital, she could not see life without him, the future was black it had no meaning, or any reason, all Annie could see for the future, was a dark hole that had no light at the end, just sorrow, and doom.

The nurse was called out of the room by another nurse; Annie put this down to that she was going to be told what was happening to Jack, from the Drs who had been working on him.

She was right; a Dr came into the room with the nurse that had been keeping Annie Company. Annie tried to work out what was going to be told to her by looking at the nurse's face, to see if it was going to be good or bad news, but the nurse had no expression at all.

Annie thought the worst; she was dreading what the Dr was going to tell her, her heart felt as if was going to jump out of her chest.

Created and written by I C Henderson

Adventure of the Mouhumes
Jack and Annie's new
Visitors

The Dr could tell that Annie was expecting the worse from the look on her face. He could also tell that she was getting upset.

So he quickly told her the news, he sat down beside her and got hold of her hand.

"Annie we have had to fight for his life…and I am happy to say we have won" the Dr told her with a smile of achievement.

Annie gasped then cried even harder than she had done before.

"Can …can…I see him…please" Annie asked with difficulty as she was still crying.

The Dr told her only for a short time as Jack was still poorly and tired; he held his hand out so that he could lead her to the room where Jack was being kept in.

Annie held the Dr by his arm, as they entered Jacks room. Annie wheezed for breath again, she could not believe how poorly Jack looked. His face was as grey he had a mask to help him breathe. Wires hooked to him monitoring his heart. Even after his accident he did not look this poorly.

Annie spent a short time with Jack and then she was asked to leave by the nurse, as he needed his rest.

Annie reached over to kiss him on the cheek, Jacks weak hand stretched out to hers and tenderly held her for as long as he could, as if he was frightened to let her go, but he had no strength, and his fingers weakened then his hand fell to the side of the bed.

At this stage the nurse came to Annie's side and held her around the waist, Annie was clearly upset, as Annie was going towards the door, she turned her head one last time to look at Jack.

Created and written by I C Henderson

Adventure of the Mouhumes
Jack and Annie's new
Visitors

Jack looked terrible, Annie could not help but worry, she had never seen anyone as terrible as what Jack was looking. She asked the nurse sobbing "he will…be all right…wont he?"

The nurse nodded and asked Annie how she was getting home? As it was 3am, she asked would there be anyone who could stay with, her Annie shook her head.

Annie asked the nurse if she could get her a taxi to take her home.

Annie sat with a cup of tea, whilst she was waiting for her lift home. A car pulled up out side near the window where Annie was sitting.

Annie looked at the nurse who had rang for the taxi, and smiled and thanked her for her help. The nurse came over to her held her hand and said that he would be ok.

As the taxi pulled up outside her home Annie looked up towards the front door, it had never looked so lonely and empty. She had come home unaccompanied before when Jack had been at work but this time it seemed it had emptiness to it. She paid the taxi driver and walked towards the back door, her eyes filled up with tears, she could not stop herself, from crying. It had been too much, she had thought that she had lost Jack; that he had died in her arms the Drs had fought for his life for what had seemed to be forever.

As she came into the kitchen the emptiness and cold hit her like never before. Was this what life was going to be like? As she approached into the living room she collapsed onto the sofa and held onto Jacks favourite jacket the smell of Jack seemed to give her some comfort.

She fell asleep, after sometime crying into the coat. She suddenly awoke not for any specific reason. Just the fact was that she had not purposely wanted to sleep on the sofa.

Created and written by I C Henderson

Adventure of the Mouhumes
Jack and Annie's new
Visitors

It was still early she had not had a lot of sleep, as she got up from the settee the coat fell onto the floor; Annie at the same time got a cold shiver down her spine. She had an inkling that there must be something wrong with Jack. She seized hold of her car keys and ran to her car.

Determined that she was not going to accept, or let her existence be like this, cold and empty she was going to make Jack get well and not let him go without a fight.

As Annie pulled up outside the hospital, she froze for a moment, what if she was going to find out bad news? How was she going to manage? All of these thoughts we're running though her head; she shook herself and headed for the main hospital entrance.

The corridor heading to Jacks ward seemed to go on for ever, as she arrived outside Jacks ward, she took one big breath and headed straight to the room where Jack had been the night before.

As she entered to her horror the bed was stripped, no sign of Jack, Annie gave one almighty gasp.

"NO…no…no…NO… please…JACK…JACK" Annie screamed weeping at the same time.

A nurse who had been passing went running in as Annie had fallen to the floor sobbing.

The nurse helped Annie up off the floor, and sat her on a chair; Annie was unable to ask the nurse what had happened to Jack, due to crying and gasping for air. Another nurse by then had come into the room, this nurse had been on duty the night before, when Jack had been brought in. so she knew Annie and she realized what Annie must be thinking.

She crouched down in front of Annie and held Annie's hand. "Annie I think I know what you must be thinking just now" she

Created and written by I C Henderson

Adventure of the Mouhumes
Jack and Annie's new
Visitors

said with a soft friendly smile on her face. "Jack has been taken to a different ward" just then

Annie cried even harder than before.

"No Annie…. he is better than he had been last night…we have to keep these beds for emergencies" The nurse held onto Annie's hand then she put her arm around her shoulder to help comfort her.

After sometime they calmed Annie down, one of the nurses took Annie up to the ward to where Jack was being kept.

As they went into the room where Jack was, to Annie's surprise Jack was sitting up and carrying on with another nurse. Who was trying to take his pulse?

He still looked poorly; his face was colourless, his eyes sunk into his skull, but he still had his daft way, the way he carried on with people.

The nurse told Annie not to stay too long as he needed his rest and also that she thought that Annie needed some time to rest, as she was also looking drained.

Annie stopped with Jack until they both fell asleep. Annie's head resting on Jacks chest, her arm holding his waist not letting him go.

Jacks arm around her cuddling her, not wanting to let her go they slept for a while before the nurse woke Annie up.

The nurse told Annie they had a bed that was being brought by the porter, so that she could sleep near Jack.

The porter pulled the bed to the side of Jacks bed; it was a tight squeeze as the room was only designed to have one bed in it.

Adventure of the Mouhumes
Jack and Annie's new
Visitors

Annie stayed with Jack as long as she could, but when the Drs came around, they convinced Annie that it would be in her interest and Jacks welfare if she was to go home and rest properly, as when Jack would be well enough would also be able to go back home, they also have to assess Anne's wellbeing, as she would be taking care of him.

They all agreed that Annie would be best resting properly at home this would be in her best interest and more in probably Jacks interest.

Annie went towards Jacks head and gave a kiss on the top of his brow. And whispered that she loved him and wanted him back home, then a tear fell from her cheek onto Jacks brow.

Created and written by I C Henderson

Adventure of the Mouhumes
Jack and Annie's new
Visitors

Chapter 38
Strange Happenings

THERE HAD BEEN no sign of Jack in the conservatory, during the day or in the evening. There had been no sign of Annie coming and going throughout the day or night. This got the Mouhumes a little worried about what was happening? The mound of clay on the lawn was still wet with the rain. There was also a ring of yellow mud around it on the grass. It looked terrible.

The weather was getting a little better. Or at least it had stopped raining. Ratty was making plans to leave the following day. Some of the Parkland Mouhumes and some of the Woodland Mouhumes had come to the shed to make plans: what way would they go? How long do they think the journey would take? They all agreed that word would be sent back to let them know where they were and how they were doing.

There was around twenty or more just from the Parkland. Tube asked them if there was anyone left. They smiled and said there was more than enough left at the park. They were right, at least double were still at the park. They had done well to recover that was done with the help of all the resources around them.

It was late evening before they saw any fairies. The light was dimming. There was still no sign that anyone was in the house. Starlight and eight other fairies were around the muddy area. Tube was under the shed. He had not wanted to go into the shed as the talks had nothing to do with him until they had decided when and where they were going. Instead, he watched what the fairies were doing. They had some paper that had been left days earlier when the mud had been tipped out of the wheelbarrow.

Starlight had picked the paper up it had been left the same time as the mud had been left on the lawn. She had known that it was going to rain but not just that they still had not decided if they were going to do what Jack and Annie wanted. They had needed to

268

Adventure of the Mouhumes
Jack and Annie's new
Visitors

wait and see if they deserved what they were asking. By what they had been told from some of the Mouhumes there was sufficient evidence to say that they were good humans. They might have lived next door for a number of years but the fairies had kept out of the way so they did not see a lot of Jack and Annie. And because they had no pets the fairies had no idea if they liked animals.

Yet they had the pond, but this was in question as the fish sometimes tried to eat the fairies if they went for a drink and lately Jack just sat looking out of the window. So they had no idea what sort of humans they were.

The fairies went about what they had started. Tube was amazed with what they had done in such a short time. He had seen nothing like it, not just the speed and work they were doing but it would have taken the Mouhumes twice as long with the same amount of workforce. He had to go and inspect it closer. Starlight heard him coming and grabbed hold of some clay and without a word plonked it on Tube's head then flew on top of the hedge out of his reach laughing. Tube without saying anything or even his facial expression changing just looked at the work that had been done. The detail was like nothing he had seen before not even the best workers in the Mouhumes community could have completed a job like this! Not in the time they had done it and not even if they had longer.

Starlight was surprised that Tube had not said or done anything as she watched from the top of the hedge. She fluttered down beside Tube. Tube, still not making any sort of response, continued looking at the work that Starlight and her friends had done.

She asked was there something wrong. He shook his head then said that it was perfect and that he had never seen or had the capability to have done something that good. He then knew that he and the Mouhumes had so much to learn. Ratty and the others might be leaving too soon. They had so much to learn too. Maybe

269

Adventure of the Mouhumes
Jack and Annie's new
Visitors

the fairies were not bad and did not have alternative motives? Maybe they just like to help?

Starlight was now looking around. At the work they had just done, it looked okay so why was Tube still just looking? It was getting dark now so she said her goodbyes. Just as she said this the lights went on in the house. Starlight looked up into the house she could not see who was in the kitchen. So she nodded to Tube to make him aware, not just that she was going now but to let him know the lights were on in the house. Tube gave himself a little shake and gave Starlight a smile.

There had been two Mouhumes looking around the garden next to Jack and Annie's. It had a lot of fruit trees and fruit bushes but was now left to wreck and ruin. What had once been a well looked after garden was now allowed to grow wild. This was not a bad thing for the Mouhumes as there was plenty of food to collect: not just the fruit that was ready now but the seeds of the fruits that had fallen to the ground, fruit that had not been eaten by the birds. The two Mouhumes looking around this garden had a lot to do. Like all creatures the Mouhumes needed variety in their diet to help keep them in good health. They did not just collect the fresh fruits but they also got the seeds still in the decaying fruits.

This was not something they liked to do but they were getting punished for something and that was their punishment. Ratty had told them what to do, so that some seeds would be taken with Ratty for his journey. In the last two days they had been doing this punishment they had collected a lot of seeds. Some had been put to one side for Ratty and those who were going to leave with him.

Tube went on that side of the garden and stood near the hedge looking into what seemed to be a wilderness trying to spot the two Mouhumes who had been banished to do the work only in that garden. As he looked he could not see a thing. The overgrown plants could hide something as big as a large dog. It would and

Adventure of the Mouhumes
Jack and Annie's new
Visitors

could definitely hide two ordinary sized Mouhumes so it was pointless trying to go in to find them.

He still stood a little longer hoping that one of them might see him but it was not to be. He would have to go to the house to see who it was and what was happening. What had been the blue light? And why had they not seen Jack in the conservatory?

Tube had told one of the Mouhumes to get some twine and attach it to a hook at the top of the window on the conservatory; he had found out about them climbing up to help the fairies. Tube knew it had all been taken down after they had made their escape, but he wanted a piece put back up and they still had not done it, so he would have to do the one thing he disliked and that was to climb the hedge. He hated climbing hedges; often if they made one mistake they would get hurt by a thorn or even get tangled and attached to parts of the hedge. That made it more difficult to try to free themselves.

As he started to climb the hedge he gave a big sigh. He began to realise that he had aged. His strength and mobility was not as it was. Not just that, but in the time they had been under the shed he had not been very active and now it was starting to show. However, he was very determined; he carried on until he reached the same level as the window. As hard as he tried to go a little higher, he ran out of steam but he was still high enough so he could see into the conservatory. The lights were on in the kitchen, he could just see someone moving around in the living room: a dark figure. He could not see who it was as there was not enough light in that room the only light that was coming in was from the kitchen and from the street light outside the front window. The curtains had not been shut.

From what he could see it looked like Annie. She was now sitting in a chair with her head buried in a coat. What was she doing Tube thought? She sat there and did not move so Tube got back down from his location. It was a lot harder going down than

Created and written by I C Henderson

Adventure of the Mouhumes
Jack and Annie's new
Visitors

up. It took him some time but before he reached the bottom, where he found some Mouhumes who had been sent out to find him.

He was complaining and groaning and moaning until he saw the Mouhumes who had been sent for him. They put their arms out to help support him as he reached the bottom. It was late now so he went to the shed and told them that it would have to be in the morning when they could carry on holding their talks. However, just as he said that he could tell by their faces that they had already made their decision. He knew they had made up their minds and he could see that a large number would be leaving. A far greater number than he thought. But, he still told them he wanted to wait, to sleep on it and wait until the morning to be told what he already knew.

Created and written by I C Henderson

Adventure of the Mouhumes
Jack and Annie's new
Visitors

Chapter 39

The Decision

TUBE WAS UP early looking at the food larder. They had taken a lot out due to the rain, the Mouhumes could not go out hunting for food as much as they would have liked. The park camp had the same problem due to the bad weather. Humans had not been there so food supplies were also lower than they would have wanted.

The woodland camp had not been as bad as the other two but they also had taken out a lot from their storeroom. Tube thought this might give him a bit time to decide what he might do himself. They could not leave today as they had intended. They would have to wait until the food provisions had been topped up. He went out into in the garden. The day looked like it was going to be better than it had been.

The warm air was making vapour come from the damp earth and helping to dry it out. This was always a good indication that it was not going to rain that day. He then noticed the lights in the house had come on upstairs. Not known to Tube Annie had gone upstairs to get changed and have a wash but he knew that she would be getting ready to come down into the kitchen. That's what they did every morning then they would look out down the garden. His only concern was this ornament that Starlight and her friends had made. What would Annie think? Would she be happy or would she be annoyed? What would it also do to the harmony that had been between them until now?

Tube was right Annie was at the kitchen window looking down the garden. He hurried back to the shed and hid under it watching up the garden. He just knew that Annie would be coming down shortly. Sure enough Annie came down the garden. She looked around. What had the fairies done? Then she made a strange noise. As Mouhumes could not understand humans he did not have

Adventure of the Mouhumes
Jack and Annie's new
Visitors

any idea what the noise meant. Was it good or bad? Then she did some sort of jump around the garden. What was she doing? Then off she went back up to the house.

Tube raced back to the shed to warn the others. They left quickly out of the little doorway. Some went under the shed, some went into the underground warren and others went into the little shed at the back of the garden. Just as Tube was about to go out the big door opened. Quickly he ran to find some cover but poked his head out to see who it was. In came Annie with a plate full of food, she started to speak to Tube. He could not understand what she was saying but her tone was gentle so Tube thought that he would come out to see what she wanted. After all she did have a plateful of food and she might want to give it away. It would be very handy as they did need some extra as Ratty and others were going to leave and they needed to take food.

Annie stood in one place looking around to see if she could see any Mouhumes that might be hidden away, behind something but she could not see. She was just about to go when she noticed something. Tube came out from behind a box that had lots of empty plant pots in. He gave a big stretch as he was feeling a bit stiff after he had been climbing the hedge. Then he crouched down beside the box and sat on the floor.

Annie started to talk again. Her tone was soft and kind. As she placed the plate of sandwiches on the floor in-between her and Tube. Tube gently took a sandwich and tried it. He liked it. This was not something he had tried before. It was freshly made, not something that had been put out for the birds and past its sell by date.

The side door opened; in came Ruddy but she stopped in her tracks when she saw Annie. Ruddy saw that Annie was looking at her. She had seen that Tube seemed to be fine so she started to walk backwards to the door. Tube, in a quiet voice, told Ruddy to stop and come forward. Ruddy, not saying a word, hesitated. Tube

Created and written by I C Henderson

Adventure of the Mouhumes
Jack and Annie's new
Visitors

then waved his hand again as if to say come forward. At this point Annie was bending down. She must have thought that Tube had been waving to her so he held his hand out to her. To his amazement Annie copied him.

Tube picked up another sandwich and placed it onto her hand. Annie was still unsure what she should be doing or what Tube wanted her to do so she stayed still, trying to look at the two of them at the same time. Ruddy still kept her distance, as she also did not know what she should be doing. She had taken on things a lot bigger than herself but a human was more than even she could handle. All sorts of thoughts were going through her head. Would this person hurt her son Glow? Should she attack the human? Could she frighten her off if her intentions were to hurt the Mouhumes?

Tube was now pointing to Annie to give a sandwich to Ruddy and for Ruddy to take it. There was hesitation on both Ruddy and Annie's part but they did with the help of Tube. Ruddy got a hold of the sandwich and took a mouthful and straight away took another. This was something far better than they had ever had.

The Mouhume's door was slightly open and some Mouhumes were peeping through the crack. Annie stood up and started to leave the shed. Once her back was turned towards Tube and Ruddy the others came in and quickly took all the sandwiches off the plate. In no time at all they were all gone. Annie looked back she had not seen what had just happened; now all she could see was the empty plate.

A Mouhume watching from under a plant, near the top of the garden, saw her smile when she turned back towards the shed. He would report this back to Tube. It was as if she was pleased to see that all the food had gone. As Annie got near the doorway of her house a man the Mouhumes had seen before but did not know who he was or his name was coming through the gate. Annie and the man stood for a while talking before they went into the house.

Created and written by I C Henderson

Adventure of the Mouhumes
Jack and Annie's new
Visitors

The Mouhume watched from his hiding place. Annie and the man went into the conservatory. The man stood at the window looking down the garden. Annie went in to the kitchen to make a drink for the two of them. She returned to the conservatory and then they sat down. As the Mouhume watched Annie and the man he could tell that what ever they were talking about was intense, just by the look on their faces. This was definitely a time when a fairy would be useful, just to help explain what the two humans were talking about. The Mouhume stayed a little longer but decided to go and tell Tube what he had seen. He also hoped to find a fairy to see if they would come back to the conservatory to see what was being said.

Back in the shed the Mouhumes shared the sandwiches amongst those who were leaving and those who were staying. They now had plenty food for the journey: maybe not as much as they would have liked but there was still sufficient and it was as much as they would be able to carry anyway. Those being left behind had enough food to last a day or two. The weather was getting better so the hunter gatherers would not be put off by the weather.

The young Mouhume who had watched Annie and the male reported back to Tube. Tube had no idea what to make of it so told everyone just to carry on as normal. Ratty and his fellow companions from the parkland and woodland camps were ready to go on their journey to find a new and satisfying land to settle in. Just like the land they once had. Could there be such a place?

They would do as they had always done: travel in small groups of about five or six. Leaving in daylight would not have been something they would have normally done but they had worked out this was the best time as humans had gone out for the day and would not be back for some time. Only a small amount of humans came back at lunchtime. They had also worked out that it would be best to leave after the morning activities had finished. It was still early so they would have to wait; besides they still did not

Adventure of the Mouhumes
Jack and Annie's new
Visitors

have all their supplies sorted out. That would take a little more time as they had just been given more food.

Ruddy had been asked if she would go with Ratty. She did not sleep for days thinking about it. She was torn between Ratty and Tube. She liked them both. They were like fathers she had never known and now she was being asked to choose. No matter which one of them she chose she would be leaving the other and likely never to see him again.

The thought of it was more than she could cope with. The biggest thought going through her head was why? Why did they have to part? Why did they have to go? Why was life so hard? Why were things not straightforward? She would have to go and talk to Ratty. That was all she could do and she dreaded it, as this was a talk she hoped she would never have to have.

Ratty was under the shed amongst those who were going. They seemed well organised, had more than enough food and some had been to the pond to collect water. It ran like a military operation. All remembering that at all times they had to move in and out of the hedging keeping out of sight from all eyes.

Annie and the other human were still in the conservatory looking out of the window. They were talking but not paying much attention to what was happening outside.

Ruddy sneaked up behind Ratty and pulled him on to the ground but Ratty was quick enough to turn around on the floor and then overturn Ruddy who had not had time to pin Ratty down properly. Ruddy was laughing so much that Ratty could not tell her off. Then he started to laugh as well. The two of them had not done this for a long time. It always put Ratty in a bad mood but this time it was as if he knew this would be the last time. A tear came down his face. He wiped it off before any of the other Mouhumes had seen him. Ruddy had seen this and what she had to say would be harder than she ever thought. Ratty jumped to his feet pulling

Created and written by I C Henderson

Adventure of the Mouhumes
Jack and Annie's new
Visitors

Ruddy up with him and as he did so he knew they had to talk. They went down into the shelter under the shed, as far away as they could from all the other Mouhumes.

Tube had gone outside, back to the top of the garden to watch Annie and the other human. He still needed to know what was happening. One or two of the fairies were in the hedging but Tube could not see them. Tube was still wondering what had happened to Jack? He had not been seen for a while. None of the Mouhumes had seen him either. Was this new human male now going to be a permanent fixture and if so, what impact would he have on the Mouhumes?

Tube started to think that maybe they should all go with Ratty. He also wondered, if Ratty and the others had gone and then they decided they wanted to come back that would be okay, at least they would have somewhere to come back to.

Meanwhile Ratty and Ruddy were talking. Ruddy was telling Ratty that they had everything here: plentiful supply of food, the humans Jack and Annie seemed okay and the shelter was good, as good as they could have anywhere. Then she asked, with a tear in her eye, why did he have to go? He and Tube had been on many an adventure together.

Ratty sunk his head. He had no idea why he said that he was going. He knew that if he went it would be unlikely that he would see Tube and Ruddy again. He sunk down to the ground, sitting on a rock rubbing his head.

Ruddy knew why he wanted to go as she also wanted to go for the adventure, but she knew Tube was too old for anything like that. His days had come and gone for that kind of lifestyle, especially when they had somewhere that was almost perfect.

The time had now come for all those who were leaving to congregate in and around the big shed. Tube had arrived to say his

Created and written by I C Henderson

Adventure of the Mouhumes
Jack and Annie's new
Visitors

goodbyes. He was still wondering if they should all really go. With a sad heart he wished them well on their journey. So many Mouhumes had come to say goodbye.

The Mouhumes from the park and from the woodland had all come too. Tube could not believe his eyes at how many Mouhumes there were. It was truly becoming three large communities. As hard as he looked he could not see Ratty. The hustle and bustle, the coming and goings and then they were gone. An unhappy Tube walked away he needed to be alone with his thoughts.

Had he done the right thing staying? He walked around under the hedge to keep out of sight, then another hedge then another; he just walked around with his thoughts.

He had never felt like this before, yes he had lost Mouhumes who he had been friends with. But this was different. Ratty was more than a friend. How would he cope without his best friend Ratty?

He finally found a place and he sat down hoping that no one had seen him. Tears were now running down his face he was sobbing uncontrollably.

Created and written by I C Henderson

Adventure of the Mouhumes
Jack and Annie's new
Visitors
Chapter 40

The fight

THE NEXT DAY felt strange. The Mouhumes went about their day as they always did. They had been reduced in numbers and now they faced a new challenge. A Challenge where numbers would be needed something they did not have so other tactics would have to be put in place. This was something that the Mouhumes knew one Mouhume would take on.

The kitten from Ted's house had caught and killed two Mouhumes earlier that morning. Some Mouhumes were still and had not known about the killing of the two Mouhumes, Tube had not been seen. He was still saddened from not seeing Ratty the day before. His friend had gone and they had not said their goodbyes. The fairies had not been seen for a while. It was as if they had been abandoned by all when they needed help most.

Ruddy was now set, she stood there dressed in her fur, her hair as golden as ever after the rain. Thorns at the ready, determination on her face, she was set to go to war with this new threat. Ruddy would not ask another Mouhume for help. This would be a fight that would or could kill her. The kitten had speed and strength, but one thing Ruddy had, was experience. Not that she had ever relied on that as each fight was always different. It was no good going into a fight with any idea other than winning.

Created and written by I C Henderson

Adventure of the Mouhumes
Jack and Annie's new
Visitors

Planning ahead as she passed another thorny bush she snapped off thorns and placed them in different locations. If she had to move around the garden she would not have time to look for more weapons. This would give her a fighting chance.

Created and written by I C Henderson

Adventure of the Mouhumes
Jack and Annie's new
Visitors

She scaled up a hedge to give her a height advantage. Then as still and as quiet as she could be she lay amongst the leaves, waiting for the kitten to come out. This was the pathway it took into Jack and Annie's garden so she had to be ready to pounce down onto it with one clean sweep.

She could hear the door being opened. Ted was telling the young cat to get out. The kitten had been getting out more now as it was getting older and Ted did not want it to be a house cat so he would let it out in the morning and let it back in lunchtime. It was learning to do what cats do and that was to hunt. Nothing more or less than the Mouhumes had done themselves.

Created and written by I C Henderson

Adventure of the Mouhumes
Jack and Annie's new
Visitors

Suddenly it was there, coming around the corner from the house it came slinking down ready to hunt. Ruddy, now with her thorns at the ready moved slowly, ready to swoop down on to the back of its neck. The kitten was moving nearer to where Rudy was. Ruddy slowly got herself into position ready to attack. She held a thorn in each hand and one in her mouth. She knew what she was going to do and what she had to do.

The young cat was getting closer now. It was also preparing to hurt or kill something, crouching down as it walked each step slowly without making a sound, it sniffed the air smelling anything that should not be there, almost into position it stopped. It stayed there not moving as if it might have known something was waiting for it. It was just out of reach for Ruddy. She still could swoop down but she would be at the disadvantage and with the kitten being bigger than her and stronger she did not want to be at any disadvantage. Her heart was not in it. She did not have that aggression that she normally had. She was thinking too much. It was not something she would do in a fight. She would generally just attack and attack and attack again until the fight was over. She gave herself a shake and told herself to stop thinking and get on with it.

The kitten changed direction and started moving again along the side of the hedge. It had not gone through the opening that it would usually go though. It was as if it was hunting something itself, Ruddy stopped for a moment to look in the direction the cat was going. She could see what it might be after. She had no time to think or hesitate. She had to move now. From branch to branch she swung jumped and leaped. There was anger on her face and aggression in her body. She jumped out of the hedge her thorns ready to do the deed

She landed just short of the back of the cat's neck onto its shoulder blades. The cat jumped up onto its back feet. Ruddy held onto its fur with one hand trying to pierce it above its shoulder but the cat was running and shaking its body trying to get her off.

Created and written by I C Henderson

Adventure of the Mouhumes
Jack and Annie's new
Visitors

Then the cat did something Ruddy had not expected and that was to roll onto its back. Without hesitation, it turned one way then suddenly another. Ruddy lost her grip and landed on the ground with a thud. It knocked the wind out of her. Suddenly the young cat was holding her down with its paw. Its claws either side of her head.

The young cat growled and with one swipe hit Ruddy's head knocking her semi unconscious. Then it picked her up with its other paw that had been holding her down and hit her again. Ruddy's body fell to the ground. The weapons she had been holding falling out of her hands. Her body lay there broken in a crumpled heap.

The cat now moved away from Ruddy it was going after the pray that it had originally intended to go after, Ruddy's son Dash. His mother had done what any mother would do without thinking and that was to defend her son. He was now hiding high up in the hedge. Dash had seen what the cat had done to his mother. Fear was something his mother had never shown, but he was feeling fear and rage as his mother was lying there not moving. From a distance you would not even think that her body was that of a Mouhume.

The cat had smashed her body so easily and now it was after Dash; Dash had learnt a lot from his mother and knew he still had a lot to learn. His hands now held a thorn, each hand holding them tight but he was fearful that he might drop one. The cat was below him sniffing the air. Dare he try and jump onto its back like his mother had tried? One thing his mother taught him was not to over think a situation, just to act without pause. Maybe that was how his mother met her end? She had not thought, but just acted. What was he to do?

Suddenly the cat pounced almost reaching him in the hedge. He almost lost his balance and had to grab hold of a branch, doing so he dropped one of his thorns. The cat quickly jumped up again

Adventure of the Mouhumes
Jack and Annie's new
Visitors

hitting the branch just below him making Dash shake, almost falling out of the bush and before he could get hold of a branch to support himself It jumped again hitting another branch, only this time he fell head first lucky for Dash his clothing became snarled on the bush. This stopped him falling to his death but now he was left hanging upside down and the cat slightly out of reach was now getting more irritated.

As hard as Dash tried to get out of that position he was conscious that if he made a mistake he would fall towards the kitten and if he fell only a little more, the young cat would be able to reach him. The only thing stopping the young cat getting him were the thorns from the hedge. The cat had another idea. It started to walk back towards Ruddys body. By now there were a number of Mouhumes under the shed watching in horror. All were frozen to the spot; they all knew what the cat would do as they had seen cats do the same thing time and time again. It would go and play with the body, tossing it up and swiping it with a paw. If Ruddy was not already dead she would be soon.

The cat now stood over Ruddy's lifeless body sniffing her. Then suddenly there was a squeal from the kitten. Ruddy, with what little life was left in her with all her might had pushed a thorn under the cats chin piercing into its mouth sticking it into its tongue. The cat sped off leaving Ruddy lifeless on the ground. The Mouhumes from under the shed ran to help her. One of them had gone to tell Tube, who was now on his way. When he got into a certain position under the shed where he could see what had happened. He fell to the ground with despair.

The Mouhumes had reached Ruddy and some were helping Dash down from the hedge. Dash could only but stare in his mother's direction, hoping that she would be ok. She had cheated death so many times. He had heard all the stories about her. She must be ok but the look on those trying to help her told him something different.

Created and written by I C Henderson

Adventure of the Mouhumes
Jack and Annie's new
Visitors

Some stood crying uncontrollably. He looked around. Then he caught sight of Tube eager to see some sort of hope on his face but he was also weeping. Dash's eyes started to fill up but he was the son of Ruddy, a great worrier, brave and fearful; he could not show any weakness. His mother told him that again and again until he could stand hearing it no more.

Ruddys body was taken back under the shed. Those carrying her were still sobbing uncontrollably. Never had the Mouhumes shown such emotion openly. Ruddys body was placed down gently with great affection.

Dash, now present along side countless Mouhumes pushed through the crowd which must have been ten deep. He stopped and took a deep breath. Even with all his strength he could not stop his eyes filling up. He bent down and held onto his mother's hand kissing it. Begging her to be ok, her body had been placed upon a brick, up off the ground it looked like an altar.

Dash still bending down felt a hand on his shoulder. He turned his head it was Ratty, Ratty had gone with the others but somewhere on the journey he knew he had to come back as Ruddy had said something to him that he could not get out of his head.

Dash stood up. Ratty put his arms around him trying to comfort him but it was also to soothe himself. He had gone into his own sleeping area and not told anyone that he was back so he was feeling guilty. He could have helped Ruddy. They might not have killed the kitten but there might not have been anymore deaths. They all stood around wondering what would happen now. There had never been anyone else like Ruddy. Not in any old tales past or present. She was something words could not explain.

Linden, Woozy, Joy and Scallop, who had been spending time in the parkland warren, arrived. The news had travelled fast and even those who had been some great distance away took no time in getting back. This news was even worse than their old

Adventure of the Mouhumes
Jack and Annie's new
Visitors

home being destroyed. Even then Ruddy had been a leader but there was never a time when she tried to undermine Tube or Ratty. Most would have followed Ruddy, as they had done when she left the warren. Even Tube and Ratty who were the leaders, left with Ruddy. That in itself, showed her strength, not just physical but everything about her.

Dash was now standing with his head dropped down to his chest, wondering about what to do next. His fists clenched there was nothing but aggression on his face. Someone or something was going to suffer.

Bang! There was a thud on the shed wall. Buster and Tilly had arrived. Tilly using her head was banging on the site of the shed to get attention, Quickly Dash jumped up onto Tilly's back, wanting to go after the kitten. Ratty told him to get down off Tilly. That the kitten had gone home and was back in the house. Dash still wanted to go to Ted's house and barge in. maybe Tilly could open the door somehow, barking or even banging at the door. She often did that at her home. She would bark and head-butt the door. Once the door was open they could rush in and seek revenge.

Ratty told him that Tilly would be destroyed and the Mouhumes would be hunted and killed, "after all Ted took care of Ruddy when she was giving birth to you" he explained

Dash could not understand why Ted had such a creature that would kill as it did. Just as he had said that Starlight came with a number of her companions. She reached out to Dash and took him in her arms. She was a lot bigger than Dash. He seemed to disappear in her wings only his feet could be seen.

Another fairy went towards Ruddy. The Mouhumes, who had been surrounding her parted as the fairy approached Ruddy's body. She placed her hand onto Ruddy's head then spoke as she placed something over Ruddy's heart. None of the Mouhumes standing near could make out what she had said. Ruddy's hand

Created and written by I C Henderson

Adventure of the Mouhumes
Jack and Annie's new
Visitors

opened ever so slightly. Those watching cheered, Dash turned around to see what the excitement was. His mother was breathing. Her chest was moving ever so slightly but moving. She had taken a beating, a beating that would have killed most creatures and one that almost killed her.

Ruddy would need to rest, she would need to build her strength up, Starlight told them that when Ruddy was ready they would have to go and see the young cat and try to make peace, just as she had done with all the other creatures in that area.

Glow arrived. She had been away with her son Capheus. It was that time, when they would part and would never see each other again. That had been the reason the Mouhumes had not seen the fairies. It had been a sad few days for them. A new male had arrived and he would be welcomed later that day, but first Starlight and Glow had to persuade Tube and Ratty that they had the best interest for Ruddy and they must do as they were asked and do only what they would be told to do. They knew they must do what ever it took and that they would have to start straight away to help Ruddy to survive, Tube, without hesitation agreed; Ratty was unsure but went along with what was being said. They would have to move her with care to somewhere they could attend to her. Glow and Starlight could not go into the Mouhumes underground camp.

Mousy came and Starlight took him to one side. She told him that he must keep everyone away except those who would be picked to help with her needs. She then pointed to the fairy that had touched Ruddy. Starlight did not give her name or even say who she was, but it was clear that she was someone important and that she held a higher status than all those who they had already met.

They decided where she would be placed and who would watch over her, Tube and Ratty were chosen to watch over her. They were told that no other Mouhume would or could enter the area that had been chosen for her. No matter what or how long it took.

Created and written by I C Henderson

Adventure of the Mouhumes
Jack and Annie's new
Visitors

Chapter 41

The Following Week

OVER THE NEXT few weeks Ruddy was in recovery. None of the Mouhumes had any idea on how to help a sick Mouhume. It would be a case of letting nature take its course and only the strongest would survive.

This time they had help, the fairy community had knowledge of sickness and ill health. They had what the Mouhumes thought, magical powers; after all they could make themselves vanish. So what other mysterious things could they do, bring back the dead as it seemed they had done with Ruddy!

Tube and Ratty had stayed near Ruddy watching over her in the small shed at the back of the garden. They had taken Ruddy there because the fairies could not go under the ground. The openings were too small for them and they could damage their wings. The fairy that had stroked Ruddy over her head when she was all but dead came every day to tend to her. But when she came in to the room Tube and Ratty had to leave. This was the only time they left her side.

They had been given strict orders of what they must do and not do. They followed the instructions to the letter. After all, this was Ruddy. No other Mouhume had been given permission to go anywhere near her, not even Dash could see his mother. Dash had asked Tube and Ratty why, but they could not answer, not even they knew why the fairies had said that no one could see her. All they could say was she was getting better each day and with every new day she was getting stronger.

Ruddy was getting visits not just from this new fairy but her old friends Starlight and Glow. They came with foods and other things. Things Tube and Ratty could not know about. They were not allowed to see what they had or what they were doing.

Created and written by I C Henderson

Adventure of the Mouhumes
Jack and Annie's new
Visitors

Though each time Tube and Ratty were allowed back in to see her they could see a difference, in a good way and each time she was getting stronger. Today was the first time they had seen her sit up. She was still looking weak but compared to just a few days earlier there was a big difference and all for the better. She was still not talking. Tube and Ratty had been told not to try and talk to her so they did precisely as they had been asked. Unknown to them Ruddy had also been told not to talk but just point to what she wanted or needed.

All would become clear in a day or two. Glow had told them that the fairy looking after Ruddy would explain all they wanted to know. As Glow told them this she had a sadness about her. It was as if she knew it was not going to be good news.

Glow went on to tell them that Dash would be allowed to see his mother the next day and they must tell him that he could talk but not to encourage Ruddy to talk. They were also told that the fairy that was helping Ruddy to recover would be there to make sure her demands would be carried out. Glow said this with manner and tone in her voice. Glow also advised them that if this was not carried out exactly as they had been told then things would not be okay. Ratty wanted to ask why, but it was as if he knew he would not be told, so all he could do was nod his head to show he understood.

Starlight and the fairy that were looking after Ruddy were in the shed. Tube had arrived back, he had been away checking up on the other Mouhumes, making sure they were still doing what they needed to do and also asking about the kitten. No one had seen the kitten since that day.

Tube also asked about Jack, whether anyone had seen him? They told Tube none of them had seen Jack, they had seen Annie coming and going out of the house but that she had not been down the garden. The other human had been once or twice but not in the

Created and written by I C Henderson

Adventure of the Mouhumes
Jack and Annie's new
Visitors

house so they just hid. The human had looked around the sheds and the garden but that was all he had done. He was just looking, he never touched anything.

Tube did not know what to make of this. Who was he and what had happened to Jack? Annie was always coming and going out of the house so that was nothing knew but who was this human?

Starlight was just coming out of the shed when Tube arrived. He asked what had happened to the young cat. Starlight told him after Ruddy stabbed it under the chin it had not been out of the house. Its chin had swollen up so it was being kept in the house until the wound had healed.

Tube reported this news to all the other Mouhumes. Once again, Ruddy had saved their lives. Once again, she had put all other lives before her own. This time it had been far more than any … number of Mouhumes could have … he stopped, he could not carry on. All those there knew what he wanted to say. No matter how many Mouhumes would have or could have stood up to the cat they could not have done any better and most would have been more than likely killed.

Tube had also asked the name of the fairy taking care of Ruddy. Starlight could not tell him, it was something she could not tell; she had been given her name many years ago. It was not something she wanted to share. Only a small number knew her name but what she could tell him was that she had spent some time with humans and learned a lot of things just by watching and listening. She was now full of knowledge.

One thing she had said was not to be too quick in trusting humans. This had Tube thinking, why then did they trust Ted so much? What was the name of this fairy he had never seen until now? Why did she not trust humans? So many thoughts and

Created and written by I C Henderson

Adventure of the Mouhumes
Jack and Annie's new
Visitors

questions were going through his head but one thing was sure, she was helping to making Ruddy better.

Each day she would bring food. Some of which he recognised and some he had never seen before. There were ointments that he had no idea about. This was something the Mouhumes did not do, treat an injured Mouhume. They would have to get better by themselves. It wasn't that they did not want to help injured Mouhumes but they had no idea how to do it or what they had to do.

A wounded Mouhume often died from wounds, if not from the wound itself, the infection would often finish them off. As for broken bones, again infection or out of place bones would be the end of them.

Ruddy was needed. They would have tried anything to keep her safe. Even though they would not have known what they were supposed to do. This fairy seemed to know what to do. She had it all in order. She cleaned Ruddy flesh wounds. She knew exactly what rest was needed, any slight exercise and when she had done too much. Tube and Ratty might not have been there when she was doing what she did but they still had some idea what was happening. They should have asked what the food stuff was and how it would help her but they said nothing.

A week passed and Ruddy was now standing by herself although she was still a little unsteady on her feet. Each day she was looking better. Ruddy had wanted to go out amongst the other Mouhumes but she was advised not to, for another day at least.

The fairy explained to her that she needed to look as strong as she had done before the fight. This would give the Mouhumes hope. Then it suddenly became clear to Ruddy. After all she had seen and done this many times before. She had seen all the signs and now she knew what had been happening. This was not going to

Adventure of the Mouhumes
Jack and Annie's new
Visitors

be a long-term fix but only for show: a show that could only be for a short time. How long she had no idea about.

Starlight came in the shed with Glow. Ruddy asked them why had they saved her? Why not let her die. Why all of this just to prolong things? They sank their heads. This was not going to be easy for them. But they could only tell her the truth as they seen it. It had started some days earlier when they were at the pond and the young cat came. All the fairies could do was to go for the dogs to help the Mouhumes. Though it had only been Buster they could get at that time and it was only then they knew that something would have to be done so that they all could live in harmony.

Starlight and Glow and even others had tried to talk to the young cat. But like all cats it was built in to them to hunt. The kitten had killed at least three fairies and two Mouhumes in the last few days when it had been allowed out of the house. It might live in Ted's house but it belonged to Ted's wife Linda. They told Ruddy that Linda had no idea about the fairies never mind all the Mouhumes. It had not been something Ted had ever told her.

"So when Linda got the young cat Ted did not think that it would hurt any of us, not even thinking about the Mouhumes but then he had just seen you Ruddy and then you had your boy Dash," Ruddy nodded. The unnamed fairy went. "Ted had helped in a way. He brought food out and let the fairies look after you, so he had not been a bad human. Jack on the other hand, had left traps that killed one of the Mouhumes then put lights in the garden that could have put the Mouhumes at risk"

The three fairies stayed with Ruddy to explain about her wounds and broken bones. What was likely to happen and that she would never be the same as she had been. Then they told Ruddy what they would like her to do and what she might be able to do once they had her on her feet … but that would be at least another day or two.

Created and written by I C Henderson

Adventure of the Mouhumes
Jack and Annie's new
Visitors

Chapter 42
Alliance

IT HAD BEEN nearly two weeks since the parting of the Mouhumes and Ruddy's recovery. Still no one had seen her. The young cat had only been out once since the fight. Since that day nothing had come into the garden that would hurt the Mouhumes.

Some Mouhumes had now worked out a routine to go between the other camps. That way they could help each other and learn about different things. The woodland Mouhumes had different creatures living alongside them, some they would rather not have had anywhere near them, while others had been a good food supply. The same went for the parkland Mouhumes. The food source was similar as the garden Mouhumes. Most of the food came from humans but they also had fish and a few different animals that they could eat and also be eaten by.

So it was good that the three camps kept in contact with each other, they were able to learn about what was happening, and what was the best way to do some things and what dangers were about. Although most of all, they were able to make sure all camps had support when it was needed. They all wanted to know about Ruddy: how she was and whether she had been seen outside yet? That was always the first question anyone asked when any of the Mouhumes from the garden camp dropped by even if they were just visiting. Sometimes when the Mouhumes went between the camps they would often stay overnight, sometimes two nights. It was something they had just started to do. That way they could learn more about one another's environments.

They also brought each other food which meant because they had different types of food; it would give them all a better diet. Not always a healthier diet but a different one. Those in the park often had leftover food from the takeaway shop: like chips, kebab and pieces of different flavoured pies but most of the time they left chips.

Adventure of the Mouhumes
Jack and Annie's new
Visitors

Parts of the parkland had berries growing but not enough to sustain the growing numbers. The food the humans threw away was more than enough to store away for bad weather. They had learned in a short time that when the weather was not good the humans did not come to the park, so they had to store as much as they could and rotating the food to help keep it edible.

Word had got around that Ruddy was back on her feet and on top of the agenda a meeting with the young cat to be made although it was unclear if Ruddy was going to kill the young cat; especially since she had nearly done so at the last meeting. This time she would have help, no Mouhume wanted any harm to come to her again.

The strongest from the park and the strongest from the woodland went to the garden where Ruddy was but when they got there they had been told the meeting was with Ruddy and Ruddy alone. This was not something any of the Mouhumes had wanted but they were told it was for the welfare of the community.

It was true enough, after they arrived and the meeting was about to start, Ruddy was back on her feet looking as strong as ever. She was covered in fur from top to bottom but unknown to any other Mouhume that was to hide the wounds and battle scars.

Ruddy went with Glow, Starlight and another fairy, not the one who had helped her back to health but another one, who looked far stronger than any other fairy they had seen before. She made Ruddy look weak next to her.

Dash stood watching his mother being led away. He had been told by Tube and Ratty not to intervene in any way. This instruction had come from his mother. Tube and Ratty, one on each side of Dash, did not know the full reason for this meeting. All had been kept secret. Only Ruddy and the fairies knew what was going to happen.

Created and written by I C Henderson

Adventure of the Mouhumes
Jack and Annie's new
Visitors

Ruddy had her thorns tucked under her fur tied around her waist. She had more covering than normal but still looked good. She walked with a slight limp but hid it well under her clothes.

As she entered the meeting area, arranged by the new fairy with the strict face, Ruddy looked around towards Starlight. Starlight was looking nervous as did Glow. This made Ruddy a bit apprehensive. She placed a hand on one of her thorns ready to pull out and attack.

The place chosen was only two gardens away. It had an area that was overgrown but also had an area with short cut grass. This was ideal for the meeting and the overgrown area would be a good escape if need be.

The kitten came. It was crouching down, as cats do when they are ready to attack. Ruddy was just about to pull out her thorn when her hand was stopped. Starlight placed her hand on top of Ruddy's. Ruddy's first instinct was to pull out the other one with her other hand but Glow was on that side and placed her hand on top of the handle. What were they doing? Why had they stopped her?

The kitten was now encircling Ruddy. Its jaw area still had some swelling around it where Ruddy had stabbed it. Its claws were already out and its teeth were showing. It was a frightening sight, not just for Ruddy but Starlight and Glow too, who had now made themselves invisible.

The only fairy that could be seen was the one who had come with them. As big as she was the young cat still looked more powerful. The fairy jumped in front of the kitten startling it. It stopped in its tracks, moving slightly back. Ruddy had seen this happen before. When cats do this they sometimes pounce forward.

The fairy put her hand on the kitten's nose with her palm over its nostrils and pushed hard downwards. The kitten seemed to just

Created and written by I C Henderson

Adventure of the Mouhumes
Jack and Annie's new
Visitors

lie down and wagged its tail with temper, not really knowing what was happening but unable to do anything. Then Ruddy was beckoned over to the kitten's head. Starlight and Glow showed themselves again but stood back, away from Ruddy.

Ruddy stood over the helpless kitten. The fairy pointing to her as if to kill it; Ruddy was a little confused. She pulled her thorn out and looked at the kitten that was now unable to move. What had the fairy done to stop this killing machine in its tracks? It had killed one, if not more fairies, so how was it, all of a sudden, helpless just by one touch?

The fairy asked Ruddy why she had not killed it. Ruddy could not kill something that she or any other Mouhume was not in danger from. The kitten's claws had been out ready to attack but now they were not to be seen. It had pulled its claws back. It could only look with its eyes and unable to move its head.

Ruddy shook her head. She could not kill it. The fairy asked again.

"Why? It would have killed you"

Then she told Ruddy that she would be dead now if not for the care she had so why not kill the enemy that had killed your kind. She asked again with a little more harshness in her voice.

Ruddy told her she did not kill for any other reason other than for food or to survive. She did not kill for killing sake. The fairy then asked what she would like her to do with the kitten. Ruddy, as always, told her the kitten could be good friends like your kind have been, like the two dogs Buster and Tilly have been and the hedgehog. She wanted them all to get along.

Created and written by I C Henderson

Adventure of the Mouhumes
Jack and Annie's new
Visitors

The fairy then reminded Ruddy that cats have killing built in them. They can't help themselves; it's something they just do. Not necessarily for badness or even to eat, it's just something they must do.

Ruddy stood for a while thinking about everything she had been told. She knew it was true but all of her new friends once, if not all, had a fight with her and almost killed her, apart from the two dogs.

She looked at the fairy and asked if she could tell the kitten she did not want to harm it and at the same time she did not want her friends harmed. She also wanted to know if it was possible for them all to get along. She said there was plenty to hunt and kill.

The fairy told Ruddy she did not need to tell the kitten anything as the kitten could understand everything that was said. She also told Ruddy that when she had put her hand on the kitten she had something in her hand that would make the cat understand what was happening and what was being said, but at the same time helpless.

"So how will we know if it will be a friend or enemy? And how will we deal with it?" Ruddy asked.

The fairy told Ruddy there is only one way we can do this to find out and that was to remove what ever hold she has on the kitten. As she said this she tapped the kitten on its head. The kitten pounced up and gave Ruddy a fright but Ruddy, unlike normal, did not pull out her thorn ready to fight. She just stood there.

The young cat, after hearing all that had been said, now had a choice to make. It walked from side to side, looking all the time at Ruddy. Both did not say a word. Ruddy did not move her head, only her eyes kept watch.

298

Adventure of the Mouhumes
Jack and Annie's new
Visitors

Then the young cat jumped onto Ruddy, knocking her down with its paws and pinned her arms. All the aches and pains she thought had gone came back twice as hard. Even if she wanted to fight she could not. It looked straight into her eyes and was only a breath away from her face. The young cat said that it liked to play and it liked to hunt.

This was strange; Ruddy could understand what it was saying. Ruddy still pinned down looked towards the fairy with surprise on her face. Obviously the fairy knew why Ruddy was looking surprised. How was it she could understand the kitten now?

Ruddy, without showing any fear, told the kitten the Mouhumes also like to play and liked to fight but they did not have to kill everything they came into contact with. The kitten let her up and then started to walk away. As it did so it said they could get along and there would be no more killing of Mouhumes or fairies.

Created and written by I C Henderson

Adventure of the Mouhumes
Jack and Annie's new
Visitors

Chapter 43

The new friendship

WHEN ANNIE GOT home she sat on the living room chair, she picked Jacks coat up that was hanging over the back of the chair, the smell of Jack gave her some comfort, she put it over herself and then put her feet on the sofa, and in no time she was fast a sleep.

She slept until she heard the clock strike twelve; she rubbed her eyes the sunlight was shining through the living room window.

Straightaway she picked the phone up to call the hospital to see how Jack was, it seemed to ring for a along time before someone answered it, Annie asked how Jack was she was told that he was still resting, he had a bad nights sleep, Annie asked what time she could go and visit him she was told anytime but the Drs were due to come and see him shortly, Annie told the nurse that it would be in the evening as she had some thing's to do.

Annie went in to the kitchen and looked outside there at the bottom of the garden she could see a fairytale castle, just like the picture that Jack and Annie had picked out from the magazine. It was damp outside she quickly put her jacket on, and went on her way to have a closer look,

"Well I never" She walked around it and it was in every detail right from the picture.

It stood about three feet high, and looked excellent; Annie clapped her hands with excitement. She almost did a dance around the garden, why had the Mouhumes done this why now and why not the other day? All theses questions where going through her head, she went on her way back into the house, on the way up the garden path she looked towards Ted's garden half expecting him popping his head over the hedge, she did not know why but she

Created and written by I C Henderson

Adventure of the Mouhumes
Jack and Annie's new
Visitors

thought that it was as if she knew that he knew more than he was letting on.

As soon as she got into the kitchen she started to make some ham and salad sandwiches, she cut them into quarters. "Right that will do it, I hope he's ready for his breakfast" then she went down the garden and into the shed, it was dull but still light enough to make things out "Right then are you coming, I know you're here and I would like to thank you for what you have made"

The chubby Mouhume popped its head from behind a box on the floor, and it gave a big stretch, as if it had just woken up. "There you are, are your friends not coming then" she bent down with the plate of sandwiches and put it on the floor just in front of her and the plump Mouhume, it looked up at her and without any hesitation got hold of a sandwich and started to eat it.

It looked like a Mouhume but it had a difference about it Annie could not work out just what it was at this stage, as she had only seen them from a distance, as she was standing another one came in from the outside in the little doorway that they had made, it got a fright at first seeing Annie stood there and it froze to one spot.

Annie realized that it must have had a fright so she did not move, she looked down at the chubby one and it waved its hand as if it was saying to come here, so Annie bent down towards it and it held its hand out as if it wanted Annie to copy, so Annie did this she held her hand out then to her surprise it shoved a sandwich in her hand, Annie not knowing what to do, did it want her to eat it or what?

It then pointed towards its friend who was slowly moving backwards, as if it was in reverse, it stopped in its tracks when Annie still kneeling leant towards it with the sandwich in her hand, and offered it out to the little Mouhume.

Created and written by I C Henderson

Adventure of the Mouhumes
Jack and Annie's new
Visitors

Annie could see the difference now. But she had to get the trust of it the chubby one got itself another sandwich, and sat down near the plate, what a good eater Annie was now knelling over it so she had to steady herself by putting her hand down on the ground. She was so near the one eating she could feel its warmth from its body, she turned her head to look at it to make sure that it was ok, as she done this the other one took the sandwich from her hand.

Annie turned her head slowly to look at it; it was standing by the little doorway with its back to Annie, which gave Annie a chance to have a good look at it, it had fur around it and what looked like a flower head on top of its head? This puzzled Annie why would it have a flower on its head, the fur around it which might be its own looked dirty and green, as if it's been in amongst the greenery, and some of the colouring of the plants had stayed on its fur.

Annie was unaware that Brian and Jack had discovered that the one they were doing the post-mortem on. Had indeed been wearing what seemed to be the skin of a rat, so she had no idea that it had no fur of its own and had to wear what ever it could to keep warm and dry, and with Annie being not happy at that time they never got round to telling her.

The one near the doorway, kept turning around looking at Annie, Annie was amazed that something so small could hold a sandwich that must be more than half its size, and even eat it all, the one near Annie picked up another sandwich to Annie's surprise it could not still be hungry she thought, it rested the sandwich on its large belly then it scurried off, the plate still had a number of sandwiches on

Annie got up and told them that she would be back for her plate later, and she would like them to be fed and looked after, if there was anything she could do for them, all they would have to do was to let her know

Created and written by I C Henderson

Adventure of the Mouhumes
Jack and Annie's new
Visitors

On her way up the garden only a few yards from the shed, she turned her head and looked back into the shed and she could see that the plate had been emptied in that short time, she then knew that there must be a lot more than the two she had seen

A hand was coming over the garden gate trying to open the catch; Annie was a little bit surprised to see this as she was not expecting anyone. As she got near to the gate she opened it and she gave a scream as did Brian, they both did not expect to see each other, Annie started to giggle "you gave me a fright screaming like that, what on earth are you doing?

"Sorry I was not expecting to see you Annie I came to see Jack" Annie explained to Brian that Jack had taken poorly and was in hospital. Brain told Annie that he had the results from the samples from the Mouhumes fur jacked, and he was right it was from a rat.

Annie was taken aback, she had no idea that they had taken samples from the poor thing, Brian could see that she was upset so he asked her if he could make her a cup of tea or something, Annie not wanting someone coming into her house and running around after her, unlike Jack. She told Brian that she would be ok, and offered to make him one.

They went into the house Brian sat in the conservatory; Annie opened the window from the kitchen into the conservatory so that she could talk to Brian without shouting. Brian started to tell her that he had been reading his grandfathers notes and discovered that the Mouhumes would make clothing from anything.

Annie came into the conservatory with a tray and a plate of sandwiches then went back for the drinks. "So Brian you say they would make garments from anything" this had Annie thinking, that's why the large one in the shed looked somewhat different, the clothing was something else

Created and written by I C Henderson

Adventure of the Mouhumes
Jack and Annie's new
Visitors

"Brian would they look different if they had…different things" she stopped how could she explain "you know what I mean"

"Well I think like anyone when we wear a suit we look different to when we wear baggy cloths… like a baggy jogging garment perhaps" Brian explained that clothing can change our appearance a lot

Annie nodded, but she was thinking about the little one that came into the doorway, it had what seemed to be a flower on its head. Was it using this as camouflage to hide in amongst the plants? She wanted to ask Brian but she might have to tell him about the ones in the shed

Brian started to ask how Jack became so poorly, and he wondered what could have made him end up in hospital. Annie did not know what to say. "We were down the garden and it started to rain Jack stood in it longer than he should have"

"Was it to do with the Mouhumes they must be back" Brian knew it had to do with the Mouhumes "look Annie it was you and Jack who brought me here…sorry asked me here so don't cut me off now" Annie knew this and got up out of the chair

"ok…ok we discovered them in the shed" Brian jumped to his feet with excitement "hold on I don't want you running down there, I want to tell you a small number of things first" this stopped Brian in his tracks

Annie explained that she wanted to keep this as quiet as possible, and she did not want him to take any for experiments if he wanted to study them he must do it in the garden and only if they would allow him. Brian agreed to all of this it was his dream come true and he knew about them more than anyone as his grandfather had already studied them years earlier. This was going to be a start of something wonderful

Created and written by I C Henderson

Adventure of the Mouhumes
Jack and Annie's new
Visitors

Chapter 44
Annie

ANNIE HAD STARTED to come down the garden again. She had been missing for a while. The Mouhumes had not seen a lot of her until now. It had always been Jack who ventured into the garden but lately it had just been Annie. Until recently she had just been seen as someone who went into the house then out the next day. She was always just seen very briefly but now she was the only one who was seen regularly.

Sometimes she was seen with another man sitting in the conservatory, both of them looking out to the garden as they chatted. That was all the man did, look out. Once he had tried to come around the pond but the Mouhumes hid away. They did not want another human near them at this time. So the man kept his distance, it was as if he knew that was what they wanted.

Annie did not just bring food for them. She also started to make clothes for them from materials she had around the house. Some things she knitted and others she stitched from old clothes. The Mouhumes still had to modify some garments but most were just right.

The fairies still kept out of sight from Ted's wife, They were still unsure about Annie so they tried to keep out of her sight. Every now and again they forgot about her and went about their jobs as normal. They watched Annie but they mostly stayed hidden away to see what was happening and what was being said when Annie was in the conservatory with the man. They still had little idea of who he was and why, when he came, all he did was to sit and watch the Mouhumes. Sometimes he had something on a stand that he had pointing towards the pond and sometimes down the garden towards the shed and greenhouse. The Mouhumes had no idea what it might be but it didn't seem to hurt anything in the garden so they weren't that concerned.

Created and written by I C Henderson

Adventure of the Mouhumes
Jack and Annie's new
Visitors

The man was coming at different times of the day and more and more with his stand. They tried to find out what it might be but when Annie and the man talked it was mainly about Jack. What they had discovered was that Jack was in something called a hospital. They had heard the man asking Annie when Jack would be out of hospital.

They had not heard what Annie had said. So they had no idea what a hospital was or when Jack was coming back. It seemed to be a long time since Jack had been seen so hearing his name was a good thing. The fairy, Lilac, was the one who kept an eye on Annie. She informed the Mouhumes what was being said and also told Starlight and Glow.

The fairies learned about the human who had been coming to the house. He was called Brian and he was a friend of Jack and Annie. Lilac watched over Annie almost all day and best part of the night. She understood most of the things said by humans but she still did not know everything such as hospital and a few other words.

Lilac was keen on learning as much as she could about human beings. It was good for her to study Annie. Lilac overheard Jack was coming home in two days. Annie had been telling Brian that he was being brought home the night before the funeral and that Jack was going to go into the living room.

Brian had been asking Annie what had happened. Annie told Brian that Jack had been suffering for a long time and being caught in the rain knocked him back. Then he went into some sort of depression and with everything else he caught pneumonia too.

Lilac had no idea what Annie had said but she could remember most of what had been discussed. She also noticed Annie looked very emotional when she was talking about this to Brian. Then suddenly she smiled and cheered her self up asking Brian to help her to move some furniture in the living room.

306

Adventure of the Mouhumes
Jack and Annie's new
Visitors

As the two of them moved the furniture around Annie was talking all the time about Jack and how he would be put in a certain position so that he could look out towards the conservatory. She had Brian moving things around then putting them back. Then she had Brian take a small table upstairs and a little while later it was brought back down again. They stopped for a drink. It was as if Annie had finally realized Brian was worn out. He was not a young man nor was he a fit man, all this hard work showed on his face. So when she asked him if he wanted a drink he was only too glad to accept.

Brian walked back into the conservatory. He stood for a while looking down the garden towards the shed. Then he looked at the little box on top of the tall stand, took it off placed it on his knee and sat down looking at it.

Lilac could not understand what he was doing but his face seemed to light up when he was looking at it. Annie came in with drinks for them. Annie asked about the little box. Brian showed it to Annie. They both smiled. What ever it was seemed to bring them happiness. Brian put it back, this time pointing it slightly towards the fish pond. Lilac shrugged her shoulders and dismissed it. Humans were strange!

Annie started to talk about Jack again and started to cry. "The things that Jack could do before his accident he can no longer do and the harder he tried the more upset he got."

Lilac had never seen a human cry before. She then knew that something bad must have happened to Jack. Lilac herself felt upset seeing Annie cry whilst trying to tell Brian.

Starlight came to the side of Lilac. Lilac started to tell Starlight what had happened, what she could understand and even what she had little idea about. She knew she had to repeat the words that Annie had said to Brian. Lilac started from the beginning. Annie had told Brian that Jack had been in a car crash a

Adventure of the Mouhumes
Jack and Annie's new
Visitors

number of years ago. He had got himself back to work but irritated part of his injury that had happened in the crash. Lilac had little idea what some of these words meant but she continued repeating it word for word. She had a good memory.

Jack needed an operation to repair the damage and then he needed another operation on his heart. Even before that he had been in a lot of pain. When moving around he would get bad-tempered or even aggressive. The more pain he was in the less he would tell anyone and the more he would try to get back to normal the less he could. It was a vicious circle. Then he would get irritable, driving friends and family away. The last few days she had spent with Jack had been the longest and that was only because they had been watching the Mouhumes … Lilac then stopped. She got a lump in her throat. This was not something the fairies had ever experienced. Could this be an emotion they had never had?

As Lilac was telling Starlight it became clear that things right in front of humans can be missed. Things they should have seen but just overlooked, much like the fairies. This puzzled Lilac. How could humans not see something right in front of them?

Brian was still in the house with Annie. He had gone into the kitchen area to make a fresh drink for Annie who had now stopped crying. To the side of Annie was a little table with some outfits on she had made for the Mouhumes. She had made tops and bottoms. They were all different. She had clearly kept herself busy.

She must have made ten or more outfits for the Mouhumes. All were put in a neat pile of tops and bottoms. Then just behind that pile was another pile but different styles and colours. She must have used anything she had to make clothes with.

She had not put them out for the Mouhumes yet. She had been distracted with Jack. It had been sudden. It looked like he was going to make a recovery but then he took a turn for the worst. It took Annie by surprise. As he seemed to be on the mend she had

Created and written by I C Henderson

Adventure of the Mouhumes
Jack and Annie's new
Visitors

not gone to hospital that day to see him. She had things to do at home and now she was feeling guilty.

Created and written by I C Henderson

Adventure of the Mouhumes
Jack and Annie's new
Visitors
Chapter 45
The Funeral and Starlight

STARLIGHT STARTED TO keep an eye on Annie. Starlight stayed with her for days on end, watching over her. She had never seen a human in mourning but it was not that different to the time when Glow parted with her son, Capheus. She could actually understand the hurt and pain she was going through.

Not all Annie said was understood. Some words were new to the fairy. There were people coming and going. Starlight had never seen as many humans going to Jack and Annie's home. They were all saying similar things and Annie continued to tell them the same account. Sometimes it was slightly different but always about Jack and how he had passed away.

Starlight had never had a lot to do with Jack and Annie. She had seen Jack before his accident in the garden. He cared for the plants and his fish. He looked like he had a kindness about him and she noticed how he liked things in order: such as his garden tools. He put them away after he had used them. He cleaned them, oiled them and did what ever else he needed to do.

The human Brian had not been for a number of days. Lots of other humans were bringing flowers and cards. Starlight could not read what was on the cards but they gave her something to hide behind, the flowers did too.

The day had come to say goodbye to Jack. His body was in a coffin in the living room. Humans came to speak to Jack in private whilst others stood in the kitchen and others stayed in the dining room or the conservatory. Even some of the humans stood outside in the garden. Starlight told the Mouhumes what was happening and what she thought it meant. The Mouhumes hid amongst the flowers.

Created and written by I C Henderson

Adventure of the Mouhumes
Jack and Annie's new
Visitors

Starlight had been upstairs in the bedroom where Annie was getting herself ready. Annie was sitting on the edge of the bed sobbing. Starlight felt the pain that Annie must have been feeling as she, just a few days earlier, had to say goodbye to Capheus.

Jack was in his coffin, they had left it open only showing Jack from his waist up to his head. Some of the Mouhumes had sneaked in to see Jack and it all became clear. This was the first time the Mouhumes and the fairies had seen a dead human. A new understanding had come to them: humans also die and they too find it hard when it happens.

Cars pulled up outside and there were men in black clothing. They walked in and spoke to Annie. Annie nodded and they went into the room where Jack was. Those in and around the other rooms went outside. They lined up along the garden footpath and some lined up the path outside the garden.

The men, who had gone into the room where Jack had been, now came out carrying the coffin, then they placed it into one of the cars. Annie came out behind them and climbed into another car; just behind the one Jack had been placed in. followed by some other humans, Ted and Linda also climbed in. The street was full of humans; they were all in dark clothing. As the cars drove off slowly one of the humans walked in front of the cars. The fairies placed themselves in the street.

The Mouhumes were also there hiding in and amongst the plants, up and down the street. This had been the first time the Mouhumes were out in numbers hidden amongst humans.

The cars took a little time to drive away. They were almost out of sight before the man walking in front got into the car. It then drove away at a slightly faster pace. The rest of the humans who had stood outside the house got into their cars and drove away.

Created and written by I C Henderson

Adventure of the Mouhumes
Jack and Annie's new
Visitors

Starlight was still in the bedroom looking out of the window, a tear rolled down her cheek. It was a sadness she knew only too well. As the last car went out of sight she went downstairs. Some of the windows were still open. The conservatory door was slightly open. Someone must have pushed it closed but not sufficiently enough for it to catch shut.

This gave Starlight an idea. How could she help Annie? What could she and the Mouhumes do to take some of this pain away for Annie? She called out for some of the Mouhumes to come into the house. They all went into the dining room which adjoined the kitchen.

Starlight asked the Mouhumes to look around the house for anything that seemed out of place. She explained what she meant. She took them into the room where Jack had been and pointed to the floor. It had bits of broken plants on the carpet.

That would be the first room they would tidy up. They picked up the broken stems from the flowers and anything else that might have been dropped on to the floor. They also picked up bits of paper and flower petals. Before they got started you could hardly see the carpet for all the bits on the floor.

They cleared it in no time, putting all the rubbish in the bin outside. As for the cups and other things in the kitchen the Mouhumes put them in the sink. Turning the tap was more than a task. They had no idea how to do it so they left it alone. At least the kitchen tops were tidy!

They did as much as they could to help Annie. Some things were just too heavy for the fairies and the Mouhumes to move so they just had to leave them as they were. Annie would most likely not notice due to her being so upset. It would give her something to do when she got back home.

312

Adventure of the Mouhumes
Jack and Annie's new
Visitors

That was all they could do for now. Just before they were leaving they went around the house to check that everything was alright: that all windows were locked and doors were shut. Then they went out of the conservatory door. That was the only door not locked. Starlight could see the door had a key in it. She asked the Mouhumes to push it shut from the outside as the door, when opened, it went outwards not inwards.

Starlight could not work out who had closed that door and why they had only pushed it so that it looked shut. Something worried Starlight. There had been people there she had not seen before. Starlight had been around Ted's for a number of years. She knew all the faces around that street and those who passed through but there had been some faces she had never seen. She asked for Tube to come with Ratty and Ruddy. She needed to see them urgently.

The Mouhume went for Tube, Ratty and Ruddy without hesitation. Starlight needed to know something. She had a suspicion about something she had seen before but she just wanted to make sure that it was not her imagination.

She stayed in the house until Tube and Ratty landed. Ruddy was not that far behind them. To Ruddy's surprise Starlight looked worried. They started to talk about the day's events. She asked if any of them had seen who was last to come out of the conservatory door? Tube had seen. He explained who it was. It was someone who often went in houses and garden sheds. The Mouhumes had seen him a number of times.

Starlight wanted to know more about this human. Tube started to tell her that he was well known to the Mouhumes. He was often seen going into houses that were empty. What he meant to say was that when a home owner had gone out he would often go inside. Sometimes coming out with items and putting them into a car waiting nearby.

Created and written by I C Henderson

Adventure of the Mouhumes
Jack and Annie's new
Visitors

Starlight then knew the Mouhumes did not know about this type of human. She started to tell them of the type of human he was and that she thought Annie might be in danger. She asked Tube and Ratty to get as many Mouhumes willing to help defend Annie's home. Ruddy just looked at Starlight. Starlight put her hand up and asked Ruddy if she would be the eyes and ears on the ground. Ruddy nodded. Starlight knew that Ruddy was still not at full strength. She was not sure if she would ever be again.

Countless fairies came. They hid themselves all around the house and outside, near the doorway. The Mouhumes came thorns in each hand. Starlight looked at them. They needed something else. Thorns in their hands would not be enough. Then it came to her. She had been around at Ted's one day: he had been watching the television and she had seen something that might be useful.

She told a number of fairies what she wanted. Quickly they flew off. The light outside was dulling and the sky was filling up with clouds. She needed to tell the Mouhumes what she was wanted them to do. She was determined to protect Annie's home.

Tube and Ratty were standing nearby. Starlight was talking quietly. Ruddy could hardly make out what was being said. Then the fairies came back. They had not been away long. They had things in their hands: some had long sticks and others had shorter sticks. How was this going to help thought Ruddy?

Starlight told Tube and Ratty she would show them what to do but she needed everything back when it was over. Tube and Ratty agreed but could not understand what all the fuss was about, they often used long sticks!

The fairies then started to bend the longer sticks. They attached some cord, turning it around so it was pointing towards the cushion on the chair. With a shorter stick they placed it onto the cord then pulled it back as far as they could then let go. The Mouhumes jaws must have dropped with amazement.

Created and written by I C Henderson

Adventure of the Mouhumes
Jack and Annie's new
Visitors

They had never seen anything like it before. They never even thought that two sticks of different lengths could be so effective. The cushion was covered in sticks sticking out. Tube was the first to go and look at the cushion. Some sticks had almost gone all the way through. Just the end of the stick was sticking out of the cushion. Ruddy stood with her mouth wide open. She was amazed by what she had just seen.

Starlight told them that she only had seven of these new killing weapons and she wanted them back afterwards. They all agreed. The Mouhumes who were going to use these weapons came forward. Starlight explained what she wanted them to do.

She showed them what to do. She held the longer stick with the string attached to it in the middle then she placed the smaller stick in her hand, attaching it to the string. She then told them to pull the stick as far back as they could. With her arm slightly bent she then told them to look down the stick to the end of the tip. Then once they saw what they wanted to hit they had to let it go.

TWANG! They hit the target with a thud. Starlight pointed to the pillow. Now it was the Mouhumes turn. Six had bows. She explained the larger sticks are called bows and the shorter stick is called an arrow.

They took their turns: some were dropping the bows after they had let go of the arrow. The string had scraped up their forearms. This was not something they had expected. Now they were rubbing their arms and jumping around the room in pain. Starlight started to laugh. She had forgotten to tell them about the string sometimes catching the forearms.

Those who had dropped the bows did not want to have another go so others had to try. Ruddy was one of them. She had seen what had happened to those who had not held the bow correctly. She picked the bow up and held it like Starlight showed

Adventure of the Mouhumes
Jack and Annie's new
Visitors

them, bending her arm slightly holding the bow. She placed the string onto the arrow groove then pulled back as far as she could. She had not expected it to be as hard to pull back the cord. It took some strength.

She looked down the arrow as she had been told then let go of the cord. Thud, it hit the target right where Ruddy had aimed for. She was thrilled with her aim. Starlight came to her side and was beaming at Ruddy's achievement.

Six of the Mouhumes who wanted to try these new weapons had now been picked. Starlight was holding one too. She told them if they needed to fire them, to do altogether. Tube asked what they were going to be shooting.

Created and written by I C Henderson

Adventure of the Mouhumes
Jack and Annie's new
Visitors

Starlight told them the man who had left the doorway unlocked because he was a thief. She had seen him go in and out of human homes many times, taking things that did not belong to him and she thought that he was intending to come back to take Annie's possessions. The next question was as important as anything could possibly be.

"Do we kill him?" asked Ruddy.

"No we just shoot him in his legs and backside area, that should put him off," Starlight said. She had no sooner said those words when one of the Mouhumes came running in telling them that a human was coming towards the house. He had come from the woodland area and through one of the gardens on the other side of the road.

They all hid away. The gate squeaked slightly as it opened. The conservatory door was pulled open. A dark figure snuck into the conservatory. The Mouhumes and fairies were all hidden away but peeping out to see what was happening. The human went into the living room towards the television quickly bending down to unplug it. As he did so the Mouhumes shot their arrows simultaneously into his backside.

He squealed a squeal that would have been heard streets away. The human's body straightened up as he screamed. Starlight with her bow and arrow was just behind him: twang … her arrow was let go. It went right into the middle of his ear, straight through. There was another yell and he was off running out the way he had come in. Not known to him, the fairies and the Mouhumes set another trap. They had string attached on to the gate posts, just high enough to make him trip on to all sorts of prickly things.

The human fell face down onto the palms of his hands and onto some sharp objects. Not just that, some Mouhumes could not resist in stabbing him in the legs with thorns. The human was up on to his feet, almost running before his feet were off the ground. It

Created and written by I C Henderson

Adventure of the Mouhumes
Jack and Annie's new
Visitors

was a frightening experience for him, one that he would never forget.

The fairies and the Mouhumes started to tidy up the footpath and in the house where they had left evidence that they had been there. It was getting late and they knew Annie would be coming back some time soon.

They wanted everything just right for her but they also did not want her to know what had gone on. This was something the Mouhumes could not understand: how one creature could do something so wrong to another creature. Starlight started to tell them as they were tidying up. She had seen a number of things that humans did to one another that would not be done by any other living thing.

Car lights pulled up outside and then the car door opened. The Mouhumes could see that Annie had returned. Annie was getting out of the car, as she did so she was talking to the driver. She then stood outside the car stretching and straightening her back but then bending slightly to talk to the driver once again.

The Mouhumes could not understand what was being said but it all seemed pleasant enough. Not moving they stayed hidden away, forgetting to go and tell those in the house. Annie was heading towards the back door when one of the Mouhumes realized that those in the house should have been told. It was not that Annie had not seen them before; it was just so they knew she was coming.

Annie walked in, almost straight into Starlight who was telling the Mouhumes to put the bows and arrows away. Starlight was hovering almost at the same height as Annie. Annie stopped in mid tracks not taking her eyes off Starlight. Starlight still hovering; looked into Annie's eyes forgetting she could no longer make herself invisible; she had used all her energy and needed rest. It was nothing she could do about it. It was something she had never

Created and written by I C Henderson

Adventure of the Mouhumes
Jack and Annie's new
Visitors

wanted, to be seen by another human. All the time she had been with Ted, Ted's wife, Linda had never seen any of the fairies.

Annie smiled and stuck out her hand, with one of her fingers pointing outwards indicating to Starlight if she wanted to rest on it she could. Starlight had seen Annie many times before. She knew she was not a bad person and her energy was low now so she rested on Annie's finger. She looked straight into Annie's eyes, Annie might have been smiling slightly but her eyes could not hide the pain that she was feeling. Annie's eyes were full of tears. Starlight's eyes also filled up, it was as if she could sense Annie's pain. It looked like it was going to be the beginning of a new friendship.

The End

I hope that you have enjoyed reading this.

Watch out for

Annie's magical friends

(*Other books*)

Jack and Annie's magical garden

The Mouhumes journey

Order in the court (play)

Homeless (play)

With thanks from

I C HENDERSON

Printed in Great Britain
by Amazon

78685394R00182